I0602563

WINGS OF TABAT

In the final book of Cat Rambo's magical Tabat Quartet, we return to the city of Tabat, a place where Humans and magical Beasts co-exist—but uneasily. The exploited Beasts, used for both their labor and their very bodies, are finally fighting back, and turmoil abounds in the city.

At the same time, Tabat is finally about to have its long-predicted elections, and multiple factions are jostling for power, all of them preparing to oust the Duke. And the mysterious Circus of the Autumn Moon has left the grounds of the College of Mages and is nowhere to be found.

Bella Kanto, once Champion of Tabat and then exiled for crimes she did not commit, has come home, carried by Dragons, to her beloved city. Now she must determine how to defend it from a menace she is ill-equipped to defeat: the transfigured Lucy, transformed by an ancient artifact into a dangerous demigod. If discovered back in the city, the exiled Bella may be taken prisoner and returned to the cells of the Duke's torturers. Freed of his curse, Bella's former companion Teo has escaped Lucy's grasp, but finds the city an unwelcoming place nonetheless.

Adelina, Bella's former lover and best friend, has married Merchant Mage Sebastiano and set up housekeeping. The two are still learning what it means to be in love with each other. But Adelina's former business, Spinner Press, has burned down, and Adelina is forced to find new ways to make money. Sebastiano, who has left the College of Mages, must also do the same while trying to rebuild his relationship with his father.

Angry at the city she feels has betrayed her and grown monstrous in her power, Lucy destroys the Duke's castle, the tram lines, countless buildings, and other vital parts of Tabat's infrastructure, raining down destruction and chaos, and threatening to eradicate the city entirely.

Now that she is reunited with her friends and family, can Bella manage to recapture her magical tie to the city soon enough to defeat Lucy before she destroys the city? Enter the world of Tabat and find out why writer Saladin Ahmed called this story an unsung gem of modern epic fantasy.

WINGS OF TABAT

BOOK 4 OF THE TABAT QUARTET

CAT RAMBO

Wings of Tabat
Copyright © 2025 Cat Rambo

All rights reserved. No part of this book may be reproduced or transmitted in any form or by any electronic or mechanical means, including photocopying, recording or by any information storage and retrieval system, without the express written permission of the copyright holder, except where permitted by law. This novel is a work of fiction. Names, characters, places and incidents are either the product of the author's imagination, or, if real, used fictitiously.

The ebook edition of this book is licensed for your personal enjoyment only. The ebook may not be re-sold or given away to other people. If you would like to share the ebook edition with another person, please purchase an additional copy for each recipient. Thank you for respecting the hard work of this author.

EBook ISBN: 978-1-68057-785-3
Trade Paperback ISBN: 978-1-68057-786-0
Dust Jacket Hardcover ISBN: 978-1-68057-787-7
Library of Congress Control Number: 2025935435
Cover design by Janet McDonald
Cover artwork images by Shutterstock
Kevin J. Anderson, Art Director
Published by
WordFire Press, LLC
PO Box 1840
Monument CO 80132
Kevin J. Anderson & Rebecca Moesta, Publishers
WordFire Press eBook Edition 2025
WordFire Press Trade Paperback Edition 2025
WordFire Press Dust Jacket Hardcover Edition 2025

Printed in the USA
Join our WordFire Press Readers Group for
sneak previews, updates, new projects, and giveaways.
Sign up at wordfirepress.com

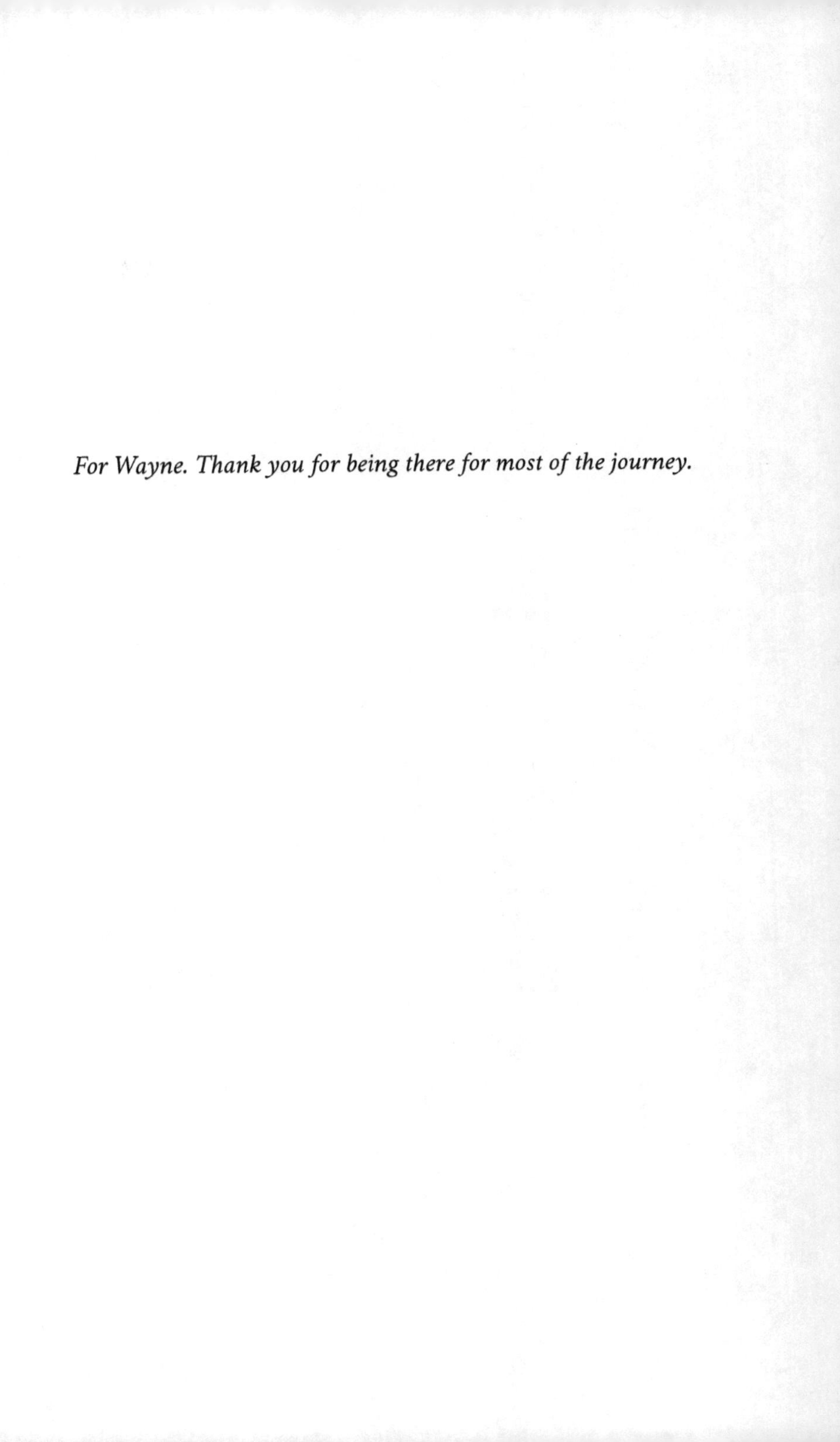

For Wayne. Thank you for being there for most of the journey.

BEGINNING

These are the last days of Tabat. Days of chaos, nights of ruin, all of them filled with fear, Adelina wrote. But that is not where it all began. It began so long ago when they built this city on the labor and literal bones of Beasts. Some claim that there's another Tabat. Far below, deeper even than the caverns, a city that a Sorcerer cursed with namelessness and threw down into the depths of the earth. A folktale, certainly, but an appropriate one.

A beautiful city, but built on a curse. Built on a price paid by others. Is it any wonder that it should fall?

PREVIOUSLY

This is the fourth book of a quartet, and you may have forgotten what happened in the first three books. While I would certainly encourage reading them if you haven't, for those who might have read and forgotten, here's a synopsis of the previous action.

Tabat is a city inhabited by both Humans and Beasts. The latter group are intelligent magical creatures, such as Centaurs, Dryads, Minotaurs, and the like. The city's economy is driven by the labor of the enslaved Beasts, as well as by its trade in their body parts, which are used to fuel magical spells and engines, such as the furnaces beneath the city, which burn Dryad logs. Humans have long justified the servitude of Beasts in one way or another, but as the series begins, for the first time a substantial number of Humans, the political group known as Abolitionists, are arguing that they should be freed.

The boy Teo has been raised in a village of Shapeshifters, beings capable of taking on animal as well as Human form. Especially feared for their abilities, the Shapeshifters must hide their identity from the Humans in order to avoid being exterminated. When Teo's ability to change his shape does not manifest in adolescence as it should, his parents decide to save his terminally ill sister's life by dedicating Teo to the Temples of the Moon Gods in return for a cure, thinking he will be safe enough there.

Teo begins the trip southward to the city of Tabat, where the major Temples are located, with the priest Grave. When Grave is attacked and put out of commission by a sting from a Fairy, Teo is sent by himself on a riverboat, under the eye of a Moon Temple lay member, the river pilot Eloquence Seaborn. The Moon Temples, which worship the world's three moons, are one of two major religious groups in the city, the other being the Trade Gods followed by the upper classes.

Teo arrives in the city of Tabat and escapes his fate of Temple servitude when a fight breaks out at the docks between the ship's cargo and the man who has come to take that cargo to the College of Mages, Sebastiano Silvercloth. Sebastiano is in an odd position; while he studies at the College and they use him to manipulate their money, they also scorn him for the Merchant ties that allow him to do so.

Adrift in the city of Tabat, Teo goes in search of the single person he knows of, the Gladiator Bella Kanto. Bella Kanto is a prominent woman who, for the past thirty years, has been determining the outcome of a ritual that controls the yearly weather of Tabat: the annual fight between a Gladiator representing Spring and a Gladiator representing Winter. Bella has won this battle every year of her career, ensuring that the city has an extra six weeks of winter every year, and people are growing tired of the pattern.

Charismatic and alluring, Bella's romances have become notorious, and sometimes complicate her life, as when she breaks things off with a relative of the Duke of Tabat, Marta, who is driven by revenge to conspire with forces working against the Gladiator. When a student, Skye, on the brink of graduating falls in love with Bella, Bella yields to temptation and is soon embroiled in scandal. At the same time, she encounters Teo on the street and takes him in as a servant.

A major source of Bella's fame are the books about her written by her best friend and former lover, Adelina Nittlescent (Nettlepurse in the common vernacular), whose publishing house is funded by the proceeds from the incredibly popular serials about Bella that Adelina writes for the newssheets known as penny-wides. publishing is considered a disreputable employment, Adelina has kept her ownership and management of the press a secret from most, including her own dictatorial mother Emiliana.

Emiliana pressures Adelina to run for public office. The city is about to move from being ruled by the Duke of Tabat, a structure established when the city was first settled, to an elected council, in fulfillment of a promise made long ago by the Duke's ancestors. Adelina does her best to duck the responsibility, but finally is pressured into making a speech—and fails in a humiliating way. Wanting to succeed, she is tempted by and succumbs to a magical drug supplied to her by a woman she's met, a photographer named Jilly Clearsight.

At the same time, she finds herself encountering Sebastiano, who has been directed by his father to find a bride and presented with three candidates: Lilia, Marta, and Adelina. She is torn between the romantic attraction she feels for Sebastiano and that which she feels for Eloquence Seaborn, who has come to her to see if she will publish his book.

Bella is tricked into killing Skye in gladiatorial combat and withdraws from society, even from her favorite cousin, the artist Leonoa Kanto. Leonoa's paintings have been stirring civil unrest, including riots, due to their Abolitionist content, and her own lover Glyndia, while not a Beast, is often mistaken for one due to the curse she is under.

Adelina is unable to comfort her; her own life has become increasingly complicated, including taking Eloquence's sister Obedience in as an apprentice, despite his disapproval. The increasingly independent Obedience renounces the Moon Temples and takes on the name Lucy, but when she inadvertently gives away Adelina's greatest secret to her mother, Adelina ousts her. Adelina is torn between Eloquence and Sebastiano, going back and forth before finally confessing her attraction to Sebastiano when she finds him talking with a potential rival, the Duke's huntswoman, Ruhua.

Confused and adrift, Bella is betrayed and drawn into a smuggling scheme of illicit magical supplies that pits her against the strictest laws of Tabat. She is imprisoned, tortured, and sent away from the city before this book begins. She is joined by Teo, although she does not realize it. Transformed into a dog by the Sorcerer Murga, the boy has been given to the Duke of Tabat and breaks free just as Bella's ship is leaving, leaping aboard it at the last minute, driven to join her.

Bella is exiled from the city she loves with all her heart, knowing that those she leaves behind face riots, political upheaval, and worst of all, the unknown forces that have been working against her. Teo is condemned to doggish form. And Lucy, after trying to find shelter with her friend Maz, a student at the College of Mages, has been kidnapped.

On a vast sea raft city, Bella reunites with an old lover, Scylla, who helps her escape from the captivity she's been forced into. Together they sail south with Teo. Along the way, it is revealed to Bella that Teo is actually a boy.

Taken to the Southern Isles as a result of mistaken identity, Lucy undergoes a powerful magical transformation. She destroys her captors and, finding herself gifted with unimaginable power, begins to use it to destroy the cities of the Southern Isles. Bored with that, she confronts Bella and takes Teo after transforming him back into his original form, intending to take him with her back to Tabat, where she means to have revenge on anyone and everyone who's ever slighted her.

As this book begins, both Lucy and Bella Kanto are returning to Tabat.

FOREWORD AND ACKNOWLEDGEMENTS

This is the fourth and last book of the Tabat Quartet, a project that I have been working on for almost twenty years now, since 2005. The first book, *Beasts of Tabat*, was published in 2015 by WordFire Press. *Hearts of Tabat* appeared in 2018, followed by *Exiles of Tabat* in 2021. I started this book in 2021, but factors derailed it. I have also written several dozen stories in this world over the course of the years; you can find a list of them at the end.

The city of Tabat started as a proposal for an area for an online game my friend James was creating in the mid-nineties. I wanted to do a seaport, and I was inspired by the building system that James had created, which allowed one to add conditional descriptions to a room, ones that would only appear if certain conditions were met, such as it being high tide, or spring, or some combination of similar factors. I loved that feature and employed it to create things like a street whose tiles underfoot changed according to the lunar cycle.

The game never came to pass, but several years later I returned to Tabat. Another online game I was working with at the time, Armageddon MUD, was closed to players every Saturday in order to allow the staff to coordinate and conduct maintenance. I suggested that a MUD (a multi-user domain) set in a very small area would allow the players to socialize and roleplay, and set about recreating the city, mapping it out and beginning to figure out some of its history. That project also never was completed, but finally in 2004 I began writing stories set in Tabat and the surrounding world, because I knew it so well.

As I've written in it, that world has continued to grow in clarity, and new landmarks have appeared, such as the Piskie Wood, the Great Tram, and the waterfall in the Duke's plaza. Its growth has been shaped by my interest in and reading of early American history. I'm very fond of Tabat, and I'd like to see it reach the heights of other fantasy fiction cities, such as Ambergris and Lankhmar.

The books have undergone a sea of changes in the course of writing, and the first book ended up getting split into *Beasts of Tabat* and *Hearts of Tabat*, so they overlap, showing the same circumstances from different perspectives.

In this series, I have tried to talk about how we demonize and infantilize those we oppress. Each of the Humans involved has to confront their own complicity in the system enslaving the Beasts. If you want a story that speaks to it directly, my "Incidents in the Life of a Beast," which originally appeared in *Realms of Fantasy*, is my first attempt to grapple with this, and it is, in many ways, an exploration of the times I'm living in and the systems that exist to perpetuate and justify economic and racial prejudice and oppression. That story appears in these books as the red-bound book being distributed by Murga: the story of Philip the Centaur.

Many people have been encouraging, supportive, and appreciative of this world. I particularly wanted to say thank you to Saladin Ahmed (I finally answered your question about the moons in this book, Saladin), Patti Bakker, Emily Bell, Jennifer Brozek, Mark Bukovec, Brenda Cooper, Samuel R. Delany, Kristine Dikeman, Deanna Francis, Lowell Francis, Jan Gephardt, Neile Graham, Caren Gussoff-Sumption, Leslie Howle, Kay Kenyon, Terra LeMay, Louise Marley, Ken Peczkowski, Nona Rambo, Wayne Rambo (thanks for being there from the very beginning), Janet K. Smith (the woman who makes castles happen), Rebecca Stetoff, Sherri Stewart, Michael

Swanwick, Rachel Swirsky, Sandy Swirsky, Jeff VanderMeer, Walter Jon Williams, and last but never ever, ever least, Connie Willis.

To my Patreon supporters—you help make it so I can write stories like this. Thank you so much.

Scott Andrews not only saw and encouraged an early version of the book, but published multiple stories from this world, including "Every Breath a Question, Every Heartbeat an Answer," "Primaflora's Journey," and "Love, Resurrected."

Most excellent editor Kevin J. Anderson, who wrote "yum!" in all the margins of the food scenes.

Peter Wallace, who said okay when I said "I've got this fantasy book, would you mind taking a look at it?"

For all the WordFire Press people who've made this happen, especially Janet McDonald, Jonathan Miller, Marie Whittaker, and Adriel Wiggins.

Thank you to my cats: BabyBear, Bruce, and Clark, who reminded me to eat and nap.

And particularly thank you to all the readers who have expressed their pleasure in this world, and who kept me going.

It feels very odd to say goodbye to this cast, who have taken up close to 500k words and two decades of thought. Adelina, Bella, Eloquence, Lucy/Obedience, Sebastiano, and Teo, it's been a pleasure. Will I write more of your adventure? Only time will tell.

—October 15, 2024

CHAPTER 1

Tabat wakes slowly and lazily on this sultry summer day. Some of its inhabitants have been up for hours already; the bread carts of Figgis are already trundling out into the streets, trailing the scent of fresh bread and sweet pastries. Birds chirp to greet the sun, then subside into softer songs back and forth while overhead gulls call out harsh commentary. Pink and yellow sea roses are blooming in almost all of the city parks, and gardeners are kept busy trimming them back along the Stairway Park.

Golden sunlight plays on the blue water and steeps the docks. The sun-warmed wood is pleasant under the bare feet of early morning couriers and errand runners, rocking gently with the ebb and rise of waves and the passage of traffic. The air smells of salt and fish and a trace of smoke from early morning fires. The gray-green tiles of the roofs lead the eye up along the terraces, scaly fish playing across a set of submerged stairs.

Chal shops across the city have already opened their shutters and doors and are serving their salty fish tea, accompanied by crisps of bread and Figgis pastries.

At the Brides of Steel, girls are jostling for position in the food line, readying themselves for another day of classes. There's a school trip planned, up to see the Duke's castle, as much a training run as an excursion, but they are all looking forward to a day of fresh air and new things to look at. Bilitia Khentor, sometimes known as "the little Khentor girl," is arguing with two friends about where a particular blue hair ribbon she planned to wear that day has gone, and who borrowed it.

In the Sea Gardens, attendants are clearing things for the day, removing the night's draping of sea wrack, checking the salt water blossoms and dead-heading any fading blooms. Along the breakwater are pots of blue irises and golden petunias, their scent heady and sweet. When the attendants finish, they sing praise to Ellora before going about their duties.

A hypothetical swallow, high above the city, or the white Moon, rolling in morning clouds, might have seen the city peaceful, getting ready for its day. The elections are next week and no one knows yet that they will never happen.

A peaceful city.

A peace that will not remain.

BY NOW SHE and Sebastiano had been living together for a month, and it was all still very new to Adelina: the cramped kitchen, and the shoulder-wide stairway that led up to their purple-painted bedroom, and the sitting room that they both shared, her desk against one wall, Sebastiano's against the other. Stacks of books intermingling, his magical theory tomes, dusty, bound in exotic leathers or rare woods, side by side with her dense histories and accounts of taxes and household budgets and customs records from decades past, printed on orange paper that started crumbling the day after it was printed, it seemed like.

She had worried very much that not having servants would impact her way of doing things. She had been raised in luxury on her mother's estate, after all, and rarely had she cooked her own meals or done her own laundry. But here in the city, it was just as cheap to send that laundry out, and it turned out Sebastiano was an accomplished cook, who did not mind making all sorts of wonderful things, just as long as she was prepared to clean up after his extravaganzas. When she queried him about the unexpected talent, he said his mother had taught him, long ago, but he'd never had much occasion to cook for another. And so he cooked, and she cleaned up afterwards, and both were pleased with the results.

They were finding out that they worked well as a team. That was something of a surprise to both of them, because neither had really expected it. Adelina's father had died before she was born, and had never been part of her life, and while Corrado and Letha loved each other, they were not the sort of single unit that Adelina and Sebastiano found themselves able to become, particularly in the face of adversity. When the landlord came to announce an unexpected rent hike, Adelina talked him out of it, while Sebastiano supplied useful facts. When there was an infestation of insect ghosts, Sebastiano read the spell dispersing them while Adelina cleaned the husks up with a broom.

Not that they did not quarrel over various things. Sebastiano kept leaving the washrag floating in the basin of morning water; Adelina's long hairs choked his hairbrush and seemed to appear with almost hallucinatory regularity in places where he did not want them to.

But they agreed on the vast majority of household matters, including the importance of books as well as their care. Sebastiano was fussier about his clothing; Adelina was more prone to buying art than groceries, but both learned to throttle the occasional flare of impatience as they learned to live with each other.

And this was a very good thing, because the backdrop of their moving in together had been the slow erosion of the city's situation.

There were riots, often involving food, but much of the time sparked by fear: fear of Beasts uprising and killing their owners, which had happened now multiple times, or so the gossip claimed, or fear of an imaginary kind, like a Sorcerer—if you credited the rumor, there were Sorcerers walking the streets to the point where every twelfth or thirteenth person must be one, and people eyed people they'd known for years as suspiciously as though they were fresh-arrived strangers.

It was Murga, both she and Sebastiano knew, behind most of the latter rumors. The Circus of the Autumn Moon had closed its gates but its tents still lingered on the grounds of the College of Mages. Sebastiano had tried, time after time, to warn his fellows at the College, but all they did was jeer at him. Old rivalries that he had thought were long buried turned out to have been taking root, underground, and were now ready to bear sour fruit.

Adelina had thought that she would try writing pamphlets, but paper and ink were both increasingly dear. The riots interrupted trade to the point of throttling it back. Farmers no longer brought wagons of goods into the city, because they feared confiscation by the Council or the Duke's forces, or co-option by some crowd with less official legitimacy but just as much readiness to resort to violence. No, pamphlets were not the key.

Public speaking was, and there lay Adelina's only secret from Sebastiano. In order to speak well to the crowds and earn the small stipend she was paid, she had been forced to resort to the powders that Jilly Clearsight provided, the magic that enabled Adelina to connect to the crowd when speaking, to know exactly what to say in order to sway their hearts. She'd tried speaking without it again more than once, but she'd always had the vial up her sleeve, just in case, and when that case came, she did not take long to resort to it. It was as necessary as the honey candies she carried in her sleeve to keep her throat from growing dry when she spoke.

The candies were cheap, but the drug was expensive, eating up half her speaking fee each time, and it was, moreover, magic that Sebastiano would not have approved of, would have set his mind to talking her out of, which was just a waste of energy. She had to do it, no matter what, and it was just as easy not to have the fight, even if it was hard at times to keep her use of it from him.

She didn't want to discuss it. Didn't want to admit that it was pleasurable as well, the drug, the way it sank into her stomach and became warmth and confidence flowering out from her core. It was a good feeling, particularly in these uncertain days, and the truth was that she didn't want to abandon one of the few things beyond Sebastiano that gave her pleasure, one of the things that might be torn away as easily, or so she told herself, as any of the other shortnesses or scarcities that plagued the city. She would give it up when circumstances forced her hand, because surely they would, sooner or later, and she might as well wait for that.

She told Sebastiano that it made her nervous when he came to hear her speak, but the truth was that she didn't want him to see her under the influence. He had shown himself much better at being able to read her than any other lover or even close friend, able to sense her moods sometimes even before she realized them and then followed that discovery by finding that he had already coaxed her out of them. So he would know, when he saw her at the podium, that the heat with which she spoke, the fire in her eyes, was something false, stolen.

She didn't let herself think what it would do to their accord if (although surely when, rather than if) he discovered it. That made it all the more imperative to keep it hidden, truly. She argued these things to herself all sorts of ways. She claimed to an imaginary interrogator that it was a valid method of keeping herself from being drained by the demands of serving the city, that it was something that almost everyone did, surely, whether they admitted to it or not. She didn't let herself look at the levels of rationalization she had achieved, didn't look too far at something that she would have scrutinized closely if it had come from someone else, like Bella.

When would Bella return? Adelina had sent letter after letter, multiple copies of some, looking to coincide with places that Bella might be predicted to be. But her friend was still in exile, and Adelina could not help but feel, deep in her heart, that if the former Gladiator had been there, there would have been less chaos. Bella knew how to handle crowds, and she'd been able to manage the Duke's ambitiousness and greed better than most nobles. She was a better politician than she should have been, given how little she listened to people, but her charisma was something that let her get away with all sorts of things.

Everything would have been fine if Bella had not allowed herself to fall for her student. But that disaster must have been inevitable. Gods and Moons, she couldn't imagine how many of Bella's students must have chased after her over the years.

How many girls had thrown themselves at her in one way or another, each requiring gentle handling and tact as Bella disentangled herself as best she could while trying to keep the girl's ego intact. Because while Bella could be—usually was—careless of lovers, the same was not true of the way that she treated students. That was a relationship that clearly felt very different to her.

Was that a legacy that Jolietta had imparted somehow? It seemed unlikely, given how thoroughly Bella had disentangled herself when it had become possible, and how little Bella had spoken of her since, even to Adelina. But someone could have an impact on a personality and still never be spoken of, that was something Adelina had found to be true.

She herself sometimes stopped to feel sad about her mother, when the way sunlight came through a window reminded her of the house she had grown up in and she heard in her mind the rustle of Emiliana's skirts. But more commonly she felt a pang of guilt that she was so happy outside her mother's house, so delighted every morning to wake and find Sebastiano beside her. Sometimes he had wakened earlier and would be on his side, regarding her with that faint, quirked smile that he saved for her. Other times she woke and watched him sleep, as this sunlit morning, until it was too much for her and she awakened him with kisses.

Their world was falling to pieces around them, but so many moments were sweet, here and now, and there was no point to not savoring them.

A distant rumble, like thunder, but the sky outside the window was bright blue and clear. She would not worry about it now. She leaned to kiss Sebastiano's chin. He came awake quickly, and pulled her down to him, and they lost themselves in each other, and did not worry about the rest of the world.

THE FIRST SOLDIER that saw Lucy only glimpsed a prick of light far up above in the vast blue dome of sky, just a glint, a hint. The soldier put her head back and stared into the sky. Drops of sweat rolled along her forehead, stung her eyes so she blinked, trying to clear them. She wondered if the glint was a bird, but no bird flew ever that high. There was something about the glint that said danger. She elbowed her fellow guard and pointed.

The six soldiers in the courtyard gathered together, murmuring in curiosity to each other. The morning had proved quiet so far, although the ever-present flow of servants, messengers, visitors, and petitioners for one case or another had been a steady, predictable trickle.

The glint dropped lower, and lower, and they realized it was just a girl.

The Duke's castle was built of green marble blocks, quarried miles away, and ferried and carried and shipped here, to build a castle that out-rivaled any on the Old Continent, or at least the stories of them. It had turrets and gambellons, bartizans and bastions, finials and merlons. None of them meant for defense, because who would attack here, high above Tabat? Any army coming up the hill would have been decimated before it reached the top.

But Lucy did not come from below. She landed barefoot in the courtyard and when the soldiers protested her presence, she smiled at them.

Then she destroyed them. Flames shot from her hands to destroy two, then another two before anyone began to scream. The courtyard was chaos, everyone running towards the nearest promise of safety, and the flames came. One quick-witted soldier managed to get to the alarm bell and sound one stroke before they, too, floated to the ground in soft gray flakes.

It took her only moments to destroy the Humans there, as well as the handful of servant Beasts. That was easy. The castle would be harder.

Rising back up to hover in the air, she studied the castle in its entirety. Built soon after the founding of Tabat, its original squat form had been embellished upon by each generation, adding turrets and balconies as well as three wings and an enclosed garden. Adelina had once described it as a history of Tabat's architecture, all in one building.

Lucy destroyed it.

Needle-thin lines of force shot out from her, hit the stones here and there. And then again. And again, and again.

The change was slow, but the stone began to falter, to slump. To slide.

More soldiers rushed out into the courtyard, but the damage was already done, the motion set into place. They died in flames. The courtyard grew cluttered with corpses, and Lucy waited for more.

CHAPTER 2

The Duke was in his throne room, hearing cases. They were boring, they were mundane, but they let him keep in touch with the common people, he often said loftily. That two hours once a month let him know what was *really* on the mind of the people, he elaborated. He did not add that he was usually pleased to confirm that what was on the mind of the people was most often how to make more money, which meant more money for him, or how to keep other people from taking their existing money, which meant paying him money for the privilege.

Today, though, the cases had been nothing like that. Someone was suing on behalf of a Beast that had been injured, absurdly, not as a matter of damaged property but a claim that the Minotaur should be recompensed for the loss of its arm by being freed. The Duke spent his time denouncing the Abolitionist tendency that had been creeping into his city—no doubt a corruption coming from the direction of Verranzo's New City, always a troublesome example of how absurd things could get.

Then some political matter with the Merchants wanting more funding for the election. And he'd be damned if he did anything to make the elections run more smoothly. He'd done his best to make sure they weren't happening, had paid money to so many people who had sworn they would subvert the process in one way or another, and yet here they were, with the elections only days away, and with them would come a lessening of his power, which was, to his mind, intolerable.

He heard the clang of the alarm, but thought it some small matter, perhaps a fire in the kitchen or a Beast gone mad and needing to be put down. But footsteps thundered along the hallway, and then two soldiers burst into the room and, before he knew it, had grabbed him up and were hustling him away, hands urgent and rough under his shoulders.

The castle was shaking so they lurched along the hallway, one side, then the other of the two holding him, pulling him. Hanging lamps swung like pendulums, at odds with the line of the floor. Was this an earthquake? But surely the College of Mages would have predicted such a thing and warned him well ahead of time. That was their purpose, to serve him.

"Where are we supposed to take him?" the shorter soldier said to the other, ignoring the Duke's demands to know what was going on.

"Cap'n said the tunnels," the taller snapped. He had hold of one of the Duke's arms, while the shorter soldier the other. The Duke planted his feet and brought them all to a stop.

"What's going on?" he demanded.

"The castle's being attacked, everything's getting destroyed up there. Captain said to get you away."

Getting destroyed? Impossible. "What's attacking?" he said. It had to be Verranzo's New City. That was the only entity on the Continent capable of waging war on a city like Tabat, well defended and well pocketed.

"A little girl," one of the soldiers said in a tone of wonder. "All she does is point, and then someone's gone."

"Ridiculous! What sort of insanity is this? Take me to the Captain!"

"Dead," the soldier said.

"Then somewhere that I can see what's going on. The southern tower."

"Fallen," the soldier said, and for the first time the Duke felt fear.

"Anywhere high up," he snapped. He pulled away fully and straightened his jacket. The hallway swayed again, and they all sidestepped to keep their balance.

"You don't understand," the soldier said. "There is no anywhere high up anymore. She's taking the castle apart."

"Why?"

The soldier shook his head. For the first time, the Duke noticed that blood and dirt caked his cheek, and gray ash clung to his armor. "She didn't say," he said. "She didn't say a word."

The Duke yielded; they moved on.

Down and down they went, past the menagerie, past levels of storerooms, past the cells where prisoners were kept, into places the Duke hadn't even dared explore when a child. The cliff where the castle perched was riddled with tunnels and caves, and only a few of them were made by Humans.

"How far are we going?" he said.

"There's a tunnel leads to the College of Mages," the taller soldier said. "Through the furnace caves. That's where we'll go." He cast a glance back over his shoulder. "They'll tell us when it's safe to come out, Sir," he said.

He patted the Duke awkwardly on the shoulder and the Duke didn't react, bemused by the audacity. "We'll keep you safe, my lord," he said. And seemed to mean it.

THE CITY WAS LUCY'S. Hers to dominate. Hers to humiliate. Hers to destroy.

Easy to destroy the soldiers. Human bodies flamed like lighting a candle wick and were gone so easily. Stones like this were a different matter. They resisted her, didn't want to be separated. But she did it, letting the force inside her lance out again and again, tightly focused. And in the end that was what tore the stones apart, sundered them, smashed them, more than any thunderclap she could have summoned.

The Duke was here somewhere. If she killed him, she reasoned, she would be the new Duke. That was how this sort of thing worked. Conquer or be conquered.

Unlike him, she wouldn't let her power be taken away. She would rule Tabat. Wisely and fairly, unlike its previous existence. But she would rule it nonetheless.

Where was Teo? He had slipped away somewhere and she hadn't noticed. No matter. He was in the city that was hers now. She could reclaim him whenever she liked.

She destroyed another tower, sliding its stones away one by one until it fell. Clouds of dust roiled around the fallen stones, and a few crumpled forms lay here and there like discarded dolls.

Rage still filled her and hollowed her out, all at the same time. It always would, she thought. She was nothing but anger now.

She didn't want to be. She wanted to be back with her family, but that was impossible because they had denied her. Had not loved her but rejected her. They, they had done this to her, had forced her and denied her and not recognized who she was.

And who else was part of that *they*? Everyone. Everyone had failed her—not just her family, even her brother Eloquence, but also Adelina, whom she had thought so kind at first, and the boy Maz who had pretended to be her friend, but was the reason she'd been kidnapped.

No one was her friend, no matter how much they pretended.

Very well, then. She would be no one's friend. She would be their Enemy, she decided. The gloriousness of that decision filled her up, assuaged the void inside for a moment. She had heard the stories of Mary Silverhands and the Princess with Copper Scales, and all the rest of the powerful fairy-tale heroes, and she was more powerful than any of them.

She smiled and turned to the next tower. By now the soldiers had stopped running directly at her and were trying missiles of various sorts.

First arrows, which she made burst into flame. Then spears, which stopped when she made one turn around in mid-flight and impaled not just the caster, but the two about to cast their own spears. Some enterprising soul brought out a ballista and that just made her laugh, and every rock thrown at her rebounded and went smashing into the castle.

It felt so good to be the one in power. She had been pushed around and that would never happen again.

She would take this machine apart more slowly, she decided, or no, she would use it and whenever anyone ran out, she would throw them in a long arc, so far! And they would sail over the city and land in the sea and drown. That would be satisfying.

But when she reached to pull a stone out, it came begrudgingly, and she felt a slow burn along her skin, as though the fire she had been casting so freely were turning inward.

She frowned. Her powers had seemed limitless, but now …

She had expended them so fast, so furiously, she realized, that she was in danger of burning herself out.

She stopped. A silence fell over the castle, only the slow sifting of dust and ash, like a muted patter of rain, and in the distance, the city bells crying alarm.

Very well, she had announced herself, and in the process learned she had limits. She would find a place to rest, and recoup her energy. Next time she would spend it more wisely.

Next time she would parcel out destruction more judiciously. But parcel it out she would.

She looked down at the city far below, the city full of so many people who had wronged her so deeply. So deserving of anything she might do—anything she *would* do.

She smiled anew, and it was not a smile that boded well for the city.

Lucy was the most terrifying person Teo had ever met, and he had met more than a few in his short life. Including Murga, who'd turned him into a dog and given him to the Duke. Lucy had freed him from that curse, to be sure, and had done it before he had become lost and unable to recover his Human form.

But she hadn't done it to be kind or friendly. She had done it because in Human form, Teo could answer her when she asked him questions.

Not that she had asked him many on that equally terrifying journey, flying unsupported by anything but the air over the depths of the ocean. At first he had kept his eyes closed, but finally he had looked, and immediately puked, which just made Lucy laugh.

And then she landed and began turning soldiers into ash, and Teo didn't dare draw her attention while she was doing that, because what if she did it to him? Instead he had stayed still, very still, while she moved, and when she had moved to a place where she couldn't see him anymore, he had taken a careful step backward, and then another, and another, until he was in the shadow of a half-destroyed archway.

If she caught him trying to escape, she would kill him.

If he stayed, she would probably kill him anyway.

He wheeled and ran. Outside the central courtyard were the stables and he ducked through those. Everything was in chaos, a few people trying to get the horses out, and more of them simply trying to get out themselves. A group of girls was screaming. He saw a face he recognized—Jilly Clearsight—and she saw him across the courtyard, her mouth opening as though to speak—

—And then a tower fell on her and the people near her, and a cloud of dust arose, and he was jostled forward before he could see the rubble clearly.

Arms and legs and chests all around him, pushing him this way and that in their panic to escape. People were shouting, a baby was wailing, and then another *crash!* as another tower fell.

He pushed forward and slipped through the crowds, ignoring the elbows and shoulders that jostled him, and joined the horde fleeing the castle, heading down the long cliff road towards Tabat. He could hear falling rock and crashes behind him, but he didn't think Lucy had missed him yet.

A long road led away from the castle, and everyone on it moving in the same direction, away, at varying degrees of speed. From here, Tabat far below looked serene, but once news reached it, surely it would be less so.

The crowd began to clear, dispersing as his haste took him past some of the earliest to flee. A few people were running up towards the castle in the opposite direction, but everyone else was trying to get away.

He put his head down and just ran.

For the first time, he let himself glory in the fact that he had his body back. He ran in long easy strides, letting the slope of the street speed his pace—so different from the helter-pelter of being a puppy—and felt his own legs, his own arms pumping. His own heart beating.

Despite the terror and chaos, he was laughing as he ran.

CHAPTER 3

I feel complete again, truly Bella Kanto. I know these streets, these buildings. I know the way it smells before a storm and that one must be blooming now, to account for the edge of electricity riding the hot summer air.

Against all odds, despite all the plans that were laid against it, I have returned. I will be redeemed.

Life will return to what it was.

Back, back in Tabat. Back in my city, the one I have come to save. Back in the place that I love and that once loved me. Perhaps someday will love me again. The Dragon set us down on the eastern outskirts of the city and flew away. Scylla has gone to the docks, to see if there is word of her city and a way to get back to it.

She says she will come see me before she leaves. She will not go without saying goodbye, she said, and did not mean it as a reproach. Even though it might have been.

I come in through the River Gate, not because it will be deserted, but because it is the opposite: a swirl of people, too many to track. Easy to lose myself in the crowd. I expected more people to notice me, to remark on me, but no one does. Everyone is watching what is happening at the Duke's castle. We do not know what is going on there, but we see one tower fall, then another, and another. I cannot imagine what is happening, but Lucy must be the cause.

"Is it an invasion?" a man asks.

"A rebellion, perhaps," a woman says, and scowls at the Minotaurs unstacking cargo. They have not been permitted the time to gawp and look that the Humans are afforded. "The Beasts are restless, and the Abolitionists stir them to violence."

"The Duke is angry with the city," someone else says. "Perhaps he has sold us to Verranzo's New City."

I snort. "The man loves his castle. If its destruction were part of the price, he would not pay that bill."

People don't seem to recognize or realize that I might have more to contribute on the matter than they. That I might have frequently visited that castle, stood inside those towers that are falling. They murmur to themselves, swirling through the crowd, but don't seem particularly panicked. The danger is visible, but not within range of touching them, and it is moreover a danger that seems not directed at them but the Duke, whom fewer and fewer hold in favor.

Nonetheless, I think, perhaps I will not flaunt my presence. I know that as an exile, the city guards are directed to kill me if they find me in the city. Not that I think they could, unless I was very much outnumbered.

But then I think that perhaps that is the thought of the old Bella, the invincible one. Not the one that wakes every morning feeling creaky and old bones that do not want to rise. The old Bella, who had magic bolstering her, making her unbeatable.

I am still not used to being a new and different Bella Kanto. I am not sure I ever will be.

There are fewer Beasts here than I am accustomed to seeing in Tabat, and the ones that I see are chained or otherwise tethered. Fear has spread in my absence, and the Beasts have not benefited from it. But they are citizens of this city, as surely as any Human is.

That thought is new to me, but it feels right after all I have seen, of the Dragons, and Scylla and all the others. And that brings me around to a thought that is not new: what would have happened if I had not told my Aunt Jolietta that I had seen the Centaur, Philip, doing a forbidden thing: writing? She would not have gentled him, would not have robbed him of his mind and sent him away to where I could never find him. She died soon after, and surely that death was inevitable, her heart giving out as it did. What if he had been there, to be my companion, perhaps, or my friend, through all my days? I stop in an alleyway's entrance and draw a deep breath against the pain of that.

I must think of the here and now, rather than allow myself to get lost in past mistakes.

Lucy seems busy enough with the Duke and his castle. What will she do after that? I haven't a clue, but perhaps Adelina will. Lucy was Adelina's apprentice for a while, after all. Only the Moons know what Adelina will think of all the events. Will she even believe me? And Adelina can catch me up on the happenings of the city while I have been gone, and help me decide what to do next.

And I will see this man, this Sebastiano, that has enchanted her so thoroughly, and if he is unworthy of her, I will dispose of him. Because how could he possibly be worthy of my Adelina? And she cannot love him all that much, else how could she have written me so many letters?

But when I get to the building that houses Spinner Press, I stop, dismayed. The building has been destroyed by fire, absolutely gutted by it, blackened timbers holding up nothingness. The buildings either side are soot-blackened, touched by the disaster. One has "to let" signs in its window and the other simply looks vacant.

She said nothing of this in her letters. But the press was her heart. Why wouldn't she have told me of it? What did she fear? Did she think it would be too much for me? That stings, the thought that she kept it from me out of pity.

There is no sign where she has gone. I knock on the buildings all up and down the street to see if anyone knows where she has gone, but no one answers. It is still early morning, but the streets are beginning to fill, sunlight bright on the cobblestones, hastening to heat the day. I wish I had coins on me. I would stop at one of the bakery carts and get a pastry.

Coins make me think of banks, and that makes me think in turn of Leonoa. She may know where I can find Adelina, and either way, I should check in on my cousin and make sure she is safe. Unlike Adelina, she has written no letters—at least, any that I have received— but I am sure that she is still where she has always been. But what of her odd lover, Glyndia, the one who moved Leonoa to paint the works that have been found seditious? I had not liked her, and it worries me that my cousin has been in her care all this time. But Leonoa is a strong spirit. She will not be easily steered.

I hear thunder although the sky is clear. Something is still happening up at the Duke's castle, and I fear—no, I know—its name is Lucy. But let her expend energy on him while I figure things out down here.

ABOVE THE DUKE, explosions shook the castle, and he and the soldiers lurched along, more than once nearly being hit by falling masonry. As they descended lower and lower, the shaking lessened, insulated by the layers of rock between them and the horrifying creature that had appeared out of nowhere, bent on destroying him.

The tunnels were chilly and damp and the floors were slippery with old moisture, which made the Duke stumble more than once, as the two soldiers hurried him along. Here the torches were unlit, and they took one and lit it, and walked until it was nearly dying, then took another down and lit it from the first. How far had they come?

What forces did he have against what had happened? No army, only his Peacekeepers, really, and he had seen what happened to them in the face of that girl. She had destroyed them without really thinking about it.

Who was she? Why was she here? Why did she hate him so much that she wished to kill him?

This was not how things were done, in polite society. If there was to be a war, you declared it. Then you fought it according to rules, disregarding the fact that most of the time you were not supposed to kill people. But in a war you could, and the gods would approve, such as they were. His own faith was an uneasy rejection of both the Trade Gods and the upstart Moon Temples, coupled with an unshakable sense that some force had chosen him to lead Tabat. It was his city, meant to be his. It always had been.

They wound through tunnels and finally entered an immense cavern, full of roaring furnaces and piles of wood. The air was hot and pressed against his skin implacably.

"What is this place?" he asked.

"The College of Mages uses this space for the furnaces that fuel their machinery," one soldier said. He pointed at a heap of lumber. "Dryad logs burn hot and hard, and the Mages say they release magic when they do so."

The Duke looked over the heaps of logs and tried to calculate how many Dryads had died. He thought about the ones that he had once in his menagerie—hadn't one escaped, helped by the Oracular Pig? When he'd ordered the menagerie destroyed, they would have brought the Dryads here to be disposed of.

There seemed plenty of logs, and brawny men and women working with the enormous furnaces and the apparatus capping them. He said, "Perhaps I should stay here. It seems safe and hidden enough."

The two soldiers exchanged glances. "That's not our orders," one said.

The Duke turned and gave him an outraged look. "Your orders would have come from your Captain, and who commands him?"

"Her," one of the soldiers said, and then followed with, "And you command her."

"I do," said the Duke.

"It's not safe," the soldier said. "Easy enough for someone to follow us through the tunnels. We were in a hurry, we didn't hide our tracks."

"I never hide," the Duke said indignantly. "That is unworthy."

"Sir," the other soldier said. "Would you rather be unworthy or dead?"

The audacity of the question! He would have had the man killed at any other time, but circumstances made him keep a rein on his temper, and that was the most unpleasant thing of all.

Still. Perhaps the man had a point. He would make his refuge in the heart of the Peacekeepers, in the building that housed both the Human officers and the mechanical ones. That was down near the docks and far away from the castle, and whatever it was that had taken it.

THE TEMPLES WERE CROWDED with people seeking answers this morning, as. *As always*, Eloquence thought sourly. Everyone wanted the Gods to take care of them, and no one offered to take care of the Gods. Maybe the Gods didn't want to be Gods, didn't want to be responsible for everything. Wanted to just fuck off and go wherever they wanted to go.

Or maybe that was just him, saddled with six sisters who needed to be taken care of, even though he'd never offered to become the head of the family, had never said, "Yes, I want to be the one everyone expects to take care of them."

Not that he had done all that good a job at that. He thought of Obedience with a pang. Where was she now? He had failed her and then she had started living on the streets and then who knew what had happened to her? He desperately hoped someone had found her, taken her in. But with every day bringing still no word, he was beginning to abandon that hope.

He stood in line with others wearing the same coin around their neck, born under the purple Moon, the Moon that brought change. Other lines snaked towards the priests of other Moons, each with a basket at their feet in which you were supposed to put money.

As though one was supposed to buy a blessing. You were not supposed to think of it that way, though. You were supposed to think of the Temples as members of your family, simply part of your life. Something you never questioned.

Part of your life that swallowed coins as greedily as did matters of rent and food and clothing and hair ribbons and all the other things that six girls required. Once he had them all prenticed out, that would be easier. Maybe then they'd even start bringing in some coins of their own, to help feed the ever-hungry mouth of Life.

If he didn't belong to the Temples, he wouldn't have to give them money.

That thought staggered him so that he actually stopped mid-step, and the fellow behind him banged into him. Eloquence apologized and got back in step, but as they inched forward, he kept thinking about what the coin in his palm would pay for.

Why should he pay anything to the Temples, after all? Did they feed or clothe him? Why, one of the priests had even tried to foist an extra mouth on him that one time, asking him to take that boy somewhere, hadn't it been? But the boy had run away and the Mage had said he was dead. Maybe he and Obedience were together in some heaven, as unlikely as that seemed.

Step forward and step again. He thought about the coin, held so hard he thought he could feel its ridges. The priest was blessing people as perfunctorily as he could, waving them through.

He stopped, and the man behind him bumped into him again and this time made an exasperated noise.

"Sorry," Eloquence said. "I just realized I need to do something." He stepped out of line and the man didn't even hesitate, just moved forward to take his place.

The moment felt like plunging into deep water, alarming, as though the entire attention of the courtyard were fixed on him, but when he looked around, he realized that wasn't true. No one was looking at him, not even the priests.

He edged his way out of the courtyard slowly at first, but by the time he reached the gate he was moving so fast that he was nearly running. He dashed down the cobblestones of the Moonway and thought to himself, "If I never come here again, I never have to give them any coins." He stopped and smiled to himself.

People were gathering, pointing up at something on the cliffs above the city, where the Duke's castle perched. As he looked, he saw one of the towers fall, and his heart, which had been full of joy, shuddered with doubt. He had turned away from the Temples and now this had happened. His decision had felt as though it might change the world, and now it had. Surely the two were unconnected— the Temples had nothing to do with the Duke, after all.

He hurried home, worried about his sisters.

CHAPTER 4

This is the mood of the city, which still does not know it is to be destroyed.

The summer heat makes people lazy, but the rumor spreads quickly. Something, someone has attacked the Duke's castle, but the details are scarce and confusing. Many fear a Sorcerer, but others claim that there are magics in place so no Sorcerer can come here. Worshippers rush along the silvery white cobbles of the Moonway and crowd the Moon Temples, praying to Toj and Hijae and the third, silvery white Moon, but the priests there seem to have no more clue than anyone else.

Down on the docks, there are more ships leaving than coming in, and some of the ones that come in turn around just as fast. Some carry everything their owner has, including families and furniture. There have been bad omens, of late, and every Oracular Pig in the city for the last month has predicted the change of everything. That was inevitably attributed to the power of the coming elections, but now people wondered if there were something else at play.

The city's Beasts work, as they always have, but sometimes they whisper to each other. None of them care whether or not the Duke falls. Most would, in fact, rather see him ended—his deliberate cruelties to the Beasts in his menagerie are as bad as any of the unconscious ones the College of Mages practice. No Beast wants to be sent to either, because no Beasts ever return from either destination.

Instead, they pass along news from the Abolitionist network. They tell each other the ways to take out of town, the rivers to follow, the mountains to cross, if they want to get to Verranzo's New City, where the Beasts are free.

And some of the Beasts murmur that perhaps this city could become like that one. Not a matter of time, they say. A matter of effort. And luck.

The College of Mages has convened a war council. Gathered in their high hall, the room's heat overpowering their best efforts to cool it, they alone of all the city (except for Bella, who may or may not be part of the city) know something of the menace. They used farscrying to watch Lucy destroy the Duke's castle, and they have already expended vast amounts of magic, uselessly, trying to determine what she is. If they know what she is, they say, they can defeat her, for their library holds all of history and how to defeat each thing that has arisen.

They do not say, what if the girl is something new? That would be unthinkable.

But they think it, nonetheless.

SEBASTIANO HAD NEVER BEEN SO happy in all his life, and that was what terrified him. It gave him something to fear losing. Before he'd been happy enough to muddle along, enjoying himself, his studies, his growing mastery over magic, but he hadn't feared it stopping. Hadn't feared losing that existence.

And now he had Adelina in his life, and that was amazing. And terrifying. Because if he lost her, it would be like losing himself entirely.

There was a fly thrashing about in the smooth unguent of his existence, and that would be the relationship between his father and himself, complicated by various factors, not restricted to but including the following:

His father's hostility towards magic as a profession suitable for his son.

Sebastiano's insistence on said magic as a profession, although he had found himself falling into compromise there, less from any desire to do so on his own than the College of Mages' own snobbery towards a member who was born into a Merchant family, rather than one of the families that had devoted generations to the pursuit of Mage or a somewhat lesser status but still quite acceptable member of the noble class, all of whom were directly or indirectly related to the Dukes of Tabat.

The results of his father's insistence that Sebastiano pursue a marital alliance with one of three women, one of whom had been Adelina. At the time that Corrado had offered her as a choice to his son, he had had no way of knowing that Adelina would soon thereafter lose the financial stature she had previously held as Emiliana Nittlescent's heir.

But not only had Adelina been disowned soon before her mother passed away and left the house to a minor cousin, she had also lost the business which might have otherwise left her well pocketed enough to satisfy his father, Spinner Press. But the press had fallen, burned to the ground, and Adelina currently made her money by printing other people's broadsides on the small hand press that had been the best she could afford.

The fact that Sebastiano had, in a rare moment of temper, destroyed the thing that Corrado held dear, the only place he had allowed his effort to stray outside the house he led, his garden. He still remembered the expression on his father's face after Sebastiano had cast the magic that had frozen every plant, a gesture calculated to hurt his father as hard and deeply as in that moment Sebastiano had felt he deserved, a fury born of a life of rubbing up against his father's standards and being found wanting.

Since then, he'd repented of that temper so many times. He'd had his own heart-deep hurt, the loss of Fewk the Griffon, his companion, and every time he thought of the Griffon—as he still did, every day—it hurt him, a gap in his life that he could not help poking at, like a missing tooth. Adelina's presence in his life was helping heal it, but every once in a while he thought about how Fewk would have loved her and it hurt even more.

There was hubbub on the streets when he went out to purchase groceries—a joint for dinner would then provide the base for several lunches and at least one more dinner, at least that was his thought.

But everyone was moving more rapidly than usual, and shoppers were buying more than they usually did, as though worried that the supplies might vanish. Prices, which had already been skyrocketing, seemed to have tripled overnight, and so he picked a smaller joint than he would have liked, and was thinking on how to augment it further.

"What's happening?" he asked the butcher as the woman wrapped up his purchase in orange paper and string.

"Some magic thing up at the Duke's castle," she said, twisting the string around the package in an expert tangle. "Maybe somefin' went wrong, maybe one of his critters got loose." She shrugged. "Maybe both. Fella's been freeloading off this town and its work long enough."

He had thought to take the package home, but perhaps first he would go up to the College of Mages and get the news. Even if he was no longer one of them—cast off by his father, cast off by the College— they'd been ready enough to contract his services so their lives could continue untainted by the presence of money and all the influences of the Trade Gods it brought with it. They claimed it muddled up magic; he had yet to find that to be true, but saying so was one of the reasons they'd been so ready to cast him off.

Thunder in the sky. He would see to Adelina first.

But when he returned, she was not there, and the note on the mantel simply said, "Gone on errands," nothing more than that, so he had no idea where to expect to find her or when to think she might be home.

THE DAY HAD BEGUN in the most ordinary of ways. After kisses and snuggles, Adelina had gone back to sleep and later woken to find Sebastian already there with pastries fetched from the cart down the block and hot chal.

It would have been entirely delightful if she had not woken thinking that she needed to see Jilly sooner rather than later, and feeling that edge of irritation that grated along her nerves whenever too much time had slipped away between one use of the sparkling crystals and the next.

Sebastiano wouldn't understand, she thought, yet again. And it was a harmless thing. It was simply that it made her more *her*, somehow. More convinced of the rightness of her own self, less concerned with what other people thought of her. It let her string together words knowing that she could weave them, and expertly, rather than the more normal sensation of sitting down to write and feeling oneself completely inadequate. It made her feel unworried.

Afterward, though, all the insecurities came creeping back, stronger than ever, and that was very much less than pleasant. Every time it happened, she resolved that this would be the last time, that she would be rid of this sensation, she would ride out the withdrawal and then be rid of this constant companion.

Perhaps she should confess everything to Sebastiano. Ask for his help, even.

But she could not bear the thought that he might think less of her. Know that she was not as strong as he believed her. It was so delicious, the way he looked at her, as though she were the center of his world and, more than that, she was safe to feel the same. He would not cool the way that Bella had. Sebastiano's was an altogether different kind of love, not loud, not flashy. Not a flame that would consume itself and die away.

Losing that would be unbearable.

No, she would continue as she was for now. Sebastiano had gone out for groceries and she had a few moments to herself. Going upstairs, she opened up the sewing kit that had once been Emiliana's, the one that she had left to Adelina, along with a handful of trinkets, and not a copper coin's worth of money. Swinging open its deck, her fingers searched among the spools of thread to find the glass vial hidden towards the back.

She tipped out a few grains and considered them, pretending that she was about to put them away. This was a new moment for her—up until now she had managed to keep from dipping into these when not about to speak before a crowd. Now she shook what she could back into the vial and, before she could allow herself time to think about it, licked up the last two grains that lingered in her palm.

Calmness seeped into her nerves, and she sat, then lay back on the bed and contemplated the ceiling, painted the same inexplicable purple as the walls. This place had been reasonable in price, but it had its eccentricities, and the bedroom color was, if nothing else, the least of it. A set of stairs in their living room led up to the roof, a relic of the building's past as a storehouse, and the windows let out directly onto a vista, three inches away, of gray-green brick, unrelieved by ornament or vegetation.

She let the thoughts of words she might use to describe that vista flow through her mind, savoring the feel and taste of them. She thought of going to get a pad and pencil, writing some down for a possible essay, but she lingered in the bed nonetheless.

Someone's knock on the front door yanked her from her contemplation.

Going to the door, Adelina found her neighbor, an elderly female Scholar, there, looking worried. She said, "I was coming home from chal and people were talking on the street. The Duke's castle— something is happening up there."

"Another political festival?" Adelina said.

"No … I don't think so," the old woman faltered.

She scrawled a note for Sebastiano and the two of them used her own personal egress up to the roof of the building. There were already a few other of the four-story brick building's tenants there, arrived through the main stairwell and all looking up and northward to the castle. As Adelina joined them, she saw a cloud of what must be dust hung around the castle and several of the towers were falling.

Her mind went cold and sharp. She was witnessing something that would matter decades, maybe centuries from now. This was history, and must be recorded, must be preserved. She said to the nearest woman, "What has happened so far?"

"Was a flash and then I saw a tower fall," she said. "Can't make out what's happening. Someone said that maybe it was something the Duke cooked up, trying to scare people into sticking by him. Wouldn't put it past the greedy bastard."

Adelina stared up at the castle, straining her eyes to try to discern what was going on. She ran downstairs and rummaged through the desk till she found the spyglass there that sometimes served as paperweight and took it back up.

But the brass tube did not unravel the mystery for her. She could not make out what was happening, though she could see that crowds were running down the road, away from the castle, escaping whatever it was that menaced the place.

Sebastiano appeared from the stairwell doorway, glancing through the crowd for her and moving to her side. "What's going on?" he said.

"You tell me," she said. "Can't you look with magic?"

"If I had taken the time to enchant something, maybe," he said. "Here." He took the telescope from her and twisted it in his hands a few times before giving it back to her. She put it to her eye and found things somewhat clearer. "That is a proper use of magic," she said approvingly.

"I adjusted the lens," Sebastiano said drily.

But despite the improved sight, no matter how it had been arrived at, she still could not tell.

"It surely is something serious," she said.

Sebastiano stared up the hill, frowning. "I will go to the College of Mages," he said suddenly.

"I thought you do not like to go there, that it reminds you of what fools they are for casting you out."

He gave her a fond look. "That is a tactful and utterly biased way of putting it. It is as though you were skilled with words."

"Indeed," she said, and nuzzled him, forgetting the rest of the world for the moment. "Perhaps I should take up some profession that has to do with weaving them."

They clung together, lost in the world they held between them, until the representative of the real one, their neighbor, cleared her throat significantly.

They drew apart.

"Will you come with me?" he asked.

She shook her head. "I will go to the Merchants' Council. There will be news there. They will have sent runners to see what was going on."

And on the way to there was Jilly's little house, and if she stopped today, she would not need to tomorrow. She would be a bit ahead. She chewed her lip.

"What's wrong?" Sebastiano asked.

"I was thinking about buying some new ink while I am out," she said.

"Do you need coins?" he asked, as she had hoped that he would. Ever since they had taken up together, Corrado had not been particularly warm towards Sebastiano, but had demonstrated his approval of this state of affairs by making sure that they always had enough to pay the rent.

She took them from him and kissed his cheek before they made their way back downstairs and off.

CHAPTER 5

All the way home, Eloquence fondled the coin in his pocket and thought about what a difference having the money that normally would have gone to the Temples would make to him. Should he tell his sisters about all of this? Perhaps not. Probably not.

After all, he was in the habit of threatening to sell them to the Temples if they didn't behave, and that was a useful threat. No, they could keep thinking that they should obey the Moons. And they should, really. He didn't need to because he was the one taking care of things, but they were being taken care of. Anything that kept them quiet was useful and should be used.

It was so hard being in charge of seven—no, six, he amended with a twinge—girls. None of them seemed inclined to hard work of the sort he had done, no matter how he tried to find them a good prenticeship. Perhaps he should start looking for matches to harder-working sorts for some of them, but he had no faith in their ability to keep a house the way such a match would implicitly demand, nor were any of them particularly beautiful or socially graceful. They brought nothing to such a match except themselves, and that wouldn't take them far in Merchant-minded Tabat.

He was turning over the notion of actually promising two of them (but which two, that would be difficult) to the Temples, and perhaps even getting a profit for himself in the process, when he turned into his street.

A man and a woman were sitting on the stoop of his house. They looked to be northern travelers, an older woman and her husband or perhaps brother, travelworn and not particularly clean. As he approached, he scowled at them to signal that they were sitting where they should not. They did get up, but not to leave, but rather to address him.

"Eloquence Seaborn?" the man said. He spoke with a country accent, and looked to be a Northerner, unfashionably pale, his clothing worn but neatly mended.

"I am," Eloquence said warily. Was this something to do with his refusal to give the Temples money? How would they have possibly realized his decision already? No, he was just being paranoid. "What would you have?"

"Our son," the man said.

Eloquence laughed. "I have no boys here, only girls, and useless ones at that." He saw Absolution and Grace, looking out through the window. Very well, let them hear his opinion of them. Maybe they would learn to be a little more grateful that he did what he did, but he suspected not.

"Our boy. The priest Grave gave him to you to look after."

Teo. Of course. Teo, who had run away into the city, and died, surely. He felt his smile falter despite his best efforts. "Have you gone to the Temples?" he hedged.

"Yes. They said you were the last to see him."

Eloquence spread his hands. "He ran away, soon as we hit the docks, before anyone could catch him. I've spent time going up and down Tabat, looking for him," he added, trying to make it sound as though this had been a daily hunt, rather than the sporadic "I wonder where he went to" look around. "It's a big city, and plenty of people looking for a smart boy to work for them," he said reassuringly. He would not tell them that the Mage had said the boy was dead. Let them keep their hopes alive, since they would not be able to confirm or deny them.

But the two of them only stared at him, as though they didn't understand his words.

"We realized it wasn't the place for him," the woman said. "I missed him. We made a promise and we would keep it but …" She looked away.

"The Moons have broken their oath to us as well," the father said heavily. "We offered him if his sister lived and she did for a handful of days, after he'd left. And then the fever came again. I did not promise my child for only a handful of days with the other. The gods have reneged on their bargain and I will have my son back."

Sympathy filled Eloquence. Like him, they were realizing that the Temples were … well, were not everything his parents had told him they would be. Had they changed over time, or had he? Perhaps a mixture. He said, "Come in and eat, at least."

He sat them in the parlor and gave them Mercy to talk to, she was chattersome enough that she'd keep them entertained. Honesty had prepared a bean soup, and Eloquence surreptitiously added more water. There was bread enough, at least, and he shared the thin beer that he had put away for some special occasion.

"I am sure you will find him," he lied, feeling the lie, lumpy and uncomfortable in his mouth as the soup's not entirely cooked beans. Personally he thought if the boy had not died, he would have been impressed as a sailor. The latter was not supposed to happen, but it did, particularly to young folk who could be trained to ship life.

"Perhaps," the father said. "We've come to the city at a bad time, it seems. Folk were saying the Duke's castle were under attack this morning."

"They say so, but half a day has passed since that happened and nothing more," Eloquence said. "It is some political trick on the part of the Duke. He does not want to be deposed, but the nature of the coming elections is such that he will be."

He launched into a disquisition upon the complex nature of Tabatian politics, and the long-ago promise that would be forcing the

Duke out of his position. They should know what sort of atmosphere they would be finding themselves in, with the elections so near. They would not be able to vote, but they should at least be informed as to the greatness of the occasion they were privileged to witness.

Perhaps since he was not supporting the Temples, he need not vote for their candidate? That was a thrilling thought. He could go to some rallies, let different groups try to woo him with sausages and beer.

The pair listened patiently to his account of what was happening in the city, but when Eloquence looked again, the woman had nodded off on her husband's shoulder, and he was valiantly fighting to stay awake himself. They had come a long way. Eloquence could shelter them for tonight.

Only tonight, though.

I KNOW the way to Leonoa's as well as I do the way to my own house, a thought that gives me a pang, remembering the landlady, Abernia, that last day I saw her. Abernia had believed all the charges despite knowing me for years. Had looked at me with disgust, while behind her people filed in and out of the house, taking away all of my worldly possessions, to be sold and the money given to the Crown.

That is something to think about. All of my money and goods have been confiscated, and how am I to pay for anything, if I have no holdings? I will go to Myrila, perhaps, after I have seen Leonoa, and offer to work for her as an instructor again.

I trot down the Tumbril Stair. Everyone is talking about whatever was happening up at the Duke's castle. That would be Lucy, bent on the sort of destruction she had wreaked in the Southern Isles.

And then where will the girl go, once she is done with the castle and the Duke? Only logical to think she will move on the city, but surely she must have some ties here, some family.

Another thing that Adelina will know, if only I can find her.

Trotting up Leonoa's familiar street, I feel myself relaxing. My cousin will help me.

I knock three times, heart surging with happiness. It has been so long since I saw my cousin, my favorite cousin. She will be delighted to see me as well. Will take me in and tell me all the happenings, catch me up on what has happened during my exile.

But the steps that come down the stairs are too light and quick to be Leonoa's and I know by that cadence who will be standing there when the door opens.

Glyndia, golden hair and feathers, the woman who claimed not to be a Beast but a victim of sorcery. Leonoa's shocking lover, the one who had inspired her to paint pictures of a new world, one where Beasts were considered just as valuable as Humans, and, shockingly, acted like them.

"Bella Kanto?" Glyndia says, startled. "How are you here?"

"I had to come back."

Glyndia glances up and down the empty street. "But surely they are looking for you?"

I shake my head. "There are other things to keep them occupied, and it will get worse before it gets better. I must speak with Leonoa."

But Glyndia does not step aside. "She is not here right now."

"Then I will wait."

Glyndia does not waver. "She is imprisoned, Bella."

"What?"

"The Duke had her arrested a week ago. For her paintings." For the first time, Glyndia does not look like the serene, beautiful and unmovable creature I first met. Now I notice a few crumpled and broken feathers, and a dullness to the golden shine of the wings spread behind her. Her clockwork hands are clasped in front of her. "The trial is next week."

"They'll never get to it."

"Why? Do you plan to break her out?"

Once I might have reacted to the sneer masking the pain under the words, but I have learned to look a little deeper. This woman loves my cousin, and she is here, watching over her studio, and more, has been doing it all this time while I was gone. So I say, "I wish I could. But the city is under attack."

Now she simply looks bewildered. "Attack?"

I point up towards the Duke's castle. "See the fallen towers?"

Her eyes narrow. This is the price Alberic has paid for distance. His own city does not remark on his falling, because it has happened outside the city limits and people believe that this city will never fall. Who would dare attack Tabat?

"Her name is Lucy," I say. "I don't know how she can wield the magics she does, but she does, and she will destroy the city."

"This is too much for me," Glyndia said. Her eyes are unkind, so unkind. She thinks me mad, perhaps. "You are a criminal and an exile, and I am in enough hot water without you jumping into the pot."

"I will get her out," I tell her. I don't know how but I am back in Tabat, and if that is possible, anything is possible.

She closes the door in my face.

FILLED WITH NOSTALGIA AND IRRITATION, Sebastiano went to the College of Mages. He'd been useful to them, had helped them build and administer their coffers, and then they'd thrown him out because he had no money to give them directly. It had been a short-sighted maneuver on their part, costing them long-term profit; his Merchantly side knew that for certain, but they had never acknowledged it.

Still, if you wanted to find out what was happening on the magical side of matters, there was no better place to go.

Cobbles gritted under his heels, and he dragged his fingers along the iron fence of the College as he walked along, feeling the bite and prickle of its warding magics. A sense of urgency rode the crowds now, particularly here. From the Duke's castle it was only a cliff's length and then a few terraces.

At the gates there were, unusually, guards. "Your business?" one demanded.

"To see Master Mage Faustino," Sebastiano said.

The guards exchanged looks. "He is too busy for visitors right now," the other said. "Come back another day."

"I am a Mage," Sebastiano pressed.

"You are not," said another person, coming up. Gley, whom Sebastiano had always disliked. "He was removed from the College for failure to pay his tuition," Gley, thin and pale and full of spite, said to the guards with the slightest of sneers.

It had been considerably more complicated than that, and in Sebastiano's mind, the College owed him a great deal more than he owed them, but when they had chosen to add the cost of Fewk's death to his arrears because he had insisted on burying the Griffon rather than letting him be chopped up for magical ingredients, he had simply quit and resolved to go about his own business.

It was a path not many took—given that it cut them off from the ample resources that the College offered—but more than one Mage had chosen that path for one reason or another.

But it was definitely a path that could be employed to forbid him the College, he realized more fully now, looking at the slight smirk on Gley's face. Before, his presence had always been tolerated, undoubtedly because he did bring some value to the College, having been willing to do trade on their behalf, despite all the maxims that said that trade and money were antithetical to magic.

He had never found that to be true, and had thought perhaps his experience differed from that of the "normal" folk. Or it might be that the Mages, conscious of their social class, had chosen to ally themselves with the longer-lined nobility rather than with the Merchant Houses that had emerged here in the city as it had progressed—through three centuries now, though, so surely the Merchants' names were well established historically, despite all the muddles that Old and New Continent naming systems had created.

"Gley," Sebastiano said, making his voice as reasonable as possible. "We are in a time of crisis at the moment, and surely the College needs everyone who has any amount of magical power at their command. If not that, then I would ask you to at least let me come onto the grounds and speak to whoever is not, unlike Master Mage Faustino, busy, because ..."

Because I might know something of what is happening if it involves Beasts, he would have said, but Gley cut him off before he could finish his sentence. "Everyone here is quite busy," he said with a politeness so perfunctory that it bordered on insulting, "You should return to your home and wait further word. I am sure that the Master Mage will send a messenger to you if it turns out he should be needing you."

In the face of such brazen disdain, Sebastiano's temper flared, but he throttled it back. For now. "I see," he said. "I presume it would be of no use to leave word with you for him."

"No use," the other said, cheerfully, but added, "Less that I would not relay it to him, but that I cannot. As I said, everyone at the College is extraordinarily busy right now ...." His eyes flickered upwards towards where the remnants of the Duke's castle could be seen. "Are you not married recently, or did I mishear? Go home to your spouse and take care of them and your household."

The unexpected warmth in the other's voice startled Sebastiano into silence.

Gley simply nodded at the lack of response. "I mean you no malice, Merchant Mage," he said, and there was weariness in his tone, "but I have sat up all night—as has almost everyone here—because all the omens were suddenly pointing to disaster. Now the Duke's castle has fallen and we are trying to figure out what is going on and how best to fight against it. If you should find out anything, I say with all sincerity to let us know."

"The circus on your grounds ..." Sebastiano said.

"Yes, I have heard that you think it a hotbed of revolution because of all its Beasts. But you are tardy in speaking again, because they have already left our grounds."

"Left?" Sebastiano said.

"Not so much left as abandoned, much of it," the Mage said. "Brand new tents and other stuff like it, left rolled and moldering in the meadow there. The cages, all of them empty, their doors unlocked, and the horses and other dray-animals unharnessed and vanished with the rest. The student Mages go there sometimes and play among the machineries and the booths full of petty competitions. All quite bewildering. What would you say of such a thing, Merchant Mage, if you were to make observations?"

Sebastiano thought. "That to abandon everything like that—and newly purchased, as you have indicated, stuff made for the occasion and never used elsewhere—would be a costly proposition. Someone must have funded all of that. And if they left—where would they be now?"

"Still in the city, by all accounts, although all of the Beasts have gone to ground. But it turns out there were almost no Humans whatsoever in its employ, or so we found when we examined the rosters that had been left behind. I think they went to ground here, split up and scattered, vanished among the rest of the crowds of Beasts that fill Tabat."

A messenger ran up to speak to the Mage, whispering quickly and urgently. "Excuse me," he said, and left without further explanation, but before he did, he said to the guard, "I was mistaken as to who it was. This fellow's all right, and you can let him in." He shrugged off Sebastiano's bewildered thanks and was gone.

Sebastiano made his way through the gate with haste, before anyone could change their mind, but on the other side, he took a moment to collect his wits and wonder again at the other Mage's change in attitude.

Sometimes people you thought were the villain of your story were only characters from their own stories passing through, he thought. More often than not.

CHAPTER 6

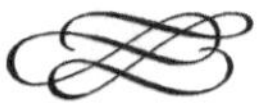

*A*delina knew where Jilly Clearsight lived, along Pipe Lane, a twisty little street of small, neat houses. She knocked at the door, its lintel scattered with purple tiles, and no one answered. She listened and thought she heard a footfall. "Is anyone there?" she called, but no one answered.

Well, perhaps Jilly was at her shop. Yes, that was probably the better bet, she thought.

But the shop was closed, and a sign on the doorway said Jilly would return tomorrow, gone on errands. Adelina sourly wondered how she could possibly predict where Jilly had gone. If she had Sebastian's magic, no doubt she could have twitched her nose and had it tingle when pointed in the right direction.

Very well, she would go to the Merchants' Council and find out what they were speaking of whatever was happening up at the Duke's castle.

THE PLACE that hosted every major Merchants' Council meeting was the Main Trade Hall, located on the third terrace of the city, close enough to the docks to make it easy to go down there if one needed to, but also convenient enough to the tram lines if one needed to send a messenger elsewhere. It reminded her of childhood trips there with her mother, back when she had thought it would ever be possible to win her mother's favor.

The building had existed since Tabat's earliest days, a large, four-story building made of white limestone that had been quarried several miles up the coast, leaving one of them substantially diminished in stature. It was an architecture whose stones spoke of no frills but attempts at elegance in the heart of what had at that time been a frontier city, albeit one carefully planned by its founders. Those plans, Adelina knew, had been met time after time by unexpected circumstances: the discoveries of the vast caverns underneath the planned city's spot being one of the largest, but hardly the only one.

The stones were not ornate, but not so the great colored glass windows depicting all the many gods of trade. Uhfawyanbi, surrounded by dark clouds. Angrato, helping load a ship. Domkepku, Adelina's favorite since a very young age, in a window in an obscure corner, slouched atop a pile of books.

The guards refused to let her in at first, but she persuaded them that if she could not be admitted as a Merchant, since she was no longer allied to the house of her birth, then she could be considered a Scholar, there to record the events of the Council for history. Every Merchant, even their guards, understood the importance of keeping track of things.

It seemed as though every Merchant in the city were there, trying to find out not just what had happened, but what the council intended to do about it and what contracts might come out of it. Right now, most of them were standing about in small groups, ranging from pairs speaking to each other to larger clusters exchanging words back and forth.

Even in all her speaking engagements, Adelina had not been in such a close press of people since the riot at Bernarda's gallery—earlier that year, though it seemed a lifetime ago now. At the engagements she was usually isolated from the crowd backstage, to be put forth before them, still at a distance, to speak, and then hustled off.

Here she was an anonymous part of the mob, jostled this way and that, trying to pick her way through the throngs, sidestepping as necessary, sometimes giving way to someone else, but always, inexorably, moving towards the center stage and the Chief of the Merchants' Council (they were never allowed to call themself the Chief Merchant, by law). At length she found a good spot near the stage but not one where the ebb and sweep of the crowd would affect her much.

She'd dreamed of the riot at Bernarda's ever since it happened, a nightmare full of the smell of spilled punch and the crowd's perfumes, fire licking at every corner as she sought to escape. Now she felt that same urgent restlessness, that heightened sense of danger. Was it because she was here unbolstered by the drug? But no, that was only necessary when she was going to speak, not just listen.

She told her heart to still, but it hammered on, an uncomfortable and disconcerting feeling. Leaning on the wall, she worked at catching her breath and ignored the proceedings.

And so it startled her when an abrupt hush fell over the crowd. She looked up to the stage where lights shone to cast the Chief of the Merchants' Council in a cone of illumination, glittering off the metallic embroidery of his waistcoat, the jeweled buttons at his cuff.

Emiliana had hoped to hold that position once, but her untimely death had prevented her ever taking it. And certainly she had—for at least a little while—hoped that Adelina would hold it, perhaps even be the first Merchant Scholar to hold the title.

But that had been a dream that Adelina had broken her mother of, after all that time of hope, by letting her know she had engaged not just in business, but one highly disreputable and at odds with her mother's dream, that of publishing. The Trade Gods that ruled her business—advertising and rumor and fickle public opinion—were not ones that her mother countenanced.

And that was fine, she thought, listening to the Chief.

"My fellow Merchants," he began, surveying the crowd with just the right note of gravity and satisfaction at their numbers and reassurance. Adelina could feel the crowd quieting a little. She wondered if he had partaken of Jilly's drug, a sharp wonder that made her look at him more closely, but no, it seemed to be a natural talent. He said, "The Duke's castle has been thrown down. The Duke still lives, but the Peacekeepers have taken him to a location which I cannot disclose."

Murmurs from the crowd, which seemed to think that was all very well and proper, but when push came to shove, they were much less concerned with the Duke's holdings than they were with their own, after all. What was going to be done, voices rose to demand.

The Chief—what was his name again? She'd gone through school with one of his daughters, so he was a Knothammer, but she couldn't remember his own appellation—spread his hands with a practiced gesture, and the muttering stilled momentarily.

"You want to know what will become of the city proper," he said, "and that is right and good, because we are all invested in it to one degree or another. The Peacekeepers are patrolling to make sure no random Beasts decide to take advantage of the chaos, you will be glad to know."

"But what about the source of the chaos?" someone shouted from the back of the crowd.

There were other cheers at the frankness of the question, but the Chief of the Merchants' Council looked unperturbed by the question.

"The force that destroyed the castle is as yet unknown, but messages from the College of Mages confirm that it is magical in nature and that they believe it to be some new form of Beast, perhaps created by a Sorcerer gone rogue, or even perhaps a Sorcerer who has decided to wage a frontal attack on the city for unknown reasons.

"In the meantime, we have created a system of tariffs to ensure that prices are maintained at an equilibrium during these difficult times. No one wants to be accused of profiteering—"

"But we all want to profit!" yelled another person towards the back of the crowd, a woman this time.

The Chief of the Merchants' Council stayed calm and patient.

Adelina had to admire the man's poise, which must have been a major factor in the decision to put him in his current role. Meric, that was his name, a pale and doughy man with the coloring of a Northerner. His house had made their start in fishing nets, and later branched out to other ropework and rigging, and then sails.

"We all want to see the city prosper," he proclaimed. "The best way to do so is stay about your business and keep an eye on any Beasts in your employ."

This all seemed far less helpful than Adelina had hoped. Although now that she thought about it, there was no real reason for the Merchants to have some special hold on how to go about business while a segment of the city was under attack.

She found herself summoning her voice as readily as she ever had under the drug. "What news from the Duke's castle?" she called. "How many are dead, and how did they die?"

The Chief gazed in her direction. "There are at least a hundred dead," he admitted. "Eleven of them our own."

Shocked intakes of breath sounded throughout the chamber. Adelina was a little staggered herself. But it made sense—not just all the inhabitants of the castle, all the servants and guards and other people who serviced the Duke's wants, but there would have been visitors as well, since the castle—or at least the gardens of its outer bounds—was a popular location for school trips and other outings. Ambassadors and officials, she thought, but still—over a hundred?

"Eyewitnesses have mixed reports," the Chief of the Merchants' Council went on. "We will be posting news here on the main boards, and you are welcome to use them to coordinate the movement of your goods. I will remind everyone that the banks are very safe and you should be ready to put your money there for safekeeping, rather than try to carry it about with you or hidden somewhere in your house in these perilous times."

Adelina wondered how much the banks were paying to have that assurance underscored. She assumed a hefty amount directly into the guild's coffers. This was all useless though. She had expected some sort of definitive word about what was happening. She hoped that there was some better information at the College of Mages, and that Sebastian's foray there would be more successful in finding out what was actually happening.

As she exited, she found herself speaking to more people than she had meant to. So many knew her from her speaking engagements, wanted to congratulate her on some speech or another. It was different from being an author, where people read your books but knew nothing of your face. And it felt as though every time she spoke to someone now, she failed to match up to their estimation of her. She saw it in face after face, marking her a very different figure than what they had expected from the brilliance of her speeches.

Making excuses to avoid further conversation, she hurried home. At her dresser, she fumbled with what she had left of Jilly's powder. So few grains! But perhaps there was more; twice she had forgotten a little vial of it only to find it later. Surely that was the case, that there was some small stash of it hidden among her small clothes. Recklessly, she tipped the last of what she had into her mouth, not thinking about what if she was wrong.

Because, she found to her later dismay, she was. Search as she might, through every pocket, pouch, or other possible hiding place, there was nothing left of the powder she knew she would come to crave soon, and the anticipation of that craving was almost as bad as when it started.

THE ATMOSPHERE of the College of Mages was troubled, clots of students hurrying here and there, others crowded together to talk amongst themselves, although Sebastiano noticed older Mages hurrying to break up such clusters.

On one corner, Master Rehallow, whom Sebastiano had always cordially hated, was preaching to a gathered crowd, the same story he had been spinning for decades: magical creatures will overtake the Humans and kill them. The sort of story that led to the tormenting, sometimes killing, of Beasts.

Habit drew Sebastiano halfway to the stables that had been his home for years before he'd been ousted, and curiosity drew him the rest of the way. The yard outside held no Beasts. He had thought to find his old quarters occupied, but the entirety of the stable lay empty and musty, and the racks were bare of feed. Only mouse droppings showed where once grain had been spilled.

The stairs creaked beneath him as he went up to the loft that had housed him for so many years. As he opened the door, there was a flutter out the open window, and he realized some small Fairies had been nesting there, judging from the scattering of flower petals and candy wrappers. When he looked out the window, he could see them sitting in the pine tree, waiting for him to leave again.

He closed the window and turned back to the empty, furnitureless room, in which he had spent so many years.

The air smelled of old hay and dust. He laid himself down on the hard floorboards to think, folding his hands over his stomach and looking up at the ceiling's bare rafters and the iron hooks that he'd hung his study lanterns from.

"Fewk," he said to the empty air. "Are you there?" He knew in his heart there would be no answer from the dead Griffon, but hope still surged in his heart. An errant fly buzzed against the windowpanes and the Fairies outside bickered softly among themselves.

"I'll talk to you anyway," he said, interlacing his fingers over his stomach and wriggling as though he could somehow make himself more comfortable on the boards. "I'm worried about the future, Fewk. And starting a family with Adelina. I want children, but I know they can never see you, and that grieves me.

"And it's not that I mean for them to ever know a Beast in servitude," he confessed. "My mother is right; what has happened is wrong. And you died while in the service of the College, and I fought to have you buried rather than chopped up. It was a fate unworthy of you."

The thought of Fewk was so vivid that it was almost a ghost itself. He closed his eyes and remembered the dusty sweet smell of Fewk's downy undercoat, the sleek shine to his hard horn beak, or the great furry voice grumbling to him as he worked at combing through Fewk's plumage. He still carried dried apricots in his pocket, telling himself that it was in case he ran across any creature that might be coaxed with a sweetmeat.

He wondered if Fewk's body had been left unmolested or if the College had lied and dug him up afterward anyway. He wouldn't put it past them.

The bell in the center of the College of Mages began to ring, harsh urgent strokes that did not cease. Something was happening in the College and for a few moments he thought of going there, to see what was happening, but they had rejected him enough for one day.

He made his way through the crowds converging on the main building, moving in the opposite direction, swimming against a strong current. He went back home and to Adelina.

CHAPTER 7

eo knew so few people here in the city. And none that he
trusted. He had been gone how long? It was so hard to
remember things from when he was in dog form—all of that seemed
hazy and unsure now, as though his thoughts had been elsewhere.

But he had seen a familiar face in the horror of the Duke's
courtyard, one that had fallen when a tower collapsed at Lucy's
gesture. Jilly Clearsight had been kind, up until the point he let her pet
Griffon out into the cold—an accident! But the creature had died
either way, whether accident or intention, and so Jilly had every right
to be angry. She had said a strange thing, though. Had said the Griffon
was her father. A figure of speech? But it had not sounded like that.

And what had the Griffon said?

It didn't matter. He could find temporary shelter in her house. She
had lived alone; there would be no one to discover him.

He wanted to avoid the College of Mages in case Murga's circus,
the Circus of the Autumn Moon—and by extension Murga—was still
there.

All along the wrought-iron fence of the Piskie Wood, Piskie heads
were impaled on the high points. He remembered waking up on the

other side of the fence, after he'd first been able to turn into his other form, the cougar. Now every time he thought about that form, the figure of the dog he had been intervened, refused to let him flow into that shape. It was an itch that could not be scratched, a bruise that refused to heal.

Jilly's house was shuttered and dark, as were most of the other houses on the street. Woodsmoke rose from the two closest to the mouth of the street, but no one stirred at the windows of either house. He hovered on the step for a few moments, looking up and down the street. No one seemed to be watching him and after a few minutes, he slipped around to the back and the fenced garden.

A statue of a Griffon startled him until he realized what it was. A placard on the bottom was illegible, but he suspected the Griffon he had killed—or rather, just allowed to come to harm—was laid underneath.

He tried the windows cautiously and found one unlocked at the back. Holding his breath, he raised it, listening intently—what if this were no longer her house? What if someone had come to live with her? What if she had acquired other, possibly dangerous pets?—But no alarm came and finally he took a deep breath and crawled through the opening to find himself in the kitchen.

The house was still full of paintings, clinging to every wall, each depicting a single ship.

He didn't want to make a fire. What if a neighbor saw the evidence of life and thinking Jilly at home, came to see her? So he was careful with light or smoke, leaving the basket of eggs alone despite their allure. Instead he carved himself chunks of the cheese and sausage from the larder, and poured himself a mug of cider from the squat jug, and ate them ravenously at first until he almost choked himself, then more slowly.

His stomach full, he went upstairs and took a blanket from the bed, brought it down to the lower room and curled himself onto the couch. What was he to do next? Jilly was gone but at some point someone would surely come to check on her house. Lucy was here in the city, and who knew what she intended, but he did not think it was a good thing for Tabat that she was here now.

No, he thought. He would find a way to go north. He would find a way to go home. There was no reason not to. Once there, surely the memory of being a dog would have faded, and he could take on his cougar shape again. He would be a Shifter as fully as any other member of his village, and that meant none of his peers could tease him anymore.

In fact, since he would be the only one of them to have ever traveled outside the village, his status might rise a bit. It would be good to see his sister and his parents, and if the Moons objected, well then, they could try to stop him on his trip however they liked. But by now he had little faith in the Moons. They meant nothing, were only shapes in the sky and a way to scare children.

He turned over and tucked the blanket around himself. He could hear the soft roar of the waterfall in the plaza, outside in the night where it was cold. There was a certain satisfaction to being warm, and dozy, and safe (for the moment). He might as well relax. For now.

He thought of the garden and the statue of the Griffon. He regretted his carelessness so much! But he could not undo it, could never undo it, and now he couldn't even make it up to Jilly, because she was dead.

As it turned out, the pair of visitors proved a welcome distraction to Eloquence, keeping his mind away from the turmoil in the city. Both volunteered to help with the evening meal, and he found that having two extra pairs of hands made the preparation a much simpler thing. Even enjoyable when the father entertained him with tales of hunting some of the same creatures he'd glimpsed in his travels along the river.

Not all of the girls came in for this meal and their demeanor was sullen and heat-addled. He wished they could eat outside, where there might be a breeze, but not with so many of them. Again, the thought of promising two to the Temples crossed his mind, and he studied the ones around him, since they were the most likely candidates, with the others encouragingly out at their prenticeships.

The mother, Etta, had not just searched Mamma's own spice drawer, but supplemented it with her own.

"Makes trail food more homey-like," she'd explained to Eloquence as she dug through the pouch of spices in her pack. "And thought, maybe, I'd cook somefin' for Teo, if we … once we find him."

She managed not to glance over to her husband but busied herself about the cooking, and so did not catch the look he gave Eloquence before launching into another hunting story.

Eloquence thought the result of their combined efforts quite fine, which is why it infuriated him that Mercy took one sniff and contented herself with bread, while Honesty and Compassion made continuous sour faces at each mouthful. He redoubled his own eating efforts and smiled warmly at Etta as he held out his bowl for thirds.

"I try, but it's not something I know well," he admitted to her. "Can't seem to make home-cooked food the way Ma used to."

One of the girls murmured, "'Tain't nothing like what Ma used to make," but he ignored her, although it was an effort.

"You have a great many hands to help you here!" Etta said, beaming around her. But her cheerful smile faltered as none of the girls returned her gaze, still scowling and sullen.

"Ignore them," Eloquence said. "They are a surly lot, and do not understand how well off they are." He pulled the bowl towards himself and shoveled it down determinedly. He said, loudly, "I wish one of the girls had such a fine touch with spice and salt, but that is apparently too much to hope for."

He did not add that it was not a skill he himself had managed to pick up with all his travel on the riverboat.

At the thought of the river, of the serenity of water flowing past, of sitting in the pilot house watching the shore and its endless, fascinating vistas, a pang gripped him to the point where he put his spoon down.

He wanted to say to his sisters that they did not understand all he had given up for them, but surely they knew! Surely they were full of ingratitude, to treat him so! He did not understand them, any of them, anymore. One day they had all been sweet girls, flocking to give him kisses and affection whenever he returned, so happy for whatever trinkets he had brought them, because he was a good sibling, and always brought something for each and every one of them, and played no favorites! And the next they were sullen, and angry, and uncooperative.

He scowled now at them, and their faces faltered as they turned themselves to the bowls. No one made conversation as they ate the last of the meal and when he had finished, Eloquence ordered two of them to wash up, and took himself out onto the stoop to watch the early evening with the father.

People were passing along the street, talking fervently.

"You've come at an odd time," he said to the man, Donas. "Everything in upheaval, I suppose you understand all that."

"We heard along the road that Tabat is changing, and not doing it graceful-like," Donas said. He took out a smoke pouch and rolled himself a small cigarette. Eloquence shook his head when offered the pouch to follow suit. "Not a habit they encourage on the boats," he said.

"Ah? You'd think it different, surrounded by water."

"Too easy for cargo to go up fast, particularly packed tight."

"Stands to reason." Donas lit his spill the old-fashioned way, sparking flint to a bit of tinder, and then using it to light the end. He breathed out blue smoke. "It's a country custom, I think," he said, leaning back against the solidity of the stone step. "But our herbalist back home uses it for medicines, too, and she claims it tests the lungs."

"Everyone to their own vices." Eloquence stretched out his legs and patted the tautness of his stomach. "After a good meal, anything that lets you breathe a bit while you digest is welcome."

They sat there watching the street until Donas said into the silence, "He is a good boy, my Teo."

The mention of the name splashed Eloquence with surprise.

"Indeed," he hurried to agree. "He worked hard aboard the boat while he was with me."

"And you have not seen him in the city anywhere? His mother claims that she would know if he was dead, but sometimes people believe what they wish to believe."

Very well, then, he would be honest. "The Mage took his coin and cast magic, and said he was dead," Eloquence said bluntly. "But is the coin the boy, so strongly that such magic is reliable? I have thought sometimes that the Mage wanted to assuage his own guilt in the boy's escape. I have talked with him since and he is a shifty sort."

He adjusted his seat on the stone, leaning forward. "Perhaps he even knew more about things than he said. Perhaps the escape was staged in some way."

"You said a Dryad attacked him and Teo ran away in the confusion," Donas said dubiously.

"A Mage whose specialty is Beasts, who knows what he could manipulate one to do? But it is only a thought that has occurred to me. A few times."

"Mmm," the man said. He took a breath and stretched his arms. "We have traveled far today," he said apologetically. "I must go in and see how my wife is doing, and then we must go to sleep, in order to renew our search tomorrow."

Eloquence felt a little disappointed. He did not get the chance for adult company, a chance to sit and talk this way, very often, when not on the boat. But he nodded agreeably, and after Donas had gone in, did not sit too long there himself.

Foot traffic had died down and the street seemed lonely and silent. Insects buzzed late-summer song in the trees, but it sounded ominous, a warning pressing in on him, saying that something was to come.

Whatever had happened up at the Duke's castle, it was not a solitary incident. Striking at the castle was striking at the heart of the city. What blows would be dealt to it by whatever menace this was, in the days to come?

SEBASTIANO HAD HOPED that whichever of them got home first would put the soup kettle on, but he found the fire cold and Adelina at the table not preparing dinner but reading over a set of notebooks.

"What are you researching?" he said, trying not to let his impatience tinge his tone. He was apparently successful, for Adelina paid no attention to it, but began to tell him about the meeting she had attended with the Merchants. He listened attentively, though he took the time to start the fire as he did so. He chopped fresh vegetables to add to the existing broth and stirred in a handful of dried fish. They had only a heel of bread left; he'd go by Figgis in the morning.

"I have been going back through some of the annals to find if there has been anything like this," Adelina said in conclusion.

"I would think you would have known about it already if it had," he said. "You are Tabat's most notable historian."

She paused long enough to reward the flattery with a kiss, but also did not deny it. "There are often things hidden between the pages in history books," she said.

He studied her. "You seem distracted," he said. There was something about her, but what was it?

She shook her head. "The Duke's castle under attack, the city full of political riots, what could possibly distract me?" She did not meet his eyes, but instead kept scanning the pages. He understood her preoccupation. Magic research was the same way. You knew a solution had to exist, somewhere in the intricacy of magical theory, but chasing it down was a matter of intuition and guesswork in assembling the information that existed. No wonder she seemed a little withdrawn.

He settled himself on the couch with several histories of his own, but he did not delude himself that he would find any answers there. Instead he found himself studying Adelina as she worked, smiling to himself. The smudge on her nose was infinitely endearing, something he'd often seen her incur while pushing her reading glasses up her nose after making a note.

She looked up to catch him at it. For just a second, her expression was not what he expected, was something slightly irritated, slightly furtive, but then she smiled back and he knew everything was fine.

CHAPTER 8

Lucy had arrived in the city at morning and by midday had slain all opposition willing to come against her at this time, though she suspected the College of Mages was waiting, thinking about how they would try her. Teo had vanished at some point, but she could always track him down later, and the longer she took to do that, the more she could justify punishing him. Maybe she'd turn him back into a dog. That would be amusing.

She had found a perch, atop the highest—and only—remaining tower, and slept there for most of the afternoon, but fitfully, waking again and again to think some foe was creeping up on her, even though it would have taken wings to reach her, and she did not think any Beast would cooperate in flying to its doom.

As dusk darkened the city, she looked it over from her vantage point. Should she explore the city further? Teo would be easy enough to track down. He would be somewhere in the city, and the city was hers now.

Far below along the shelved terraces, the aetheric lights glittered harsh; something about them put her off. She'd destroy those, and the trams, and then the staircases leading from one terrace to another, which would make it difficult for her opponents.

Tiny lights bobbed out at sea—boats fleeing or reinforcements arriving? If she destroyed the docks as well, any reinforcements trying to enter that way would be hampered.

She reckoned factors coldly in a way she never had before, able to see the information inside her mind in a manner that was unfamiliar, but welcome. It came to her that this was an outgrowth of her new powers, the reforging of her soul and spirit in the depths of the world, far under the Coral Tower, that those powers were not just an outward thing, but an inward one as well, a reshaping of her spirit into something bigger. Grander, she thought with satisfaction. No wonder she had no need of anyone else.

She turned her introspection outward and back to the city. She wondered what her family was doing. What they were eating. Did they miss her?

Of course not. She had been gone all this time, and they probably hadn't even looked for her.

They didn't care, and so she wouldn't either.

Tabat was her city now. Her possession to play with, and she intended to do that.

The city had not given her a good life, and now turnabout was justice. In her head, it was almost as though Tabat were a person, a woman who was a mix of Adelina and Bella Kanto and all of her sisters, a woman who had not just failed to be kind, but been actively cruel, as though trying to destroy Lucy for spite and malice and petty reasons.

She would remove Tabat's resources, the things that gave it strength, as surely and cruelly as a cat removing a spider's legs, one by one, to toy with her.

The Moons gazed down at her from where they rolled, and she grinned at the white Moon where it shone low in the sky.

"You are powerless," she whispered to it, and then spoke her heresy louder. "You are nothing, a glimmer in the sky, and yet you pretend to direct people's lives, to be sending them here and there when it is actually all chance, all collisions of nothingness with other nothingness. Try to stop me, little piece of light. There *is* no stopping me. The city is mine, and never even was yours. Try to stop me."

She laughed, and it was not a happy laugh. It was loud, and echoed down the rocks, and haunted the dreams of everyone that heard it.

How can this city be so familiar and so strange, all at once? I walk the warm streets in the hazy early dusk, and I can see the swallows flitting back and forth among the terraces. Despite all the noise and hubbub up at the Duke's castle, there is surprisingly little attention being paid on these lower terraces. As though folks here believe that this is a matter that concerns only the Duke, not the ones he views as his figurative and literal lowers.

Will Lucy pay attention to such distinctions? I do not think so. For one thing, when she listed all that she felt had done her wrong, the Duke was not even mentioned among that crowd of folks. No, Lucy is young and powerful and petty, petty enough to seek out anyone and everyone she thinks has done her wrong.

Tomorrow I must look for Adelina and find where she has gone.

I stop in a chal shop near the docks. Here, so close to the boats, there is a different mood, and I notice that some ships are even now slipping out of harbor, despite the superstitions against setting out on journeys at nightfall. I chew knots of spicy bread, dipping them in the salty tea—there is nothing like this, in no other city. If there were one flavor that expressed Tabat, it would be this one, each time different according to the whims of the kettle where it was brewed, and yet unmistakable, every time.

Where should I sleep tonight? I think about sheltering with friends, but in the end, it seems expedient to spend a few of the handful of coins Scylla gave me.

I am oddly reluctant to seek her out. I must take care of the city first. I must find out why and how I have been sent here, and why the Moons—or one of them, at any rate—believe that I can defeat whatever it is that Lucy has become.

I find a traveler's lodge house, one lower on the scale than I would have normally chosen, but I do not have that many coins, after all. This one seems clean enough, although the basin is cracked and there is no glass in the windows, only wooden shutters to close out night-flying things. My room has a double set of bunks, and I take one of the upper ones, going to sleep early, despite the attempts of one of my fellow travelers to draw me into conversation.

Let her think me unfriendly, it is no matter. I need to think and so I lie there, wrapped in a blanket that scratches at me, unable to get fully comfortable, putting an arm outside the blankets to cool myself off, drawing it back in when I am too cold, an uncomfortable dance that keeps me awake.

What will tomorrow bring? What will Lucy do, now that she has moved on the castle? What of Alberic, has she killed him? Does she mean to rule over the city in his place?

I must find Adelina and warn her. And consult with her, truth be told.

And reassure myself that she is well, and that she has not been damaged by her associations with me. It has come to me that perhaps whoever burned down the press did so in my name rather than in any attempt to injure her, and maybe that is why she has not told me of this loss, this thing that has happened to her, to hurt her. Normally she would have told, would have taken comfort from me, would she not have? Instead she has this new man, this Sebastiano, who cannot hope to understand her as I do.

I roll over and try to put the pillow comfortably under my head. Another roommate is snoring, though not unpleasantly, and the other two have collected in one bunk and are amusing themselves very quietly, in a way that suggests the quiet is part of the game. I've played that game, myself, back in the day.

Where is Selene? Will she come to me in this city? When you love a goddess, you wonder every time if it is the last time you will ever see them. Deities are notoriously fickle after all, and certainly they have plenty of responsibilities, if I understand how such things work. And to be the white Moon, what does that involve? Does she move that round of pale stone across the sky, rolling it like a mill wheel, putting her supple shoulder to it?

The thought makes me smile and it's as though I hear her whispering in my ear, her breath warm on the hairs of my neck, "Silly Bella, I will come to you again, and soon."

It is all I can do not to reach for her, but I understand in my heart that if I do, she will be gone, will flee away from me because that is her nature, no matter what else she is. Instead I breathe out, so soft no one else in the room can hear me, "Why not now?"

This time all I hear is a scrap of laughter, and lips touch just below my ear, a butterfly's kiss would be more forceful, and then again those words, "and soon."

I would lie awake and think of her, but she has brought me peace enough to sleep now, and so I slide, I tumble, I fall into welcome darkness, still feeling that kiss.

CHAPTER 9

The curtains are drawn so nothing comes in the window, the white moonlight presses against the fabric in vain, unable to penetrate, unable to enter the darkness. Adelina lies awake—or is she asleep dreaming she is not asleep? It is an unsatisfying sensation in either case.

Perhaps she is dreaming. She is moving through the city, looking for something. Not a person—not Sebastiano, not Bella, not her dead mother, who has never come to speak to her in dreams. No, she is looking for a thing, a gleam around the corner, a sparkle of light that pulls at her, and which she fears at the same time, fears with all her heart because she will fall into this thing and lose herself, she will become nothing, something other than what she is and was and will be.

Dream logic, she thinks, and the phrase brings her the realization that she is dreaming, that she is lying in the dark bedchamber, still so much smaller than the ones she has been accustomed to, and what's more, sharing it with another body—her husband, who would have thought she would have such a thing!—beloved and wonderful and yet somehow still intrusive.

She wants the drug, and is dreaming of wanting it.

That comes to her with a brutal clarity that almost—almost but not quite—forces her awake with the shame of it. This is a craving, an addiction. A dependency. A weakness. This is not like wanting chal in the morning, or liking a particular kind of pastry that only came from Figgis carts. This is like a sickness, or like living with a fact of her own body, something that most people did not know or think about. This feels wrong, and at the same time she cannot imagine giving it up. Can think with one side of her head that it is necessary—so necessary! What will happen when Sebastiano realizes what is going on, which he must, surely, if things continue in this manner? And the other side of her mind thinking of it wholly as an exercise in speculation, not something that would ever really come to pass, would ever become part of her existence.

In her half dream she comes around a corner and is confronted with the golden glow of the drug, part of her wanting to leap forward to embrace it. But another part of her, deep in the pit of her stomach, writhes with shame when she looks that dependency in the face, and the force of it drives her to her knees so she cannot move forward....

"Adelina." A hand on her shoulder, pulling her awake. She opened her eyes to look up at Sebastiano's concerned face in candle-light. "You were lost in nightmare," he said, touching his fingertips along the curve of her cheek as though to reassure her and himself that they were both still there.

"I was," she said. "Thank you." She tilted her chin to kiss his fingers.

"What were you dreaming?"

Her heart sank at the thought of explaining it. She hesitated and then thought how to explain that hesitation and said hurriedly, "It's all a muddle. You know how dreams are, falling apart when you try to remember them." She chose to play an unfair card. "My mother ..." She let the words trail off—Sebastiano had been in some ways more upset by her mother's death than she had been, had been solicitous in a way she knew was motivated by how devastated he would have been by his own mother Letha's death. She had not tried to explain to him how fraught and complicated the relationship with her mother had been, how she had ever disappointed Emiliana in her path in life, how Emiliana would have been disappointed even now, except for those moments when she was speaking in front of a crowd, playing her mother's Merchant daughter, in a way that Emiliana would have loved.

That was a complicated thought, that her mother and the drug might be somehow tied up together in her psyche, and she did not have time to entertain it, she told herself.

She reached up for Sebastiano, who was still watching her.

"Come," she invited him, "help me chase away the remnants of the nightmare."

He leaned, smiling, to the task, so both of them forgot everything else except each other.

THE CITY IS TROUBLED as it begins to go to sleep. The day has been hot, which was unremarkable. It has been humid, which is also unremarkable. And it has been troubled, which is not unremarkable. Buzz fills the late night chal shops. No one knows what has happened up at the Duke's castle, what caused all the noise and devastation. Rumors have filled the streets, each one stranger than the last. Some even say that they have seen Bella Kanto, returned from her exile, ready to set the city to rights again. Others claim her in league with whatever force or forces attacked the Duke's castle, since it was the Duke who sent her into exile after all.

Down at the docks, the ship captains watch the color of the sky with worried eyes. They've never seen it that shade of glassy green before, and the air feels thick with some energy. Things are wrong, they can feel it in the too-still air, and many of them are already figuring out how to leave as soon as possible, even if it means not picking up goods here. *Better one's life than a profit* is the Merchant saying, and it is a wise one.

Scylla has gotten herself lodging with distant cousins who live down near those docks, part of the vast family network that has been part of all her life. They greet her enthusiastically when they can, but most are preoccupied with trying to figure out the threat to the city and how soon they should leave. They have felt the mood in the city; they have heard and sometimes witnessed the ugly flareups that happen when a Beast is found in the wrong time at the wrong place.

Most of them are already figuring out how to best cut their losses and return to the One Story city.

She finds herself in a hammock in the guest rooms and lies there wondering what is happening to Bella and reminding herself that there are many things in life that she cannot control and that her former lover is one of them.

At the Brides of Steel, the dormitories are scarcely tenanted, and Myrila is beside herself. Thirty students and three teachers went up to the Duke's castle; none of them returned and she knows rather than fears the worst. They would have come back if they could have. That they didn't means they are dead or trapped, and she doesn't think any of them trapped. She paces in her office, trying to figure out what to do, how to make sure the rest of the girls are safe from whatever is happening.

She has a list of thirty-three names, and she must send word as soon as possible to parents and families regarding what has happened. Already two notes have arrived asking for assurance that all is well there. She knows this, but the pen sits untouched on the desk. To write this down without knowing exactly what happened … no, tomorrow she will go to the Duke's castle and look for herself, and then she can write.

Although she wishes she could sleep, there is no hope that sweet surcease will come. Too many thoughts are crowding themselves through her head, occasionally spilling out in a mutter that she catches when she notices it.

She thinks of Bella, so far away, and wishes she were here. Bella would have ideas about how to save the girls; she would have done it through sheer force of will. She could do the impossible when she wanted to; Myrila had seen it more than once over the years. That shy, diffident girl who worked without ceasing, got up early for extra drills, never spoke back. She'd flinched at first when someone spoke to her softly, as though it might be some trap.

Myrila had feared the other girls would bully her, but that sorted itself out. She grinned to herself, remembering the look on Neffa's face, trussed in that tree. *Bella* had sorted that out.

"I wish you were here," she says softly to the room. Through the open window, white moonlight spills and coils, and Myrila wishes she was a follower of the Moons, that she could find comfort in this light, or the Trade Gods, who would tell her that cycles come and go, and that everything is, at its heart, predictable as coins. But she does not, and so she continues sitting, worrying at her thoughts.

CHAPTER 10

The city's mood is odd today; news of what transpired at the Duke's castle has buzzed all throughout the previous night. Down at the docks, more ships are leaving than coming in, and several that arrive turn around as quickly as they can.

Several political rallies are due to be staged this day. Adelina is meant to speak at one, down near the docks. The organizers intend to push ahead—if they don't, their opponents will, and this is a race that will be close, they think. Two speakers turn out to be missing, having been up at the Duke's castle the day before on some meeting, and they are believed to be on the list of the dead.

At the Brides of Steel, Myrila has managed to scrape up a few hours of sleep, but she is awake now, and making sure the remaining girls have breakfast, even though both of the cooks have deserted her. She has flavored the porridge with certain calming herbs she knows, harmless ones that she has been known to use to help a girl sleep or deal with too much anxiousness, but even so the mood in the dining hall is restless and skittish. Two girls ask her if they can leave and return home and she agrees to send messengers to their parents, to see if it is acceptable.

No one asks her about the girls who are not in the empty chairs. All of them try hard to avoid looking at those chairs.

At morning breakfast with Eloquence and his sisters, one of the visitors says something about the number of them, and Grace blurts out something about the missing Obedience. Shush, Eloquence says sternly, not wanting them to know he's lost not just their boy but his own sister! He sees the softening in the mother's eyes and shame threads at him further, feeling it undeserved.

Bees hum in Jilly's garden, picking their way through the flowers there. There are no Fairies in this garden, though they are plentiful elsewhere in the city.

Including down at the Sea Gardens, where the attendants are trying to ignore what is going on in the city. Tomorrow is one of their peak festivals, when the singing lilies, another of Ellora's wonderful creations, open, and everyone will come to listen to them. The lilies are kept in great stone planters, which must be laboriously loaded onto little carts, and trundled into place, and then set among the salty rocks today, in preparation for tomorrow. The blossoms are white and amber pods right now, almost ready to split and flower, so fat they look as though they might burst open at any second. But their timing is part of Ellora's ancient magic, as predictable as the Moons.

A swallow—or better yet, a Dragon—flying over Tabat and looking down would have seen much with its keen eyes: the marks of Lucy's attack on the Duke's castle, all but one of its high towers torn down, the surrounding buildings flattened, and everywhere, corpses, all through its grounds and some along the roadway leading down. No one has dared come to collect them yet, but farther down in the city, a group of Peacekeepers is being prepared for the task, addressed by a solemn-faced officer while the Duke seethes upstairs, having been told he should stay out of sight for his own protection.

The red Moon and purple Moon roll in the blueness of the sky. The white Moon seems to be elsewhere at the moment.

EARLY IN THE MORNING, Lucy rose, and went to explore her domain.

If she could find the Duke's body, she wouldn't have to worry about him raising some sort of force against her. But she didn't really know what he looked like. He would be well dressed, she supposed. She didn't remember much from when she'd seen him at the arena. That day he'd just been a distant dazzle and there had been so much else to look at.

They had all gone away and left the castle empty, at least what was left of it. Lucy wandered through corridors, looking at things. Alcoves held marble busts of former Dukes and Duchesses, and she amused herself tipping each one over as she passed with just a tiny push of magic. Petronius the Third. *Smash*. Etalberta, Fifth of her Line. *Smash*. Chadba, sometimes styled The Righteous. *Smash*.

Each time she passed a richly dressed body, crushed by rubble or some other act of her devastation, she examined it carefully. Surely the Duke would be wearing some sort of regalia, a crown or something like that? But would that be how he was dressed if she had caught him unaware, perhaps in the middle of some ordinary, everyday activity? She paused to think about what sort of everyday activities he would have been performing, and shook her head, and kept looking.

A mirror reflected her, head to toe, and she looked in it once, then smashed it to a million tiny pieces and went upstairs to find a bathing chamber. She soaped herself and washed her hair, and dried and curled it with another wave of magic. In a nearby room, she found a closet full of elaborate court dresses, silks and satins colored like flower petals, and chose a dress of multicolored, sheer silk, with matching, ribbon-wound slippers.

The dresser held several boxes of mixed jewelry along with a scattering of white leather cases, each holding a different matched set of necklace and rings and earbobs, two with tiaras and a jewel-inlaid comb. She draped herself in the glittering baubles until she was almost too loaded down to move, and then she shook her head and let it all slip off, all except a band of gold around her head. The Duke wore a crown and so would she, to show her supremacy.

What would they do next, to try to drive her away? She probably should not linger in this space. But curiosity drove her, and finally she moved to the lower levels.

The first space she found was the menagerie. But it was empty. Although she did not know it, the Duke had finally grown uneasy with Beasts so near and had them all killed, down to the Oracular Pig.

In another level beyond that, she found prisoners in cells. They were insignificant, fleeing when she opened their doors. *Let them run,* she thought. *And spread word of me.* But in one was a little woman, smaller than Lucy even, who sat on a cot and ignored Lucy looking in at the doorway.

And Lucy looked longest here, because the cell's walls were covered with pictures, drawn in charcoal on the rough stone. The harbor covered one wall, boats and gulls and water, and next to it was Ellora's Garden, the sea lilies in full bloom, velvet pistils blowing in the wind. A full-sized Figgis Bakery cart on the back wall, so real it looked almost ready for someone to reach in and take out a handful of pastries and cookies. The last time Lucy had eaten a Figgis pastry, Adelina had bought it for her, and the memory was dry and bitter.

And plenty of people as well, mostly the same beautiful woman, but a few others that Lucy recognized: Bella Kanto and Adelina.

"Hello?" Lucy said curiously.

The woman on the cot raised her head and looked at her. She had something wrong with her, her body was twisted in on itself.

"Did the Duke do that to you?" Lucy asked.

"Do what?" the woman said. Perhaps she had been driven mad by torture.

"Did the Duke make you like that?" Lucy repeated.

The woman looked down at herself. Then she laughed. "No," she said. "He hasn't done anything worse than taking my paints away. I was like this before." She looked back at Lucy. "Bonewrack fever, in childhood. And who are you?"

"I'm Lucy," Lucy said. "I'm replacing the Duke."

The woman tilted her head to one side, studying her. "You can't be worse, I think," she said. "I'm Leonoa. An artist."

Lucy had expected more than that, particularly since she was capable of freeing the prisoner. Maybe a little groveling or at least some begging of the kind the other prisoners had engaged in.

"Should I free you?" she asked. Maybe the woman just didn't realize that Lucy could. Maybe it needed to be pointed out to her.

"Should you?" the woman said with interest. "I guess that depends on who is deciding the should or shouldn't side of things. That would seem to be you, so I think you might be the best source of answer."

Was she making fun of Lucy? When Lucy could destroy her with a thought? Or just leave her here to continue rotting? She considered, waiting to see if Leonoa said anything more, but the little artist stayed silent, studying Lucy with interest. Perhaps she meant to draw her.

That thought of being immortalized decided her. She would free the artist and the artist would document her victory over the city. She might not have the power to knock down the castle at the moment, but she had enough power to keep the woman from running away, particularly since Leonoa did not look capable of much speed. She lifted the heavy bar on the outside and let the door swing open.

"I see the decision is yes," Leonoa said cheerfully, and grabbing a small bundle from near the bed, she limped out into the hallway.

"You will follow me," Lucy told her.

"Will I?" Leonoa said thoughtfully, but did so nonetheless, although at a slower pace than Lucy would have liked. She contemplated healing the woman, but that would take a lot of magic and the destruction of the castle had drained her. It would take time, probably hours, before her wellsprings replenished themselves—by now she knew, if not understood, the flood of magic inside herself. Perhaps later. If it seemed as though it might be worthwhile. Perhaps it could be used as a promised reward. That would motivate her without Lucy having to expend much energy beforehand.

"Where are we going to?" Leonoa asked.

Lucy made no answer. She wasn't entirely sure herself. She wanted the Duke, but he had vanished. Where had he gone to? Only the faintest thread of him seemed to still remain, and it led down into the tunnels.

But she led Leonoa down, deeper and deeper. Sometimes she thought she might be walking in the Duke's footsteps, that she felt his presence, as though he had passed through here recently. She could see footsteps in the dust as they descended into places few people came. There were gaps in the lines of torches where the people she was following had taken one.

She could feel the thread that was the Duke now, and it tugged at her, but she kept pace with Leonoa. There was plenty of time, and she needed to recover her strength as well. The Duke had chosen his hiding place down here? Very well, Lucy would too, and would shelter in the darkness for a little while before she re-emerged to take Tabat. And when she did, and she was revenged on the Duke, there were plenty of other targets as well: Adelina and Sebastiano, who had failed her, and the College of Mages, which had rejected her, and above all, her family, who had cast her out and blamed her so unfairly for the death of her mother.

Every time she thought of the revenge she would enact there, she smiled to herself in the darkness.

Eloquence had feared that the pair might try to stay—after all, didn't Eloquence owe them a little, having lost their child? He tried to describe how Teo had run off, and blamed the confusion of the docks and the fighting Beasts, the arrogant Mage who had been responsible for it, after all, having somehow provoked the Dryad to attack him.

But when Eloquence let his eye flicker meaningfully to the doorway in the morning, the man simply nodded, although his wife looked as though she wanted to say something.

"Go to the Moon Temples," Eloquence urged them. "I haven't heard any word of him showing up, but I don't know that they would have sent to me, after all. If anyone in this city is likely to know where he might have ended up, it would be them."

"We have lost a little faith in the Moon Temples," Teo's father said.

The sudden savage glint to his face almost made Eloquence take a step back. Instead, he squared his shoulders and spoke forcefully, "If we doubt the Temples during times of trouble, we are faithless."

"I did not doubt the Temples in a time of trouble," the father retorted, "and now they have taken my son and given me nothing in return."

Eloquence was troubled when he went inside, and when Mercy asked him for money to go buy pastries at Figgis, he snapped at her, asking if she thought he was made of money. "Particularly when I am prisoned here, watching over so, and cannot ply my trade," he almost shouted at her and then, in the middle of the resulting startled silence, he went upstairs.

CHAPTER 11

In the morning, sunlight came in through the kitchen window to slant inquisitively across Teo's face and wake him. He lay very still for a moment, absorbing where he was. He had not woken safe and warm for so many days that he tried to savor the sensation even while it was slipping away, and being replaced by worry about Lucy.

She wouldn't like that he had run away. She might not like it so much that she would just kill him, to keep him from doing so again, or she might punish him terribly, and by now, from watching her, he knew that Lucy being terrible was indeed terrifying.

He finally unwound himself from the blankets and scavenged breakfast for himself: cheese and bread, and two apples that had been sitting on the table. He washed them down with water from the tiny well in the garden, when he sunned and stretched himself.

A thought occurred to him about his inability to change shape. He had been able to turn into a cougar, and then someone—Murga—had turned him into a puppy. Could he turn himself into a dog again? But what if he got stuck in that form again? He shook himself all over. No, that would be unacceptable. He would stay Human—for now—and maybe once all the turmoil was past, he would have enough time and peace to figure out what he was and what he could actually do.

Following the Northstretch river up north would be a much harder trip than coming down it by steamboat had been, but it would be doable. When he got to the mouth, there would be people who could direct him. Could he survive by himself in the wilderness? Well, he had survived Lucy, and that, he rather thought, meant he was much better at surviving than anyone had ever thought. Maybe that was what Bella Kanto had seen in him, after all, when she had brought him into her service. Maybe it had been some inkling of his possibilities rather than pity. Yes, that surely had been at least part of it.

He felt unexpectedly cheerful, to the point where he cleaned up the kitchen neatly, making it look as though he had never been there. He scavenged through cupboards and packed himself a small bag of food, and then thought and went upstairs and found a satchel. Jilly was dead, after all, and he might as well take advantage of that, even though the act made him feel as though spiders of guilt were crawling on his skin.

He brushed them away and set to business. He packed two bottles of ginger drink, and the last of the cheese, and upstairs he took a change of clothing, and even found a pair of boots to draw on over his bare feet. They were a little too large for him, but he added a pair of thick knitted socks over his feet, and then they fit very well.

He rummaged through the dresser, blushing at some of the items, and found a thin pouch of coppers, which he counted through twice. It was not much, but it was more than he had ever had in his life. Money was power, he knew that. Money was the chance to do what you wanted to do, rather than what other people thought you should.

He washed his face in the rain barrel and chewed two mint leaves from the plant that budded in the barrel's shadow, relishing the fresh green taste, feeling cheerful and resolute.

He would make for the docks. It meant going back up, and in the general direction of the Duke's castle, but he would work his way east and away from it at the same time. That should get him in the general vicinity of the docks, at least. From there he could find out what boats were leaving. Now he had enough coins to buy a berth aboard one, he thought, and if not, he could say that he had worked as a cabin boy. He knew enough of life aboard boats for that.

He thought, once everyone realized what Lucy was and what she intended for the city, a lot of boats might be leaving. They might already have left.

STAYING AT THE PEACEKEEPERS' was far from optimal. For one thing, there were few that could be co-opted as servants and even fewer that were actually willing to be.

The truth was that the Peacekeepers were not treating him as their Duke, their leader and ruler. Outrageously so. They acted as though he had already been deposed by the elections, and it occurred to him that everyone was, in fact, convinced that he would be deposed, which was a conclusion that he himself had somehow managed not to come to. How could anyone think that Tabat would be better off in hands other than his?

He took the head of the officers' office, and might have been resisted more if that head had not been much more concerned with defending the city than his offices. Occasionally the Duke would venture out and offer to confer with the Peacekeepers but for the most part they had no time to humor him—and it was increasingly clear to him that they saw interacting with him as much the same as humoring a small child.

The Duke felt as though he were such a child, foisted on the Peacekeepers for safekeeping, and he resented it deeply and fiercely. It was not a position he had ever experienced in his life before and it outraged him to his very core.

A flurry of messengers and urgent talk about the caverns hosting the furnaces beneath Tabat. Something happening there, words of casualties, explosions. The trams brought to a standstill. The aetheric lights extinguished. Something about the mushroom caverns.

"Is she there?" he demanded of a messenger, but the man simply shrugged and said, "I must make my report," and went off to do so as though he had not even recognized the Duke!

He managed to find enough coin to send a messenger to the College of Mages, inquiring where they could house him. They had been very ready for him to go to the Peacekeepers and for the first time he found himself doubting their motives. Mages were tricky, after all. They dealt with subtleties of magic and words.

Their reply reinforced this, for they regretted, very much, being unable to accommodate him at this time. They were not sure when they would be able to meet with him, due to the "current chaotic situation."

"Balls," he snarled, and crumpled the paper in order to throw it across the room.

TEO DIDN'T INTEND to go anywhere near the Circus of the Autumn Moon or the grounds of the College of Mages. What if Murga saw him, captured him? Turned him back into a dog? But the Tumbril Stair lay along one edge of it, and without money for the Great Tram, that was the best and easiest way. He would come close—a few blocks at the nearest point, but surely he could manage to remain out of sight.

Easier said than done. As he neared, he was frightened to notice some familiar faces among the crowd, circus folk he recognized. He ducked into an alleyway to avoid the Amazing Rappinos, and thought he'd been successful in not attracting attention, until he felt a tug at his sleeve.

"I thought that was you!" Maisie cried. "Where did you get to all this time?" She was dressed much as always, but currently carried a small leash, the other end leading to her Clovian winged rabbit, which seemed content enough to scamper about her heels, although it paused long enough to sniff Teo with a dubious expression.

"Maisie!" he said. He couldn't help it, he looked around for Murga or any others and at the expression on his face, her own became significantly less happy.

"What's the matter?" she demanded.

"Maisie, you can't tell anyone you saw me," he said. "Particularly Murga!"

Her eyes narrowed and he expected some interrogation as to what he had done to fall afoul of Murga, but instead, surprisingly, she said, "He made you disappear, didn't he? Didn't seem startled to find out you was gone, nor sent anyone looking for you. Didn't seem right, any of that, and now I understand it."

"He …" Teo paused. How to say *He turned me into a dog*? She'd know the subtext—that Murga was a Sorcerer, one of the most dangerous people in the city. So he said, "He sent me away."

"Through magic," she said flatly, and he realized that he might actually have allies in the circus, rather than unanimous enemies, from the expression on her face. Others had fallen afoul of Murga, and similarly disappeared, he thought, and Maisie seemed to have had enough of that.

"He'll be coming along this way soon," Maisie said. "He goes and visits that chal shop there. Get moving! But at sunset—meet me at that park there and we can talk." At the look on his face, she said urgently, "I won't let him at you again, I swear."

He felt a surge of trust in her that he might not have felt for a Human, at least any that were not Bella Kanto. "All right," he said. "You won't tell him, you promise?"

She looked insulted. "Said I wouldn't, yeah?"

"Yeah," he said, with a rush of gratitude. She was still his friend, and that meant a great deal to him, because it meant that not everyone in the circus was automatically his enemy. He had made a few friends there, and he realized now that he missed them, had done so even while he was in Bella Kanto's service.

Maisie touched his hand, perhaps in response to the look on his face. "Come at sunset," she said again. "We can talk then." With a look around her, as though she might be afraid that anyone could be lurking in the crowds passing around them, she stepped back and vanished.

Teo took a long breath. He had feared and dreaded the first confrontation with the circus, the circus whose master had changed his life so radically, so un-understandably. He thought about the Dryad that Murga had transformed into a monster and wondered what had happened to her.

The circus had been a part of his life for a brief time, but it had been his first real experience with the vastness of the city, with how you could walk in a crowd there and not know anyone, not anyone at all, even though you were walking with dozens and dozens of people. So many faces, all of them distinct and recognizable, and none of them knowing who you were, which was strange, and freeing, but mostly strange.

LEONOA'S PACE considerably slowed Lucy, but she found that she didn't mind. For one thing, the little woman had a wicked, barbed tongue, and listening to her describe the Duke and all his foibles was as good as listening to a storyteller in the Salt Market. She gathered that Leonoa had been taken in for creating seditious art.

"Seditious how?" Lucy asked.

"Showing Beasts in a new way," Leonoa said, more than a little out of breath from her exertions.

When they entered the cavern full of heat and glare, she could feel the magic in the air, thrumming from the furnaces. She looked at the piles of logs. Each held magic, she could feel it, and she could use that better than the Mages did. For one thing, she needed no furnace to extract it.

She reached out a hand to touch a pile of logs, extracting everything ruthlessly. The wood softened, flaked, fell away into ash, the transformation flickering over the surface of the logs, tracing the outline of the bark with silvery fire before it faded into nothingness.

"What are you doing?" Leonoa asked.

"Eating," Lucy said, and licked her lips, looking at the cavern. She would have no need of rest after all. The Duke was not here but she could feel that he had passed through. And this would give her plenty of power with which to catch him.

Power coiling in her like a worm at first, then a snake, then becoming a Dragon's worth of energy, threading through her as though she were made of magic. Before her transformation in the Southern Isles, she would not have been capable of this, she would have burned like a torch if she had tried it. If she had even known how to.

Now it was easy to gulp it down, store it away. She felt as though she were ballooning outward, pushing outside the confines of her own body. She was a thousand tightly coiled flaming threads; she was a million sparks lurking inside a fire. It took her a moment to figure out how to use the power to contain itself before it exploded outward in a storm that would have destroyed Lucy—and the city—utterly.

A shout somewhere outside herself made her look away from that internal conflagration. A crowd of workers running at her, waving staves as though they thought to threaten her. Once men like this would have terrified her; but now they were laughable, like ants trying to swarm a cat to take it down.

No matter. She had plenty of energy now, and she ate her attackers too, reducing them to the same ash and extracting the minute traces of magic their bodies held. More than she would have predicted. She wondered what consuming a Mage would be like. These Humans must have that tinge to them because of their exposure to these logs, constantly working near them, and the transformation that changed them from things into fuel for the city.

What would the inhabitants of the College of Mages be like? She thought of consuming Sebastiano and a smile crept over her face. Oh, he'd regret not helping her. He'd led her on, after all, being so nice at the Gladiatorial Games, giving her food, treating her as though she was a peer and then when she went to the College, trying to get him to help her find an apprenticeship, he'd turned her away!

It had all been a joke to him, but he would find out it was a very expensive moment of fun. He would pay everything for having mocked her. Now that she thought about it, didn't her memories of that moment show him privately laughing, laughing to himself when he had thought her too innocent, too naive, to understand what he was saying? Yes, that was it. He had been her enemy from the first moment, but he had gulled her, let her think him kind, because he knew he would find it amusing when she realized the depths of his deception.

There were twenty workers and three months' supply of Dryad logs in the cavern, and Lucy consumed them all, Human by Human, stack by stack. Leonoa stood to one side, careful to stay out of the way, and what she thought of it all was something that she kept entirely to herself.

Lucy blasted machine after machine, and in the city streets far above, aetheric lights went out and the trams ground to a halt. The engines that kept air circulating in the mushroom caverns ceased, and the workers there took the ripe trays and left, knowing that soon enough the air would be too stale there to breathe. They didn't take the fungi to the city kitchens that served them daily; instead they divided up the trays and took them home to their families. Starvation would soon be upon the city.

The summons had come in the early morning and it was a puzzling one. But nonetheless Sebastiano kissed Adelina at breakfast and prepared to depart, despite her irritated protest.

"You are no longer in the employ of the College of Mages," she pointed out. "Why hurry to answer to their call? They have not treated you well enough to deserve such loyalty."

"This is something very large," Sebastiano said, pondering the sweetness of the crease that formed between her brows when she was concerned. "Not just me. But everyone with any sort of formal magical training is being summoned, even those with only the barest rudiments."

"This is connected to whatever has destroyed the Duke's castle?"

He shrugged. "What else could it be?"

He kept his face calm. There was no need to worry her. But a summons like this was unprecedented, had not happened in all his time at the College.

THE COLLEGE WAS CROWDED with people, all hurrying to the large auditorium to which they had been summoned. The long, tall windows at intervals cast bars of light across the gathered faces. He glimpsed Gley through the crowd, but the other did not see him. He saw other faces he recognized, many that he did not. Some, like him, were Mages that the College had rejected, and he wondered if they felt the same mixture of truculence and pride that he had at being resummoned, that they had thought his magic worthy after all. If that was what was going on.

Arianis appeared, Master Mage Faustino Landoro leading him by the elbow. Sebastiano's eyes widened a little. Few ever saw the elderly head of the school, who was long past his days of teaching, and devoted himself to arcane research that few ever saw.

The old man walked slowly, but deliberately, with the care of the aged who are upright and proud of it, and intend to remain so. His robes were of burgundy velvet, so ornately embroidered with spirals and comets and other strange stars that they might have been able to stand upright on their own. He made his way to the podium and placed his hands atop it, pausing to scan the gathered faces in silence. Faustino stood beside him, also surveying the assembled faces.

What they read there, Sebastiano was not sure, because it did not seem to reassure either of them.

"Children of the College," Arianis said. "Instructors and alumni, any Human with a whit of magical power, all gathered here."

Silence. Everyone was waiting to hear what he said; the only sound was the crowd's breathing and the occasional movement of restless feet.

"A menace has come to Tabat, as you probably already know. We do not know much about it. The Duke's castle was destroyed, and the survivors have said it was a girl. Some had described her as flaming, others as shedding bolts of lightning from her hair and fingertips. Others insist that she is an ordinary girl in appearance, and unremarkable."

He paused before saying dryly, "A plain little girl, and unremarkable." He shook his head.

"One who destroyed the castle!" someone shouted from the back, and the remark launched a buzz of controversy and contradictions that drowned out what the Speaker tried to say next. He tried to speak and failed and finally Faustino slammed his hand down flat on the podium before him. The motion created a sound larger than it should have been, a boom that shook all the space and demanded quiet. The crowd's hubbub lessened and ebbed, finally faded back into silence as Arianis stood there, looking at them.

"There is worse," he said. "The store of Dryad logs beneath the city is gone."

"Gone?" several people shouted, followed by various demands to know where they had gone to and who had taken them and what the College meant to do about it.

"Consumed by the child," Arianis said. "The girl. And when I say consumed, that is what I meant, because she now holds all that power. The city is running on its reserves, and those cannot last more than a day and a half longer—if we are lucky and she does not have some way to drain those reserves as well."

Sebastiano gaped. The city was absolutely dependent on the power that the College of Mages provided with their magical furnaces. That power drove the tram lines, and the city lights, and a thousand other things, including the caverns where Ellora's fruit was grown and harvested, and fed so many.

Adelina. He needed to get her out of the city and to someplace safe. But where would that be? His uncle had a small estate outside the city, near the salt marshes. Was that far away enough to be safe? And his parents. Would his father consent to being evacuated? And Letha, with her ambitions of abolitionism, would she be willing to leave?

He turned his attention back to the Speaker.

"We must work together in this," the Speaker said. "Tomorrow at dawn we will convene, and I will draw on you to cast the spell to drive this interloper away." He spoke as though there were no chance that the spell would not succeed, but Sebastiano was not so certain. "You will return home and prepare yourselves. Cast no magics until that time, and do whatever you can to augment your own. If you have placed power in devices, retrieve it. Bring anything of that nature with you. We will need every bit of what we are to do this."

He looked over the assembly and did not ask for questions. Instead he said, "Dismissed," and left despite the words seeking to hold him there.

Sebastiano raced home, thinking about the plan. This was foolish. Would it work, so many Mages in tandem? Something like that had never been attempted, but he also knew that it was the study to which Arianis had devoted so much of his life.

Adelina was at the table, writing. She had ink on her nose and a small frown on her face, making notes in her neat, cursive hand. She was intent on her work and oblivious to his entrance. He paused to contemplate her, feeling a surge of love shake him down to the bones. How had she become so important to him during the time they had shared? And better yet, she felt the same about him, which still seemed incredible. He could not survive if she were harmed.

"Adelina," he said gently, trying not to startle her.

She laid her pen down and looked at him. "What news from the College?" she demanded.

"We were right. They are attempting a collective magic against the creature that has destroyed the Duke's castle."

"What sort of creature is it?"

"A girl. Human, by all accounts."

"A Sorcerer pretending to be a child?"

He shook his head. "I don't think so. She seemed to be able to wield magic as though she were a Beast, as though it were a part of her."

"So she's a Beast?"

"I don't think so. The only Beasts that can appear Human are Shifters, and their power lies in their other form, usually."

"So you will go and help the College defeat this … girl."

"Maybe," he said. "I'm not convinced this plan will work. But that is not the point of things, Adelina. We must get you out of the city."

"Must we? But why?"

"Because you are in danger here and I could not bear it if you were hurt."

"So instead you will send me away and stay in danger yourself, without caring whether or not I could bear it if you were hurt."

"Unfair," he protested.

Her eyes were clear and luminous and kind. "Life is unfair, Sebastiano. But no, I will not leave you."

He played another card. "I was hoping you would take my parents to safety."

A good gambit, and one she clearly respected. But she chewed her lip, then countered, "Are you sure that they will go? Your mother has lived all her life in this city."

"You will help persuade them," he said.

She hesitated and he pressed his advantage. "Letha likes you. She will listen to you if you advise that they leave. There is a small estate outside the city, a silk-mothery that my uncle runs. You will be safer there, the three of you."

She seemed about to relent, her mouth softening.

There was a knock at the door.

CHAPTER 13

It has taken me a while to find her, but eventually one of the people still working in Printers' Row gave me her new address, although I had to press hard for it. I do not know this neighborhood so near the docks, but it bears every sign of being shabby and not the sort of place she is used to. She was raised a Nettlepurse, Nittlescent in the old tongue, after all, and is used to an estate, servants, a carriage to take her wherever her whim might want to go.

How dare this man not keep her in the style she deserves?

I wrinkle my nose as I smell piss in the entry hall. This is definitely not a place worthy of Adelina, and so when the man who has brought her to it opens the door, I am already predisposed to dislike him.

Moreover, I cannot see what she might see in this one. His nose is too narrow and his forehead bulges as though his brains might spill out. He wears the formal robes of the College of Mages—at home, no less, and this seems more than a little pretentious to me, as though he were worried that Adelina might forget his stature.

I scowl at him, but he does not scowl back. His eyes widen as he recognizes me.

BELLA KANTO, Sebastiano thought. *Of course she is somehow part of all of this.* But he forced a smile and stepped aside. Adelina, at least, would be overjoyed to see her.

He did spare a glance up and down the street. It was, after all, highly illegal for her to be in Tabat, since she was an exile. *Typical of the woman, to give no thought to the danger she might put them in, all for the sake of a brief encounter.*

He let none of that enter his expression or tone.

"Adelina," he called. "You have a visitor."

ADELINA CAME DOWN the steps slowly. *Who would visit her?* Most of her relatives had rejected her on her mother's behalf before her mother had passed. Her old authors did not come to see her anymore, now that she couldn't print their work. She hoped it wasn't someone trying to dun her for some bill from before the fire that had destroyed Spinner Press.

And then she saw Bella.

Older looking and more ragged. But Bella. Bella Kanto, with that same crooked smile that had caught Adelina the very first time they had met.

They embraced while Sebastiano looked on.

I STILL THINK this place unworthy of my Adelina, although I can tell she has made it hers with the piles of books. If they are all hers. It does seem to be a mingling of her historical texts with more arcane volumes, bound in fancy leathers, some of them with tiny locks on the pages.

"When did the press burn down?" I ask and she shrugs in a way I had not expected. She loved that press. Had put everything of herself into it. Surely losing it was a great blow. But she shows no sign of it.

It makes me think a little better of the man, that he has clearly comforted her and helped her through such troubles while I was gone.

"It was while you were going into exile, a few days after you set sail," she says.

"You told me nothing of it in your letters."

That startles her. "I thought they would not reach you until you were there at the frontier."

"They came in a most peculiar way," I say. "Your old apprentice delivered them."

Her eyes widen. "Lucy? She disappeared and her brother has been seeking her everywhere. He blames me for her disappearance, and I confess that I was angry with the girl, but when I went to look for her again, I could not find her."

"I do not know what sort of adventures she has had, down in the Southern Isles, but they have changed her," I say.

"How so?"

"Have they told you much about what has attacked the Duke's castle?"

"A girl," Sebastiano says. "A Human girl."

I nod and wait for them to parse it out. I am annoyed to see that Sebastiano sorts it out first, but Adelina is not far behind him.

"How can it be Lucy?" he demands and simultaneously her words "But how did such a thing happen?" fall from her lips.

And so I tell them the story, of leaving Tabat and coming to the Raft City, and escaping to the Southern Isles. Of Scylla's accompaniment (I see Adelina's lips thin a little at her name.) and our feast of goat flesh, there in the sands with Dragons all around us, conferring. Of the ride to the Coral Tower and what we found there. The revelation of Teo's true nature. And the confrontation with Lucy.

I leave out many things. I leave out Selene, for one, because I do not know how to say, "The white Moon is my lover now," without sounding insane. I do not think Sebastiano notices my omissions, but

I am fairly certain that Adelina does, because her eyebrow quirks in a way I definitely recognize. She does not press me on this, though.

"The College of Mages means to defeat her," Sebastiano says. "But from what you say …" He breaks off, shaking his head. "Ancient magic, strong enough to kill a Dragon! That is very powerful indeed."

"There must be a way," Adelina says. "If she is the product of some artifact that she discovered in the Southern Isles, if that is what changed her, surely there must be an object that would change her back, for example."

"I would think that the College of Mages would have tried that already, if it were feasible."

"Perhaps it is something whose powers they do not realize," she says stubbornly. "I am sure they have plenty of artifacts squirreled away, which they have not bothered to share with history."

Exasperated, Sebastiano says, "This is not some penny-wide, where the solution drops from the sky, unexpected. If there were such a thing, how would any of us know it?"

"Don't shout at her," I say, and he rounds on me.

"Who are you, to tell me how to speak with my wife!" he demands.

"Someone who holds her dear as well, and who has known her far longer," I snap back.

"Enough, the both of you!" Adelina says. "I do not need to be sheltered, Bella, and yes, Sebastiano, I realize that this is real life and not a pretty story, but I have faith that things work out as they should, always and ever."

I say, flatly, "Yes, everything has gone as it should, I am sure. Including killing my own student."

It is the first time I have actually said it out loud, and the words are like an explosion, leaving silence in their wake. Once again, I see Skye's face, first lost in love, and then twisted, dying of her own poison, but inadvertently given by my own hand.

They both stare at me, and I realize there are tears on my face, come there without my noticing, and that more are following.

"I …" and I falter, because I do not know what it is that I should ask for.

But Adelina, dear Adelina, knows as I thought she might and she says, gently, "You are tired and overwrought, Bella. Come. I will fix you some food and then you will sleep, and then we will think again."

It is tempting, so tempting. But I say, "First, I need to find Leonoa."

"She was arrested," Adelina says.

I gesture dismissively. "Yes, yes, I know that. But where would she have been kept?"

Adelina's face is pale. She says, "Think, Bell."

My eyes search her face. "Think of what?"

"She was arrested for preaching abolitionism, which the Duke likens to sedition," Adelina says. "He keeps—or kept, rather, I guess—those prisoners close at hand."

My stomach drops as the import of her words begins to dawn on me.

"Close at hand," I echo, and each word is a thud of despair falling to the ground.

She does not need to say it, but she does. "Close at hand. In the cells beneath the castle."

None of those prisoners will have survived the castle's fall. But I start for the door, nonetheless.

"Where are you going?" Adelina protests.

"To the castle," I say. Where else?

THE DOOR SLAMMED SHUT after the swiftly moving Bella Kanto.

Adelina and Sebastiano looked at each other. Adelina said, "This is a lot to process."

"It is," Sebastiano agreed, "a conglomeration of strangeness wrapped in a riddle."

"Lucy! Who would ever have thought that Lucy would become … whatever it is that she has become."

"And who would have thought Bella Kanto would return from exile simply to play messenger to you?" Sebastiano said, his tone dry as sand.

Adelina said, "You know she and I are friends; you have known that all along."

"You and I were friends once."

"And moved from that to lovers, where we stay, and where no one can depose you, even Bella Kanto."

Love surged in him to match her fond tone and he stooped so they might kiss, before he said, "I understand Lucy, at least as far a part as she plays in this so far. But Bella Kanto?"

"Someone stripped her of the magic that sustained her, by unlinking her from the city," Adelina said. "What if the Dragons think that it can be restored to her and thus be the one to defeat Lucy?"

"Why would the Dragons want to save Tabat? Some of their own have been imprisoned here, over the centuries."

"Not so much to save Tabat as to destroy Lucy," she said. "They fear what she might become."

"But how do they think Bella's magic can be restored?"

Adelina thought. "She was linked to the city," she said. "But how does one restore that? It cannot be as simple as the Duke annulling her exile. Not that he would be likely to do such a thing. If he is still alive to do so."

Sebastiano gazed at her. "Adelina," he said. "There is something that concerns me more. How do you think Lucy feels about you?"

"Not particularly happy," Adelina said. "She held grudges, that child. But how would she know where to find me?"

"That child has magic power enough to level a castle, and you think it may be the case that she could not find you? No, it will occur to her sooner or later. So it is even more urgent that we must get you —and my parents—out of the city."

"If she has enough power to level a castle and also to find me in Tabat, why would she not find me elsewhere?" Adelina argued in turn.

The truth was the thought of leaving Tabat in the middle of all this significant history occurring horrified her. A scholar of history did not get to experience its events as often as they would like, and she would be in an unparalleled position to write an account of it that had a good chance of becoming a definitive one, one that people looked to when writing on the subject. That was her secret pleasure, and it was one of the reasons she pursued her histories, although she would not have admitted it.

So she could not, would not leave just yet.

And Jilly's powder—she must still be able to find it somewhere in the city. There would be not even a possibility of it, outside of it.

"No," she said. "The more important thing is to figure out how we are to do this."

"I do not think the Dragons tossed her to you like a ball."

"No? Perhaps they are relying on chance and making it better when they can. Think, Sebastiano. An expert researcher, an expert Mage. Who better to figure this out?"

"Where would we start?"

"At the library of the College of Mages," she said.

"Where neither of us would be admitted."

"You have a better chance than I," she said. "You know the place and perhaps have friends left there who may abet you."

"Perhaps," he said dubiously.

"And while you do that, I will look to history and see what I can discover of Tabat's founding. It may well be that this is something that has stood since the city was first formed."

CHAPTER 14

Perhaps if he could not persuade Adelina to leave the city for her own sake, she could be persuaded to do so for the benefit of his parents, particularly Letha, whom Adelina had taken to as though she were her own mother, or more accurately, a mother with whom she got along with better than she ever had Emiliana.

The Great Tram was no longer running, nor any of the other trams. People choked the stairways, going up and down, many of them carrying gear or household belongings, on their way to find escape from the city. Few Beasts were in evidence; those that were followed their Human owners closely, and kept their eyes down, as though afraid of being challenged. Unsurprising, when the city was in such turmoil.

But then, coming up the stairway, he became aware of a hush around him, a pausing in the crowd. He looked to see what everyone was staring at.

A Minotaur, an older one than Sebastiano had ever seen before, stepping down slowly, flanked by two much younger of his kind. All three towered over the crowd. The trio moved in concert, not looking at the Humans, but their disregard was more one of fearlessness. It was that moment that made Sebastiano realize—none of the Duke's guards or Peacekeepers were in sight. There was no one there to enforce laws against free Beasts.

He found himself grinning to himself. It was good to see them walking without fear, it was what hidebound Tabat deserved. He would tell his mother about it, and she would enjoy it as he had.

When he arrived at his parents' house in one of the most respectable parts of Tabat, he was surprised. Elsewhere in the city there was a certain amount of chaos and more than a few were vacating the city before trouble came calling. But here it was serene and quiet, as though nothing were out of the ordinary and nothing to be feared.

He did note fewer servant Beasts than he had seen before here. Abolitionism had brought plenty of changes to Tabat, even as a secret movement, and one of them was that people did not trust Beasts as they once had, particularly when rumor had maintained that recent mysterious killings had been the result of one.

Truth was that killer had not been a Beast, but rather one twisted into a monstrous shape and then sent out to destroy. The Sorcerer Murga had schemed from the beginning to bring confusion and chaos to Tabat. A task for which he had been paid by the Duke, who hoped that if the crisis were severe enough, the people would forestall the elections and keep him as leader.

Another sign of how out of touch the Duke was. If he had been a leader, perhaps, like some of his predecessors … But Alberic had never shown any sign of being outside the norm, unless it was in the amount of his vices, which were many. He had been a figurehead that thought himself the whole of the ship, that was the problem.

A servant showed him into the parlor where Letha sat with a basket of small jesses, mending them. He did not engage in preamble but went straight to the point. "Mother, Tabat is in danger of falling. There is no one to keep order. You and Father need to get out now."

She bit off a thread before replying. "Sebastiano! I have heard the rumors, but everyone thinks it is the Duke causing chaos. One last thrashing attempt to have his way."

"Would he have destroyed his own castle?"

"If he thought it would allow him to keep his position, one that would later be able to rebuild it? Of that I have no doubt."

"The College of Mages acknowledges it a real danger. We go to fight it tomorrow."

He had not meant to tell her that, but he wanted her to know that the College was taking it seriously, and that she should as well.

"They discharged you, Sebastiano! What is this talk of *we?*"

"They have called everyone in, Mother. Everyone with even the slightest scrap of magic. To band together in order to repel the danger."

She rolled her eyes. "So the College of Mages is colluding with him. That is nothing new. They, like so many others, fear change."

Sebastiano knew his mother was a staunch, if secret, Abolitionist. Like her fellows, she believed the current system unfair, and felt that the Beasts should have their justice. He had even thought she might be involved with Murga's doings at one point, and had been relieved to find his suspicions unfounded.

"Here's the thing," he said. "I want Adelina to leave. To keep her safe. And if she thought that she was going in order to keep you safe, that might persuade her where I cannot."

His mother's eyes brightened. "Oh Sebastiano! She is with child, and you wish to protect her!"

He turned bright red. "No!" he said. Well, certainly she could be, but they were avoiding that sort of complication at the moment. But either way, he did not need his mother thinking about him and Adelina doing the sort of thing that led to one becoming pregnant.

Letha looked disappointed. "No?" she murmured. "Well, one can continue hoping."

"Mother!" Sebastiano said. He could feel his ears turning red.

Letha laid down the work in her lap and folded her hands over it, looking straight at him. "Sebastiano, I have no intention of leaving the city I have always lived in, and I suspect Adelina doesn't either. And neither of us are children, to be shipped from one place to another against our wills."

Pulled by the sound of their raised voices, Sebastiano's father appeared in the doorway, furrowing his brows.

"What's all this hubbub?" He scowled at Sebastiano. Despite the fact that Sebastiano was following his wishes in pursuing Adelina, he had not forgiven his son his previous intransigence, or the incident in which Sebastiano had destroyed his beloved garden.

"You need to evacuate," Sebastiano said.

To his surprise, his father nodded. "I have been thinking about that," he said heavily. "But I do not think it is possible, Sebastiano. If everyone flees, the city will fall to chaos and looting, even without any other menace. Our holdings are mainly here, in the city. And so we will stay to protect them."

"Your lives are worth more than those holdings," Sebastiano protested.

His father smiled at him. "They are your holdings, too," he said. "They are not mine or your mother's. They belong to our family." Behind his words lurked a long procession of Silvercoins, all dedicated to the house in a way that Sebastiano had never been.

"Very well!" Sebastiano snapped, and saw his father's smile slip away as though it had never been. "But this is foolish beyond measure!"

"It is the Duke, I tell you," Letha began, but was interrupted by the sound of thunder.

The sky had been quite clear when Sebastiano entered.

WHEN SHE EMERGED from the caverns, Lucy blinked in the daylight, but soon adjusted. Sunshine was pouring down on the city, and it was as if she had destroyed nothing, as if she had not brought down the Duke's castle, as though she had not consumed every Dryad log the city depended on to drive it. The energy from the logs burned in her, restlessly trying to pour out. She must use some of it soon or die.

She had decided she would keep Leonoa as a pet and although the woman was not consulted on the decision, she seemed resigned to it nonetheless. Lucy put her where she would be safe, a crack in the rock face above the city, a space no one could reach unless they were capable of flight. She said, by way of explanation, "You will be safe here."

"Safe from what, I wonder," Leonoa murmured but made no other objection.

Lucy didn't worry about her any further. She spread her arms and leaped into the air again. The sky this morning was a brilliant kingfisher blue, a few wisps of clouds already being boiled away by the sun.

She shot up into the sky so fast only a few saw her, gaped after the sight, not sure what they had seen. She found herself lost in a roiling white cloud, plunged through its nothingness and then was higher yet, far above it. She hovered, took a breath, stretched out her hands, spread her fingers.

The city looked calm far below.

She would change that.

Hanging in the air, she reached out with invisible senses, invisible arms that stretched for miles and beyond. Wind roared around her, rushing in at her pull. On the southern horizon, an edge of gray appeared.

She could feel the water and electricity in the air around her. Reaching out to tug it closer, she yanked it harder and harder until it rushed inward to boil in a dark cloud at her feet, spreading quickly. Thunder rumbled as she did it, and the citizens of Tabat glanced upward at the darkening sky, unnaturally fast, unnaturally dark. Those who could sought shelter against the sky's violent promise.

She pulled harder.

Clouds raced towards her, dark and full of rain; lightning flickered around them as though in outrage at their summoning.

Within moments, the clear sky was dark. She hung in the boiling clouds, and threw her head back, and laughed, almost giddy with the chance to finally release some of the magic harvested from the Dryad logs. The city had thought to use the magic of the Dryads for sustenance. Like a tick, a parasite, a thing that could not exist without the lives of others to feed it. Very well, let that very magic it had gathered to sustain it be its destruction.

The first lightning bolt hit the ancient tower near the Brides of Steel with a *CRACK* that echoed across the city. For a moment it was outlined in light brighter than any actinic streetlamp, and then it crumbled inward.

With an enormous flash of lightning, the power whipped out and slammed into a cathedral towering over its neighboring buildings. For a moment it seemed to hold together via the thick ivy covering it, but then that crumpled inward, and there was only a cloud of dust. Another bolt struck at a ministry building, catching it solidly in the stonework carving about its double-doored entrance, smashing it inward as though a giant fist had punched at it. Yet another streaked towards the highest tower of the College of Mages, but there blue fire leapt to meet it, a protective spell that drove the energy away to crash into the cobblestones of the street outside the College grounds, creating an enormous rocky divot in the ground.

Lucy didn't pay attention to that. She could tend to the College later. For now, she was glorying in destruction, flinging handfuls of lightning down towards the city with every sweep of her arms. She could feel the magic rushing through her as though it wanted to be expended. As though it were yearning for destruction and always had been.

Another crack, this time at the arena. This one hit sideways, took down a back wall but left most of the structure intact. Then the Temples of the Moon came in for their turn, and more, because Lucy's anger at them ran deep. She leveled the Temples, and the priests and their worshippers fled the falling buildings. Not everyone escaped. She kept pummeling the buildings, not leaving off until they were shattered, torn asunder. The Moon Temples had been the first to injure her, declaring that she was her brother's to decide what should be done with her. The Temples had encouraged her apprenticeship because they wanted money from her. The Temples made no sense, and she did not fear the Moons, because if they held power, surely they would have stopped her by now.

She left off throwing lightning bolts when it became boring.

That certainly seemed to have stirred things up. She smiled with satisfaction like a cat licking cream, and left off for now. Let them fear she was about to return.

She had softened up the city, caused chaos. She had destroyed the Duke, who must have died in her first attack, although she had found no body that she thought was his. She had destroyed the Temples and now she thought it might be time for some individual revenge. Her sisters, for one. Wouldn't they be surprised to see her? Maybe she could even pretend to be friendly at first. To have forgiven them. Smile at them. And then, when they would be most surprised by it …

The thought stopped her. Did she really intend to *kill* them? She had grown up with them. They were her family and the Temples said she should love them.

She remembered how they had blamed her for their mother's death. How they had struck her, even *pissed* on her. Her lips firmed.

No. They deserved to die.

She would spare Eloquence. Once he saw how powerful she was, he would appreciate her. Would want to serve her, even. She'd be the head of the family then, and once she felt she had punished him enough, everything could be the same again.

Yes, that was exactly what to do.

The rain began. It was the hardest rain Tabat had ever known in centuries of coastal storms. It slid over the roof tiles, prying handfuls loose, it beat the vegetation in the parks flat and trees leaned and cracked in the driving wind. Householders sprang to fasten windows, fighting the wind that seemed to try to pull everything from their grasp. Carts blew sideways, the bakery carts scattering trails of pastries.

Bolt after bolt after bolt, each one tinged with the blue fire that filled Lucy's veins, each one magic and natural energies combined in an irresistible force that struck and punched and battered the city, until Lucy felt herself hovering near the point of exhaustion, was alarmed to realize she had reached much deeper than she had meant to. Hastily she pulled her power back in, used it to push herself through the air, hidden by the clouds, until she regained the safety of her cliffside cave.

Leonoa was toward the back, having retreated from the storm's wrath lashing at the cavern's entrance. She was huddled in on herself, looking small. For a second sympathy stirred in Lucy's breast—she remembered huddling under the statue of Sparkfinger Jack, feeling as miserable and alone as this woman must. And then she remembered that this was Bella's cousin and therefore part of her revenge on Bella Kanto, and throttled down all sympathy, hardening her face as she landed.

She did not fear any violence from the little woman, so she ignored her and sorted through the pack of food she'd brought up from the Duke's stores and ate ravenously, trying to fill the void inside her.

Leonoa remained where she was, hunched over herself. Was she still alive? Lucy got up and strode over to her. She toed the little woman in the side, not too roughly, but definitely firmly. "What's wrong?"

Leonoa unhunched a little. "The cold and wind makes my bones hurt."

"Hurt a lot?" Lucy asked. She wished she hadn't expended all her energy. If she'd had enough left, she could have healed her here and now, and bound the woman to her forever with gratitude. That would have been good.

Oh well, it could wait. She had enough to sweep her hand and summon a flicker of fire in the center of the cave. The space must have housed a lookout in some former time, the only remnants the neatly stacked wood and a rusty lantern devoid of oil. "There."

Leonoa hobbled over to take wood and feed it to the fire. She spread her hands to the blaze. "Thank you," she said, her voice sincere and without a single note of "I wouldn't be here in the first place without you." Lucy wasn't sure she could have resisted the urge if she had been in Leonoa's place.

She sat down beside the fire and Leonoa sat on the other side, and they sat without speaking while outside the storm slowly died, ebbing more and more every time Leonoa fed the flames. After a while they both fell asleep.

CHAPTER 15

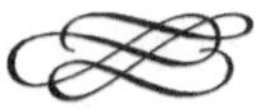

The suddenness of the storm took everyone by surprise, and three ships foundered in the harbor before anyone realized what was going on. The first strike of lightning, aimed at the clock tower, screamed through the sky as it came, hit with a *BOOM* that sent stones from the tower flying, shattering windows, knocking down trees and lamp posts, and showers of sparks flew everywhere as though the destroyed lamp posts had become fountains.

The storm ripped across the city, smashing into walls, knocking down trees, leaving devastation in its wake. Where Lucy's attack the previous day had been one of bolts directed at specific targets, this was more indiscriminate damage, hitting the houses of the poor and the rich alike, Beasts and Humans, uncaring who or where it hit.

The Duke's plaza was deserted, the machines that drove the marvel of a waterfall that once filled its center now stilled. Where once speakers clustered to address the crowds, there was no one, only bits of trash and crumpled feather cockades scudding across the cobblestones, driven by the wind.

Every window in the Duke's Teahouse smashed inward at once from a stray bolt, showering the panicked Humans crowded into its confines to take shelter.

Down at the docks, waves crashed against structures, a confusion of boats sent this way and that, at least those that were left, that did not make their escape earlier in the day, a choice their captains and owners were now regretting.

The same fierce waves reached into the outskirts of the Sea Garden, tumbling and smashing into the vases of the lilies so they fell, one by one, into the sea, despite the best efforts of the attendants to save them. As they fell, each flower opened and wailed its dismay, a long shrill lament drowned out by the cacophony of stone and water.

The furnaces below the city were cold and dead, and their reserves, already depleted, were completely destroyed. A group of terrified Humans were trapped in the Great Tram, watching lightning fly around them until a bolt hit the cage directly. Some people sheltered in their cellars and basements, praying that the spaces would not become their tombs. Others foolishly ventured into the storm, hoping to flee the city. Only a few made it; the winds were fierce enough to pick up a child now, and people clung to each other as they scrabbled along.

A bolt hit near the Peacekeeper offices. If Lucy had been aiming for it, she had missed, but the strike set the building to shaking, including the chamber where the Duke huddled while his soldiers and officers had almost forgotten him, trying to figure out what to do. The Duke could hear shouts and people running up and down the stairs.

The terrifying child—he had peeped out a window and seen her glowing in the sky—was striking at the city, his city, and surely she wanted to destroy him, its leader, its center. He would not look out the window again until the storm was over. She would have no way of knowing where he was.

How to escape the city, by boat or by land? Which route would be more likely to elude her notice? Would she even care about him? She had the city, after all. That made him relax a little, just a little.

Surely he would be low on her list of priorities. After all a child would not understand what a leader, a real leader, could do for a city. He puffed himself up, just a little more, recovering his normal equilibrium. Perhaps this would all be to his advantage and he could, somehow, emerge the hero of the city in a way that would make it clear it was best for Tabat—for all of them—if he continued to rule.

More shouts, more footsteps. The scrabble of mechanical limbs, his hounds, once his pride. It was amazing that they were still sticking with the city, the ones that were. Why were they doing it, other than some sense that they should be protecting it?

In the sky, green lightning bolts flickered and played around the distant figure of Lucy, and thunder growled continuously, not stopping, like an angry animal.

I COULD HAVE FOUND shelter with Adelina and her consort, but I have other things to do. First, before anything else, I must find my cousin Leonoa. They claimed that she was in the castle, in the Duke's dungeons. Very well, then, I will seek her there.

No one is going up the road towards the castle. I wonder where Alberic is, whether he died in the attack. It seems as though his death would have been more remarked, but who knows?

I walk quickly, without worrying about cover or who notices me. No one recognizes me. And if they did, well, I have flown with Dragons, I have faced down foe after foe. I have been exiled and return. I am and always will be, Bella Kanto.

I am halfway up the road when the winds begin. I have never felt anything like their strength; I must cling to things as I go, to avoid being swept away by the force of the gales. This is no natural storm— Lucy must be causing it somehow. I would wonder what it is that she intends to do, but I already know. Storms hold lightning, and that will rain down on Tabat. If there were only some way to warn people. I stare up at the sky and for a moment I think I glimpse the girl hanging there low among the clouds.

The first lightning strike hits the tower near the Brides of Steel, the one I used to take students to for climbing practice, with a clap of thunder so close it hurts my ears, and I see it fall. At least I know that bolt touched no one that I love. I cannot pick out Adelina's house from here, nor Leonoa's, nor any other small detail. The wind is too fierce, it scrapes cold fingers across my face until my eyes are streaming with tears.

At least, I tell myself that is why I am crying as I stand huddled in the shelter of a rock crevice and watch bolt after bolt fall on the city I love. Perhaps I am lucky to be severed from it now, because surely those hard blows would hurt me too. I try to find my connection to the city, even so. I was once Tabat's heart, and now I am useless.

The storm dies down quickly, almost as quickly as it appeared. The bruised sky clears, and I don't see Lucy in it. I press on and when I reach the castle's courtyard, everything is quiet. Gritty, wet dirt and ash coats everything, the legacy of falling and sundered stone. Alberic was proud of those towers. He used to love to go up in the southernmost, the one almost hanging over the cliff face, and look down at the city and call it his.

It is Lucy's city now, I think.

What will she choose to do with it? The child I spoke to in the Southern Isles was full of hate and revenge and anger at those she felt had wronged her.

How do I tell her, sometimes it is not a person that wrongs you and puts you where you do not want to be? Sometimes it is simply life that does that to you, and it is hard to imagine it is not personal, because an impersonal universe is the hardest thing to bear of all.

I look down at the city, and wonder, where is Selene? If she is a goddess, is it not time for her to act? Why would she depend on a frail mortal to enact her will? That makes no sense—gods are all-powerful, by definition, more powerful than any mortal.

I am very afraid that she is a delusion, a crutch my mind has created for me, a thing that my ego has animated into a puppet to console itself for my lost stature and position. Is this not all ego on my part? Who am I, that the white Moon would climb down from the sky to kiss me?

I take a breath and steel myself, leave doubts behind as I used to do, launching myself into the fight with only resolution and determination in my soul. I am Bella Kanto; Bella Kanto is sufficient unto herself. That, I have begun to learn.

IN THE MIDST of the chaos, the craving crept up on Adelina.

She had only taken Jilly's drug when speaking at first. It made her words take wing, made them soar and convince, cajole and persuade in a way she had never been able to do with the spoken word before. That was exhilarating.

Now there was no question of rallies in the face of all this devastation, and that meant nowhere to speak.

She had eked out the drug, grain by grain, but it had gone faster than she would have liked, nonetheless. She kept it in a drawer of underclothing, reasoning that Sebastiano would be unlikely to run across it there. The last time she had unfolded the cloth around the paper packet, she had opened it and found only a few grains left. She licked her finger and painfully, slowly, transferred every grain she could find to her own lips. It had been barely enough.

They were huddled in the cellar along with some of the building's other tenants. Sebastiano had his arm around her and that should have been enough, the warmth and comfort of that arm. And instead, she could feel the urge bumping up against her, the craving slowly crawling over her. She could sense the long hard hours waiting ahead of her, the constant companion that would be at her elbow, tugging at her sleeve.

She cursed the day she had tried Jilly's powder. She had paid enough for it by now that Sebastiano should have noticed that somehow she never seemed to have enough coin. But he trusted her. She laid her head on his shoulder and tried to think of other things.

The worry that the devastation would prevent her from finding Jilly again came to her and she thought with a trace of panic, *No, there must be others who know of the drug and can sell it to me. Who else, though?* She ran through names in her head, digging deep into childhood friends, girls she'd been to school with. Tetsy BarkBramble, she'd always been a little wild. But where would Tetsy be, nowadays? As lost to her as Jilly.

"It'll be all right," Sebastiano whispered in her ear, his breath warm, his fingers stroking along her back. She realized he had mistaken the source of her trembling for fear.

"Of course it will be," she said, and was reassured to hear her voice strong and steady, betraying nothing of her internal turmoil. This was not the time to admit weakness.

SEBASTIAN HAD NEVER SEEN Adelina afraid before, but here in the crowded cellar, smelling of roots and the other bodies huddled around them, he could feel the strain in her body. He patted her back and soothed her as he would have a nervous Beast. "It'll be all right."

"Of course it will be," she gamely echoed him. What a brave soul she was.

They both flinched at a nearby strike, a massive boom that made the walls shake.

"It must be Lucy," Adelina said. "This isn't a storm that came from nowhere."

"Yes," he agreed. "I can feel the magic in the air. She's expending enormous amounts. I don't know where it all could be coming from."

"Bella had Tabat's magic backing her," Adelina said. "Is Lucy somehow drawing on it too?"

He shook his head with a definiteness that he did not entirely feel. "Certainly not. She's attacking Tabat, not trying to absorb it. If she wanted that power, she would have to …" He paused, considering his words. "Have to seduce it, in a way. Not literally. But make it love her."

"Is that what Bella did? I thought it was the magic that made everyone love her."

He smiled briefly. "No. Little as I like Bella—"

"You have no reason to be jealous of her."

He brought her fingers to her lips and kissed them. "I thank you for that reassurance, though it is not necessary. No, I do not like her for a multitude of reasons, but she is your friend, and so I will not express any of that. But as I was saying, she is Bella Kanto, and the force of her personality does not, I think, have a supernatural origin. Some people are like that. Larger than life."

"She is that," Adelina agreed. Bella had always been larger than life, as long as Adelina had known her.

Another blast, so close that dust sifted down from the roof above them, and everyone held their breath, waiting to see if it would fall. It creaked but held, and there were soft murmurs of relief.

Sebastiano, trying to distract her, teased, "Are you sure that I have no cause for jealousy? I saw your face when she mentioned the woman Scylla."

Adelina sniffed indignantly. "It is not that at all. It is me realizing that she left out parts of the story when she first told it to me, and as a historian, I have certain objections to that."

Seeing his smile, she said, "I am not in love with her any longer, Sebastiano, not even a little. But I will always feel friendship to her and more than that, I have listened to her stories and written them down."

"And improved them, more than once, I suspect," he said. "How much a part did you play in her magic, I wonder? Every citizen of Tabat that read your stories adding their own little thread of magic to her."

Adelina stared. He said, "That hadn't occurred to you already?"

"I didn't understand magic could work that way. You say the thing that marks the difference between Beasts and Humans is that they are magic, while Humans wield magic. How does that notion reconcile with this?"

He sobered a little, glancing around at the others in the crowded basement. "Perhaps not the time to speak of this, my love."

"I don't think the Peacekeepers will be patrolling for Abolitionists right now," she said.

"Abolitionists!" the man said beside her. "That's how we got into all this mess, I'll be sure. Messing around and riling up the Beasts." He glared suspiciously at Adelina but Sebastiano said, smoothly, "Indeed, and that is why my wife and I are so worried."

He put an arm around her and said, "There, there." Adelina resisted the urge to hit him and instead leaned into him, but privately resolved that he had not heard the last of this.

CHAPTER 16

When the storm hit, Teo was down near the docks, scavenging for fish or other scraps despite the fierce competition from gulls and other street urchins. But the chill wind tugged at him, claiming his attention, and when he saw the clouds racing across the sky, unnaturally fast, alarmingly dark with rain, he thought, "Lucy."

He looked around himself at the panicked surge of sailors securing their ships, shop owners bustling wares set outside in the sun back inside now and closing their shutters. As the first drops of rain began to hit, he ducked into an alleyway and sheltered in a doorway there.

He was not the only occupant. Two slim Fox-kin sheltered there. When he first came in, they started to leave, but he said, "It's all right, it's all right," realizing that they thought a Human would not want to share shelter with them. They exchanged a silent glance, and did not reply to him, but they did not leave, either.

The rain drove down like icy needles, and all of them drew together. When the lightning strikes began, Teo bit back panic. What if Lucy were looking for him, what if she meant to throw these lightnings at him? She must be angry, so angry that he had run away from her. He thought of all the things he had seen her do, all things that she could do to him, and the thought scared him so deep down he could barely keep from pissing himself.

The Fox-kin, who seemed to be sisters, had their arms around each other. When he let out a little whine under his breath at a loud clap, one reached out and pulled him into the embrace. He didn't resist. If he had still been in puppy form, his tail would have wagged. He held the other two close, and they him, and together the three of them rode out the terror of the storm.

THE LANDSCAPE WAS a strange one when Adelina and Sebastiano emerged, along with the others, its familiarity overwritten with changes. An entire block of buildings gone, just twisted rubble, and another cluster of them burned and black. A Figgis Bakery cart overturned, rats and street children running away with the spilled contents. A limping Peacekeeper hound, one back leg mangled, escorted by a Human soldier, also limping.

A peculiar quiet to it all after the thunder of the storm and its attack, as though the streets were holding their breath, as though people were afraid to make noise and draw attention to these surroundings again.

The skyline reshaped, almost every tall building cast down, Was this what it was like across the length and breadth of the city? Everyone else was setting off as though they had some destination to go to. She looked at Sebastiano and he looked back.

"I need to go to the College of Mages," he said, "and find out what they intend to do. Will you go with me? It may be as safe as any other place."

She shook her head, thoughts scurrying in the back of it. "No," she said, "I have cousins I want to check on."

He frowned. "Cousins? You've never spoken of them."

"We were estranged when Mother cast me out, but I would like to make sure they're all right nonetheless."

A half truth, half lie. She did have cousins, and she'd go past their estate if she had time, but first, she would see if she could find any of Jilly Clearsight's friends.

"Very well," he said. "Will you come to me at the College later, then, or I meet you there? Or elsewhere?" He looked wryly at the remnants of their building. "Not here, I think. Is it worth trying to salvage anything from the apartment?"

Salvaging would have meant trying the staircase, which hung half-torn away. She shook her head and patted her pack. "I grabbed what I needed, didn't you?"

"Of course," he said. "But all those books. Including some of yours, love."

"Paper is paper, and you and I are flesh and blood, and we are alive," she said. "That trumps anything that we could salvage. Perhaps this is a chance to start fresh. We can go a-journeying, up to Verranzo's New City."

"Very well," he said, "But in that case we should definitely take Mother."

"Your mother! I totally forgot her. That's where we should meet."

"If it's still standing," he said grimly, but nodded acquiescence. He grabbed her to him and she sank into the kiss, his lips so soft and firm all at once, demanding and loving, and fiercely hers.

He pulled away, still looking into her eyes. "Don't do anything dangerous," he said.

"You too."

As the rain finally began to die away, Teo and his companions drew apart.

He saw they were preparing to leave, no longer looking him in the face.

"I'm Teo," he blurted out. "I'm not … I'm not …" He let it die away, not sure what to say, how to convince them. Say he wasn't Human? But Beasts surely feared Shifters as deeply as any Human did.

Again the two exchanged that silent glance. They were almost identical, their fur a deep russet, their eyes flaked with gold, but one had a blaze of white at her left temple. She was the first to speak.

"I am Kitta," she said. She indicated her companion. "My sister, Miba." She faltered, then said, "Would you like us to guide you somewhere, sir?"

"Not sir!" he said. "Never sir. Just … just Teo, please." He tried to give them a smile. "Or 'Boy' if it suits you, I have heard worse."

That silent communion once more before Kitta turned back. "Teo," she said cautiously, as though tasting the name for any sign of a trap.

He nodded enthusiastically.

"Would you like us to guide you somewhere, Teo?"

"I have nowhere to go," he confessed.

This time the communion was much longer than before, but at length Kitta turned back to him. "Teo," she said, and hesitated and swallowed, and then finally said, "Would you like to come with us?"

He could have collapsed with joy but he tried to keep that from his voice, although he suspected he did not entirely succeed. "Yes," he said. "Yes please."

They led him along through alleyways and side streets, and he noticed they kept out of the way of Humans, despite the confusion and chaos of it all. They seemed to know where they were going, though, heading north along the docks, and then along the beach.

He remembered this beach, and the bonfire where the Beasts had turned him away. Were they leading him to the same place, and what if it happened again? At least these two would vouch for him, and they seemed to have no doubts about where they were leading him.

It was not the bonfire, although it was the same general area where that encounter had taken place. He saw that since then a tiny cluster of buildings, made of scrap lumber and discarded things, had sprung up, although now the storm had wreaked devastation on the tiny encampment.

As they approached, they saw other Beasts gathering up detritus and making repairs: a Minotaur carrying up logs that had washed onto the shore while beside her a Centaur carried buckets of water. Everyone was working, even the smallest child, rebuilding this space.

He was the only one of them who looked Human, but none of them questioned him when he stepped up and began to help them rebuild their homes.

WHEN THE STORM DIES AWAY, as suddenly as it came, I finish searching the ruins of the castle. It has been razed; I do not think Alberic will ever be able to rebuild it, assuming he is still alive. Too bad. It was always one of the most beautiful things in Tabat, that long stretch of cliff, and atop it the lacework of the towers.

I do not find Leonoa anywhere, though I find the cells where the prisoners are. Some still live, saved from the onslaught by the stone that imprisoned them. Others have been crushed by falling stone or died by the fire that must have swept through here, started in the kitchens and then leaping from rug to tapestry, from bookcase to bed, blackening the interior.

This is no place to be a prisoner. I free those who still live without asking why they are there. Perhaps some of them are dangerous criminals, but I am too tired to care, and I will not see anything imprisoned any more. There has been enough of that in Tabat.

I find Selene sitting on some steps as I turn a corner. She smiles at me in greeting. Her white robe is far too clean for this place; I cannot understand why none of the soot has rubbed off on her, but such is the nature of gods, it seems.

She says, "You have had a strange return to your city, Bella Kanto, but returned to it you have, nonetheless."

"Some return, if I am not actually returning to the city, but to its ruins," I say.

She shakes her head. "It has not reached that yet. And it will not, if you can save it."

"I?" I say, astonished. "I no longer hold Tabat's magic. What can I possibly do?"

Her eyes are bright and clear as stars. "Take back the magic. Murga held it for only moments and now it thrashes about, looking for you,

Bella. It remembers you. It will come back to you, if only you can find it."

"Find it where?"

But she shakes her head again, pressing her lips together. *I can tell you nothing further*, the gesture says.

I scowl at her. "What is the good of bedding a god, if they cannot tell you things?"

Someone else might have been insulted, but she laughs. "Surely the bedding is worthwhile in and of itself," she says.

"Perhaps," I say loftily, but she can see right through me and it only makes her laugh all the harder. Finally she leaves off, and says, more soberly, "You should not linger here. It is one of the places the girl comes and you cannot think to defeat her before you have been reunited with the magic."

"Where should I go to do that?" I ask, not expecting an answer. I already have an idea where that might be. And she only smiles at me as though to say I might be right.

CHAPTER 17

It has been months since I danced this city, but I know the way I am going. Once I have said goodbye to Selene and descended the long road from the castle, I pass through a trade square and start my dance. I run along a railing, ignoring startled faces, and leap and roll to land on a bench and without pause from it over a wall to the top of the Tumbril Stair.

I could do this in my sleep. And I have, I have dreamed it over and over again while I was gone.

I run now, running down the terraces one by one. I pass within glimpse of the house I used to live, Abernia's boarding house, but I resist the urge to look at it as I go by. Abernia has scorned me, as has the city. If I gain the latter back, perhaps I will have her as well. If I still want my old apartment, but I am not sure that I do.

I run along rooftops and banisters, I leap and roll, and to my joy, my body does not play me false but rises to the challenge. Is this a sign that my magic is returning? But when I do a final roll and twist, as I come finally to the gates of the Brides of Steel, my wrist gives way and I half tumble.

Not broken, but sprained, and badly so, the flesh immediately becoming angry red and puffing up.

Carrying this reminder of the loss of my invincibility, I go to the gates, with their pattern of crossed swords. They hang asunder, though it seems not as a result of the lightning strike that hit nearby, carving a crater in the street. Something else has wrenched them away.

A face appears between them, one I recognize, one that is not smiling.

"As I live and breathe," Myrila says. "Bella Kanto."

SHE HAS an ointment for my sprain, of course. She always does. She leads me without speaking to her stillroom, rolls up my sleeve, and applies something that smells like wintergreen and has a cool burn on my skin, soothing away some of the throbbing pain, making me sigh with relief. Unsmiling, she wraps it in a bandage spread with the same salve.

"Where are the girls?" I ask.

"I sent them away at the first sign of trouble," she says. "There is a training camp up the coast, the one where we were teaching them swimming and long archery, aye? I sent them there for now,"

"Was there trouble?" I ask.

Her green-eyed gaze is sharp and she barks out a little laugh. "Trouble? What kind of trouble might befall a school that trained a traitor to Tabat?"

"Is that what happened to the gates?" I ask.

She drops a quick nod. "Indeed. And before that, enrollments dropped to a trickle. There were not that many girls to send away."

I have to know. "Do you think me a traitor?"

"I think you vain and foolish enough to be tricked into something," she says, when I had been expecting a firm denial. That takes me aback and the shock of it shows on my face, apparently, because she laughs outright at me. "Admit it, Bella! You drink in flattery as though it were wine."

She sobers and pats my shoulder. "I do not blame you for it, after years of hearing things far to the contrary from your Aunt Jolietta. But you cannot live your life making up for the privations of your childhood."

"That is not what I have done!" I protest.

"Is it not?"

"It is not," I mutter, but I can see where she might be coming to such a conclusion.

"So you are back now, and I presume you are unpardoned," she says. "You know that anyone even speaking to you risks sharing your exile?"

I had known it, but I must admit that in the excitement of the return I had forgotten all of that. I've put more than one person in the same danger that Leonoa seems to have disappeared to.

"It is no matter," Myrila says unexpectedly, watching these thoughts play out across my face. Her voice is gentle ratherhs than bitter. "You cannot help being you, Bella. I cannot imagine you as anyone else, exasperating and irritating and annoying and thick-witted and vain and all manner of things, but still Bella Kanto. Who the students love, because she is kind to them and remembers what her own student days were like, and treats them accordingly, rather than with cruelty or hardheartedness, as some others have done."

These words undo me completely. They take me apart to the bone in a way I have never experienced, and all I can do is bury my face in my hands and weep.

"I failed my students," I say. "And killed one, Myrila, and that I can never undo, never atone for. Never forget."

"And that is how you learn to be an even better teacher," she says. "Are you returned to Tabat now? I cannot think that in all this chaos they will be chasing you, but on the other hand, you are notorious, Bella Kanto, and Alberic would know that you could prove a rallying point for those who would move against him."

"He has larger things to concern himself with right now," I agree. "Surely he would not be so petty ..." I trail off at the look in her eyes. We both know that he would be.

"So why are you here?" she says

I meet her eyes. "Why else?" I say and feel a touch of delight in the declaration, a bit of the old braggadocio creeping back. Here in this city I can be who I am, without apology, because I am Bella Kanto. She has come back to me.

"To save the city, of course."

WE BOTH DECIDE that food is necessary and adjourn to the kitchen. Myrila gives me chal, and fresh bread. "They made the delivery before I thought to cancel it," she says, and scowls down at the basketfuls. "Very well, I might as well let the girls left here eat their fill of pastries."

Now that I have failed to find Leonoa, I must figure out what it is that I am supposed to do. The Dragons have told me nothing.

It occurs to me that I left Adelina too early. She may have some idea how it is I am supposed to defeat this impossible, powerful child.

But no—what can history have to share that might help me?

CHAPTER 18

At sunset, Teo slipped away from the Beasts to meet with Maisie. He told Kitta and Miba he'd be back, and they nodded without question.

Maisie was waiting for him with her Clovian winged rabbit in her arms.

"Why did you bring him?" Teo asked, petting the soft fur under its chin.

Maisie looked uneasy. "People been disappearing," she said. "The Rappinos were saying that they thought Murga was causing it all, and then they vanished, which didn't convince anyone they were wrong. Now we moved out of the College of Mages and down near the Slumpers, everyone split up."

She shuddered. "I used to think the circus was home," she said. "Close as a home ever got for me, and I ain't the only one. Plenty of folks were sheltering there. But then things started to get … well, dark is the only way I can describe it. Too many strangers coming around. The Duke's men, every once in a while. Jonas said something to one of them, and they beat him bad. He went off to the hospital and no one's seen him since. His mouse went with him."

Teo's throat tightened at the thought of the gentle man he'd helped clean the circus's grounds.

Maisie continued. "We even stopped performing; Murga said we'd lost so many people we couldn't go on, but that wasn't the truth of it. We'd worked on shoestring lines before, we could have done it again. But when we left the College of Mages, it was like he gave up any pretense of us being a circus. We still get fed, but there's no money other than that. The ones still here, well, they're ones who didn't have much other choice. Like me."

She tried to give him the rabbit, saying she was afraid Murga might do something to it, but he refused.

"Come with me," he urged, and at first she shook her head but then, eventually, she acquiesced and followed him back to the seashore camp.

THAT NIGHT WATCHING Maisie and the fox girls play with the rabbit, Teo thought that perhaps he might stay in the city after all. They were kind to him here, and they didn't question him. They were generous, in a way people had not been since Bella brought him in from the streets. Fed and clothed him. Treated him like a person. And they were insignificant. Lucy would not come here, they were not a grand lot of people for her to throw down and lord herself over.

But the north—his village—still called to him. If nothing else, he wanted them to know that he had learned how to shift. That he had not been a failure, that sending him away had been unfair. He wondered how his sister was, and if she ever thought about the sacrifice that he'd been forced to make on her behalf.

He missed them all, but he was still so angry with them for sending him away.

Waves washed in towards the shore and the bonfire they had built there, setting skewers of fish and braid of kelp to roast. There was not a lot of food, but what there was, was shared freely and without question. He chewed on a salty knot of grilled kelp, savoring the charred flecks, the tang of brine, and debated what he should do.

IN THE BRIDES OF STEEL, Myrila is less pleased to have Bella Kanto back than she might have thought she would be. This is a haunted Bella, a Bella who does not have the same assurance that her business partner always had. There is a hesitancy about her, less trust that the Universe will provide whatever and whenever is demanded of it.

At the same time—is there not some secret side of assurance that glints forth, every once in a while? The old Bella, who always knew herself loved. It was a Bella she had not thought to see again, after all that had happened. Not that she ever expected to see Bella again, after the sentence of exile had been pronounced. She did not believe the charges, but a business owner must sometimes acquiesce in the name of keeping clients.

She has never reproached Bella for what happened to Skye. She knows Bella will chastise herself more unerringly, more relentlessly, than Myrila ever could.

While Myrila is correct, Bella is not currently chastising herself. Instead she is asleep; she has always been excellent at falling asleep instantly.

The docks are awash in debris and shattered planking, and mer-creatures have come into the harbor to take what they will before heading back out to the less turbulent waters.

Sebastiano and Adelina are both awake in their bed in the half-repaired apartment, but believe each other asleep. Sebastiano is trying to think what avenues may lead to Lucy's defeat, but nothing Bella has said makes him think that this will be easy. Adelina started by thinking about a similar subject, what historical records might show, but now the longing for Jilly's drug is consuming her, is fire seeping through her veins, making her twitchy and restless.

After an hour, Sebastiano has fallen asleep and is heading towards dreams. Adelina is still awake.

Lucy and Leonoa are both asleep in their rocky crevice. Leonoa's face is resolute, even in her dreams. Lucy's is more restless, changing from moment to moment as she dreams.

The Moons, looking down on Tabat, move back and forth in the sky.

TEO DRIFTED through dreams like green water, layers of meaning and obscurity, fish colored like memories moving through tangles of green and blue weed. In the water near his eyes, constellations of plankton and brine shrimp, jellyfish and octopuses the size of pinheads, swirling against his skin in almost imperceptible touches, sparks of life.

There in the distance, something slowly moving towards him, what seemed an immense bulk at first revealing itself something smaller and closer, the curtains of water giving it a strange and shimmering appearance.

The Oracular Turtle from so long ago, and on it, riding it, a figure he remembered so quick and hard it shot through him like a knife: his sister. One hand holding onto the turtle's shell where it gapped to let the turtle's neck protrude through, the other holding something that he recognized as it came closer, the wooden carving he had given her.

He tried to call out, to greet her, but water rushed into his mouth, tasting of salt and fish-tang, filling it completely so he could not even close it, let alone utter words.

The turtle and his sister grew closer, so close he might have reached a hand out to touch them, but the thought came to him as he saw his sister's paleness, the wildness of the curls that floated in the current, "She is dead."

He knew it in his heart for a truth the moment it came to him. It sank into him like a harpoon, the hurt of the thought that she was gone, and on its heels, the hurt that all his sacrifice had been worth nothing to the Moons, after all. That his parents had wasted him.

His sister and the turtle opened their mouths together, and their words were silver bubbles in his ears, filling his head, so tight and close that he thought it might explode. All that was were the words around him.

"Go and find your coin," they said.

But they would have had it back at home, wouldn't they? He had swapped coins the night he left, exchanged his true one for the coin of his Shadow Twin, who had died in birth. The coin would be there at home, with his parents. Was his sister trying to tell him to go home?

He woke and found himself in the warm sand of the beach, other Beasts around him, Maisie in a puppy pile with the two fox girls, all of them close, close enough to feel like family.

He rolled on his back and stared up at the white Moon. What should he do?

CHAPTER 19

The handful of girls left at the Brides of Steel, whose families have not come or sent for them for one reason or another, rise at their usual hour and eat their fill of pastries. Most of the servants and teachers have gone: it is the five of them, Myrila, Becca, the quartermaster, and two cooks. They all eat together in the common hall and conversation is subdued. They are all on edge, all listening for another peal of thunder, another announcement that the sky is opening to rain down devastation.

Myrila is considering. Should she trust Bella to resolve all this and stay in place, or should she take the girls elsewhere? If they left the city, they would head west along the road and then, somehow, away from Tabat, find better transportation. She rubs a knuckle between her brow, hoping to rub away the dull ache of anxiety, but it is still there, no matter what she contemplates.

Very well. She will stay here. This is her school; this is her city. There are worse ways to toss the dice, and she has made much more good coin from betting on Bella than from the opposite.

Adelina has woken early, but rather than get up and make breakfast, she waits for Sebastiano to do so. She feels achy and drawn.

She wishes she had not given way to the temptation of the drug, so long ago. She wishes she had put aside more.

She wishes she knew where Jilly is, or anyone that might be willing to help her. At least in all the chaos, there are no more public gatherings for her to speak at, so there will be no one to hear her stammer and halt where once she had been fluent, eloquent, even compelling. She had enjoyed those moments of knowing she was doing something difficult well, and it was at those times that she thought she might almost understand what it had been like for Bella, being the Champion of Tabat, and winning time after time.

But Bella had cheated, hadn't she? It was the magic that had made her invincible. Well, then, even more similar to the drug Adelina had grown so habituated to. She lies in bed and thinks dire thoughts while Sebastiano sings in the kitchen, putting together biscuits which he will drizzle with honey.

Much to his surprise, Adelina will not eat any. They are dry and boring to her, and she tries to avoid hurting Sebastiano's feelings, but nonetheless she does. He does not stay to press her; he must be at the College of Mages at dawn to help with their spell.

Eloquence has risen early. As he always does, having no choice in this house with his loud family. He has repented of his earlier insanity. He will go to the Moon Temples and find out what he should do. Food is already growing scarce, since those that can afford it are buying and hoarding whatever they can find.

AFTER A TIME, Teo wandered the transformed Tabat. His dream had said to go and find his coin, but surely that was still with Murga, in whatever remained of the Autumn Moon. But that was not really his coin, but that of his Shadow Twin, the one who had died. He pondered again. Did the dream mean to go home, where he had left it? But how? It would be such a long journey, and he had so little money.

He went down the Moonway, and the tiles underfoot were no longer lustrous, gleaming in accordance with the state of the Moons, but instead blackened and charred as though they had been burnt. The apricot trees lay smashed to the ground, splotches of juice showing where fruit had rolled in the gutters before being collected. The air smelled of rotting lichen and broken stone.

He passed through what had once been a high archway, and paused, picking up a fragment of rubble carved with half moons, then tossed it away from him.

Lucy must have been very angry at the Temples, because she had destroyed them utterly, flattened them with blast after blast of lightning. This was the section of town that had borne the brunt of the damage, presumably because it held the Moonway and the Temples. The buildings which had housed the clergy were torn asunder as though a hand had reached down to claw them apart.

Here and there people were moving dazedly among the ruins. It was different here than it had been in the Beasts' camp, where they had not stopped to wail or wander about looking sad, but immediately set their hands to the track of rebuilding. But Teo joined the swirls of people and pretended to be wandering.

He hoped to find the coin the priest Grave would have had, but realized soon that it was not a realistic dream. Too many buildings, and no way of knowing which of them might have housed the storage space he sought.

Then as this thought crossed his mind, he stumbled, and saw a glint of light in the rubble underfoot. He fell to his knees and dug through the rocks.

There. He grabbed the chain, pulled it up towards himself. A coin dangled on it, but before he could examine it—

"Teo?" a voice said, a familiar one.

His head snapped up. Eloquence stood a few feet away, wide-eyed.

Panic surged in Teo and he started to scramble away.

Eloquence stepped forward, holding up a hand. "It's all right," he soothed.

But it was anything but all right. He had to get away! Had to escape before the man that had been appointed to bring him to the Temples in the first place recaptured him and delivered him to them after all.

He wheeled and ran, as fast as he could.

"Stop!" Eloquence yelled after him, and then, "Stop that boy!"

Hands reached out to grab at him, snatch at him, keep him there, but he ducked and dodged his way to the gates, shouldered past the people there and escaped out into the street, strides so long he was practically flying. No one grabbed at him here but they watched in wonder the long-legged boy fleeing the broken building, and more than one tried to think what his story might be. Then they shrugged and went about their day. Because life is life after all, and went on no matter what, and there were so many other things that needed to be worried about.

ELOQUENCE STARED after the boy and cursed. He could have told him that his parents were looking for him, but before he'd had a chance, Teo had wheeled and run.

Not doubt thinking that Eloquence meant to recapture him, force him into the Temples' service that he thought to have escaped. Eloquence almost laughed. Well, he had escaped that servitude himself. And nothing that he was seeing here in the courtyard led him to feel any differently.

The Moon Temples would not save the city. They hadn't even been able to save themselves. He had thought they would be standing as always, ready to serve, ready to help those harmed by the storm, but they had fallen just like everything else.

He'd come to the Temples out of habit when summoned, and had continued onward when he realized what he was doing, so as not to be remarked by other worshippers. It was one thing to be contemplating leaving the Temples in the privacy of his own mind, but he did not want it known at large.

But the Temples' destruction now … it only convinced him that he was right. The Temples had no power other than what its worshippers gave it. There was no point in pretending otherwise.

"Eloquence!" someone shouted, "Just the man I wanted to see!"

Graciousness, the priest who had given each of his sisters his coin. Beaming now at Eloquence as though he were not standing in the shattered remains of the Temple he served. Graciousness was a great bull of a man with a wispy white beard that seemed to curl in every direction at once.

"You'll want to bring your sisters, lad! We must all lend a hand in the rebuilding. And there will be a tithe soon, as I'm sure you realize with all this …" He gestured around the courtyard.

Eloquence stared down at the dust at his feet. "My sisters are working," he said. "All of them are prenticed."

"But they have free days," the priest said shrewdly, "And I cannot believe that all of them have masters who have escaped the devastation and need their service today."

That was entirely too much, that the man be pressing him like that. Eloquence looked him straight in the eyes and said, forcing the words out, "They will not be coming."

Graciousness cocked his head to the side and studied Eloquence. "You are having a crisis of faith," he said. "That is reasonable, who would not doubt the Moons a little after the last day? But they always have a plan, and they move according to it, and not randomly."

Words, words, words. That was how the priests convinced people. But he knew words himself, and he would not allow himself to be persuaded by them.

Still, there was no point in fighting publicly about it.

Instead he said, as politely as he could, "Surely you are right. I will return home and see what I can do."

"I will go with you!" the priest replied.

"Oh, there is no need of such." Eloquence ground his teeth. This was insufferable. But he did not want to be denounced in front of everyone here.

"But it will be a delight to see your sisters and your house. I have not visited since the death of your mother."

"The girls don't keep things up as they should," Eloquence said. "We are not prepared for visitors."

Graciousness waved a hand in an airy gesture and smiled. "I am not a visitor. I am a priest."

He smiled at Eloquence effulgently, ignoring the other's scowl. "Let us go."

The College had escaped much of the storm's devastation, no doubt shielded by a thousand protective magics. But the pine trees that had filled its campus were flattened, and many had, in falling, damaged the structures around them. Crews of subdued students were out, gathering fallen debris and sweeping the sidewalks, supervised by junior faculty, all of whom had their attention more on the sky than on their charges.

Sebastiano trotted up the steps of the Great Hall as the sky began to lighten. He was part of a crowd of converging figures. When he had said that the College was summoning anyone with a trace of talent, he had not been exaggerating. There were plenty of faces he recognized, but even more that he did not. He glimpsed the healer that had helped him with his Fairy bite, long ago, but the man vanished again in the crowd before Sebastiano could hail him.

The entrance led to a vast lobby and beyond that, an even vaster auditorium, layered with spells to maximize the acoustics. This was where the College's major public-facing events were held. The Duke's box, high off to the side, had been co-opted, and currently held a number of senior faculty members.

When he was leaving, he would swing by the stables and stop for a moment by Fewk's grave. He had managed to keep the great body out of the hands of the Mages who would have rendered it to its component bits by paying an outrageous ransom for it, and the school had sworn that it would not be touched in its space near the roses in the courtyard that Fewk had used to eat, meditatively but methodically, so Sebastiano would come out to find all the day's new blossoms already snipped off as neatly as though by shears, from the bushes there.

"Could you not even leave me a single one to pin on my cloak?" he would complain, and Fewk would not answer, just butt his head at Sebastiano's side to see if he had dried fruit in his pockets.

He always did. Even nowadays it was still reflex to slide a few bits from anything likely that he ate into a pocket, a habit that had made Adelina declare, quite firmly, that she would never be doing his washing alongside hers.

He rubbed at his eyes and found his place in the auditorium, near enough the back that he could entertain himself by watching the crowd.

The clock that sounded was not the Duke's bell tower, fallen last night, but a handbell that a solemn student stood up to ring. The murmuring among the assembled died away a little, and Arianis was helped onto the stage, a lesser Mage at either of his elbows, helping him move.

He paused, looking them over. The murmuring continued to lessen until it had died away entirely. Sebastiano found himself holding his breath and straining his ears.

"Friends and family of the College," Arianis declared, looking out over the audience. Although his voice was soft, magic carried it to everyone's ears so they could hear as clearly as if he had been standing just beside them. Worry and dread carved his face, the bones beneath it seeming to leap forward to foreshadow what they all feared. "You know by now that a menace faces Tabat and that we mean to move against it. I am here to tell you what we have learned so far, what measures we plan to undertake, and what part all of you play in that scheme."

What they had learned so far ... It came to Sebastiano that he, having listened to Bella Kanto's account of who Lucy was and how she had come here, was the best-informed person in this hall. He should tell them what he knew. He tried to move sideways, but the crowd was too thick.

"Excuse me," he murmured, and managed to shoulder his way towards a side door. He would go along the wall, find someone who could grab Arianis' attention.

People ignored him as he squirmed past, transfixed by the ancient Mage's words.

"As we know, the Duke's castle has been destroyed. The Duke is safe, and has sheltered with the Peacekeepers, some of whose buildings and stations escaped the devastation last night. All of the army that was stationed at the castle is gone. A full half of what was left are dead or missing to last night's attack. The storm has destroyed a great many buildings."

Sebastiano ducked behind one person. Elbowed his way through a small gap. Sidled sideways between another pair of Mages, who paid him no attention.

"The cause is a single magical creature. We believe it may be a singularly powerful Beast, because divination says that it is infused with magic, rather than someone who is wielding power outside itself. But it does consume magic. It has done so with all of the stores of Dryad logs beneath the city."

That almost brought Sebastiano to a standstill. He thought of the logs as he had seen them when showing them to the boy Maz. So many! All of that, taken in by one small girl? But surely she was not a Beast. She had started as a Human and had somehow become something more than that.

He remembered now turning her away when she had come to ask to become an apprentice. Even being amused by her impudence, and worse, letting her know he was amused. And she had not deserved that of him, not after the time they had spent together watching the fight, or after what had happened to her mother. What would have happened if he had acted better? If he had been kinder? All of this would surely have been averted.

It was not entirely his fault, all of this. The fault was big and complicated and some of it was built into the way the world worked. But he had played a part in what had happened, nonetheless.

"After the castle was destroyed, the creature stayed there for some time and then vanished to a location we do not know. All attempts to divine that location were unsuccessful, repelled by the creature's nature, no doubt. Then yesterday in the late afternoon, a storm appeared that was evidently magical in nature."

He gave up fighting against the crowd, but kept trying to edge his way nearer the stage. He would listen to what they planned and then, in the aftermath, when the crowd had thinned, he would be able to seek out one of the higher Mages and tell him what he had learned.

Which was, in truth, not that much more than they already knew. He did not know what had happened in the Coral Tower to change Lucy. Locations like that had not been his field of study, and truth was he knew little of the Southern Isles, other than the Beasts that came up from such locations, were-apes and shark-folk, and many of the more delicate mer-creatures.

"Now the creature has disappeared again and once more is untraceable. We know only that, having attacked the city twice now, it will surely move against it again. Much of the energy it consumed would have been expended in its manipulation of the storm."

Sebastiano paused to judge his distance. He did not seem to have gotten any closer to the stage.

Arianis continued. "We intend to combine everyone's magic through an apparatus we have assembled, and direct it against the creature when it next appears."

That … sounded improbable. And dangerous.

Sebastiano was certainly not the only person having that thought, because immediate hubbub and shouted questions broke out.

Arianis held out his hand, palm flattened, towards the crowd. When that failed to quell the noise, he lost his temper visibly, retracted his hand while closing his fingers together and then flung invisible force out with a pushing gesture that sent a thunder crack across the room.

The buzz of voices died abruptly and there was silence again.

"This is not a time for discussion," Arianis said. "This is not a time for debate. This is a time for trusting in the wisdom of the College and repaying what you owe to it."

Sebastiano's eyes narrowed. Having been tossed out of the College, he was not convinced that he actually owed it anything that needed to be repaid. It had taken plenty of money from him over the years, and even more work, all the while sneering at him and making him feel less because he came from a Merchant family rather than one of the illustrious lines that had spent generations producing Mage after Mage.

And the wisdom he was supposed to trust in … He had reason to doubt that as well. He knew little of the science of draining and storing magic, but he did know it was risky. It was easy to drain a person too deeply, to remove their magic entirely, or even kill them in the process.

He maneuvered himself into the side corridor and hesitated. Would Arianis even listen to him, assuming that he could even get to him?

Something tickled his ear. He swatted at it, and his hand came away with something tiny clinging to the fingers. A Fairy? Was it trying to sting him? But no, it was gesticulating at him, trying to get his attention.

He let it flutter back to its perch. Its tiny voice buzzed in his ear.

"The Queen … the Queen would see you."

Was this an emissary from the hive he'd freed?

"Come, come," it said, and so he followed. At least it got him away from the hall, and that was the first step in avoiding having his magic drained.

CHAPTER 20

Sebastiano had gone to the College of Mages, and as soon as he was out the door, Adelina slipped out herself. She would try one more time to find Jilly. Surely by now the woman would have returned home, and even if she had none of the drug—which she surely would, because she had always been well supplied—she would be able to tell Adelina where she might find more.

But no one answered at Jilly's house, no matter how much she knocked. Finally a neighbor stuck their head out the window across the street and shouted, "Wasting your time! She's dead, that one."

The word hit Adelina like a slap to the face, so hard that she was amazed her outer body did not flinch. "Dead? But how?"

"Had gone up to deliver daguerreotypes to the Duke," the woman said. "All proud she was, first time she'd had a royal customer." She shook her head sorrowfully.

Adelina's thoughts raced through possibilities and permutations. "Her friends," she said. "Her close ones, I mean. I'd like to commiserate with them. Do you know where I can find them? Will there be some sort of burial for her?"

"No one's burying anyone in the city right now." The woman

seemed to speak with a touch of satisfaction. "But go down to the chal house on the corner, that's where she was, often enough."

One of Jilly's friends might also have connections to the drug. The question was how to communicate that she was looking for such a thing without coming and saying it outright to someone who might be the wrong person.

A Fairy was buzzing around her, no doubt in search of something sweet. She slapped half-heartedly at it and moved along.

The chal house was very small, and a little grubby. Adelina ordered a bowl and said to the server, "I'm looking for friends of Jilly Clearsight. Are any of them here?"

The server shook his head. "She be dead."

"I know," Adelina said. "Her friends, though. I wanted to speak with one of them."

He studied her for long enough to seem suspicious. She tried to look like herself, not some secret agent of the police, but wouldn't they be trying that as well? She felt a little bewildered by all this subterfuge, and some of that must have shown in her face, because the server's softened in turn.

"Not here now, but coming in later today surely, though," he said. "Always show up round past noon, that's when you'll find them. Few hours from now."

She could wait that long. She would have to, at any rate. She sipped at her bowl. The cook here adhered to the school of spice over taste, and there was a sourness to it all that made her unwilling to finish it.

Tension in the crowd, she could hear it in the muttering rustling between the tables, and the server was slow, not from rudeness, but due to his preoccupation with watching the street. Whenever someone that might have been taken for a Peacekeeper went by, they flinched, even though there had been no Peacekeepers or guards on the streets anywhere, as far as Adelina could tell.

She pushed her sour chal away. She was too restless to keep waiting for Jilly's friends. She left a message with the server, and enough coin that she was reasonably certain it would be passed along.

That was plenty of time to look elsewhere and then return here if nothing panned out.

She wandered the quarter. Three Coins Tailoring, one of Bella's favorites, was one of the shops that had taken the brunt of one of Lucy's levinbolts and it was only a pile of bricks and sodden rolls of fabric now. She wondered where the owner and her daughters had gone to.

Everywhere she went, it was the same. Lucy's wrath had wreaked great holes on the city, and where she had failed, the storm had worked destruction for her. People seemed dispirited and frightened, not knowing what was coming next.

Would the College of Mages be able to defeat Lucy? She worried that they would not be able to, and that Sebastiano, caught up in their schemes, would be lost to her. But she did not think she could persuade him not to go, or at least she was still unwilling to engage in the sort of strategems that might have worked, such as begging him or breaking down into tears.

She had not meant to come this way, but she realized she was standing in front of the pile of blackened wood that had once been her press, the proudest thing in her life. Now it was gone, and she still hadn't mourned it properly. How do you mourn a press, though? A building didn't have a face or voice or life. And it was not the building she mourned, anyway. It was the existence of a business, of something that she ran and ran well.

She forced herself to smile. She would persevere. Someday she would run another press. Someday her life would return to normal.

But when?

THE PRIEST CHATTERED ALL the way to Eloquence's house, going on about this or that point of philosophy, and the result was that Eloquence could not focus enough to figure out a strategy for getting rid of him.

If he confronted the priest outright, announced that he and his sisters were quitting the Moon Temples, there would be scandalous talk and the disapproval of his neighbors. For the first time he wished that they lived elsewhere, not surrounded by people who would be shocked and even angry at their defection. But they did not have the money to swap houses, and their own was in disrepair, the roof tiles loose and the walls shaggy with ancient peeling paint. No, they would continue to have to deal with these neighbors, much as he might prefer other ones.

That was why he had intended to just slide away from the Temples, slowly drop away without anyone noticing. The girls wouldn't object to skipping Temple visits; they'd be glad enough to do so, and by the time they realized they were not going back at all, they'd never miss it. He wouldn't be the first person to do that, and as long as the decline was slow enough and gradual enough, it would be unremarked. No, he should still pursue that course, even if it were frustrating.

The streets that they passed through were crowded with people talking, some repairing the buildings devastated by last night's storm, others clearly preparing to leave. The mixture seemed to be half and half, but he realized that there were other elements missing from that blend that he would have expected.

The Duke's Peacekeepers, for one, were something that everyone was used to seeing on a daily basis. The mechanical automatons, created by the College of Mages, were what maintained order in the city and now, when surely they were most needed, they were nowhere to be seen.

For another, he saw not a single Beast, and that was very odd indeed. He knew that more and more owners had been divesting themselves, fearing uprising, fearing violence, particularly after those shocking murders only a handful of purple moons ago. Beasts did so much of the city's work but now there were none, not even among the work crew repairing a warehouse that they passed, not pulling the overladen wagons that creaked and rumbled past them as they walked down Falling Water Way.

And the trams were still overhead, none of them moving, which was another reason the streets seemed a little crowded. What had stopped them? Perhaps the College of Mages had diverted that power elsewhere in the city's defense, somehow.

No matter what, it was clear that the Temples had done nothing to protect its followers, or their city.

They came to the house, and Eloquence, who had been mulling over everything, said, "I thank you for accompanying me, but I do not wish to keep you. What if I bring my sisters, the ones that are available, to the Temple, later this day?"

He could do that, and leave them there. He could foist them off on the Temples and then go off himself, knowing that there was someone who would see that they were fed and housed and that at some point a gainful employment could be secured for them. And then, years after that had all been settled, he could come back, make his excuses and apologies, and resettle into things.

Or stay on the river forever, writing pages about the slow pace of the trees gliding past, an owl calling to her mate in the soft night hours while he stood watch. His thwarted romance with Adelina might have put him off the notion of publishing what he'd written, but nothing would ever stop the urge to put words down on paper, regardless of whether or not others would read them.

The priest's eyes narrowed and Eloquence could see he was debating whether or not to press the matter. But in the end, he did not, simply bowed, with a trace of stiffness to signify his displeasure, and went about his business.

Eloquence straightened his shoulders and decided that after all that, he would do what every Tabatian did when their soul was troubled and they needed to think. He went to the nearest chal shop.

And stopped as he entered, hit to the heart like a knife by the sight of Adelina.

She was talking to the owner, there near the back, and as he watched, the owner pointed towards an empty table and shook their head.

She sagged, and turned, and met his eyes. She looked the same as ever, and his treacherous heart surged in his chest, even though he had always thought that if he met her, he would snub her. But how could he do that to her, when she looked so sad and disheartened? He had been in love with her once, and some sparks of that fondness still lingered. He suspected that if she wanted to, she could fan them back into flame. If he cared to give her the chance.

ELOQUENCE LOOKED the same as always, a little disheveled but somehow shaggily handsome. Despite herself, Adelina felt a surge of affection. He had proved too unlike what she had thought him, had been overfond of his Temples and bound by tradition, but still, his words had been so beautiful, living up to his name.

He was unsmiling when he looked at her, but stepped forward to greet her.

"I had thought that surely we would meet every once in a while," he said, "given that we live in the same city, but I had not thought to look for you in a place like this."

"I was looking for a friend," she said with a touch of constraint, and then thought, *well, why not*, and said, "Jilly Clearsight. The photographer. Do you know her?"

He shook his head.

She said, "I have to tell you something. About Lucy."

His eyes narrowed, "Obedience, you mean. My so badly named sister."

She said, "She is here in the city. But I do not think you may wish to claim her any longer."

She drew him to one of the tables in the back. They ordered chal, which came accompanied by a pair of bitter, chalky biscuits. Adelina tried hers and discarded it; Eloquence simply shoved his in a pocket. Adelina thought it might be to share with his sisters, if they were suffering from the same high costs and lack of supplies the rest of the city was enduring.

She thought. *How do you tell someone that his missing sister has showed up and her first act has been to destroy the city?*

"This is something very serious indeed," he said, watching her face as she fought to figure out how to tell him, "for you to put so much thought in how to frame the words."

She nodded and began. "Let me tell you the tale as I had it from Bella Kanto."

He startled at the name and started to ask a question, but she held up a hand to forestall him. "Here," she said, and began to unfold the story she had for him.

CHAPTER 21

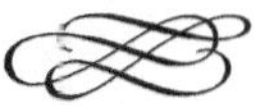

Eloquence listened and felt as though he were running among falling rocks, one of which might tumble and strike him dead at any moment. How could Obedience be doing such a thing?

"You're wrong," he said at the end of her account. "Bella Kanto has played some trick on you and is trying to blame an innocent child. No sister of mine would behave so."

"A child who has lost her mother and was blamed for it," she said. "Lucy told me that. A child who was forced into a prenticeship she hated and then …" she faltered. "Finds another she loves and is forced from that in turn. And then we do not know all that happened when she was snatched, or what the intention was. Only that your sister has returned with both a terrible anger and a power to match it."

"I will not believe it!" he shouted at her, face ablaze with anger.

"Then you are a fool!" she shouted back, and everyone in the chal house fell silent, turning around to stare at them at their table.

He shoved himself away from the table as he stood, so roughly that it banged into her, and did not apologize even at her noise of pain.

"You are a liar and seducer of apprentices!" he yelled at her. "You are filth for thinking such things!"

No one spoke to intervene with their argument and she could feel their eyes on her, wondering if it were true. And she thought, I came in here to find one of Jilly Clearsight's friends for the sake of illegalities, who is to say that is not as bad as some—only some—of the things he is shouting?

He paused for breath. She said, with chilly dignity, "I have told you what you need to know. Believe it or not, it is yours to deal with and none of mine." She stood in turn, and left coins on the table to cover the cost for both of them.

Head held high, she exited the chal shop with as much dignity as she could.

Outside on the street, she wanted to weep, but hailed a pedal cab as quickly as she could, and waited till she was in it and rattling her way home before she gave way to tears. Everything was wrong and she could not right it. All she wanted now was the comfort of the drug, and it could not be found. Despair rode her bones and when she got home, she struggled up the half-broken stairs and curled into bed, glad for once that Sebastiano was not there.

It is silly to play at tourist now, but there is still a great pleasure in wandering these streets that I have missed so sorely, even if so much of them lie in painful shambles. I do not go past my old house again, but I visit other places I have frequented. Three Coins Tailoring is no more; I remember its proprietor and her daughters, dressed to go to a political rally. I wonder where they are now; I hope they have escaped successfully.

The trams hang motionless overhead, gulls and pigeons jostling for position on the metal roofs and railings. There is a ladder dangling from one, perhaps how its occupants were evacuated when the tram stopped. Their lack of motion means there are other lacks in the city, other vital mechanisms that are stopped now for lack of fuel.

Is that a terrible thing, when that fuel was the lives of Beasts? Dryad logs made the furnaces roar as they burned and released magic to run the city. None of us thought much about what was happening in order to keep our lives running smoothly, comfortably, with lights in the city to make sure no one stepped wrong in the darkness, with Ellora's mushrooms to feed the city dwellers, and Peacekeepers to make sure no one hurt anyone else. Even though we were hurting others to maintain our comfortable lives.

The thought makes me uneasy. Does Tabat deserve to survive?

I think it does. But it must change, must become a city that serves all of its people, rather than one that relies on one class to serve another.

Is that something I can help it do, if only I can regain my tie to it?

After listening to Adelina and Sebastiano argue about magic and how I was tied to the city, I have formed a simple plan. I will act as though I am the city's Bella Kanto, and sooner or later the city will take me up again.

It must work. Because it has to.

At some point it occurs to me that maybe, if I am to be Bella Kanto again, then perhaps I should recover something that belonged to Bella Kanto once. Winter's Armor, the thing of silver and gilt and moon-steel that I wore every time I defeated Spring.

That is something that I might have thought to go back to the castle for, but I have been thinking about the Ducal box at the arena, and the case at the back of it housing ancient weapons and a single suit of armor, the armor his ancestor wore when he founded Tabat. Alberic has ever been a trophy seeker, and where better to house a trophy of his victory over me than in the place where it would be the most suitable, one he would see, and be able to gloat over, whenever he came to the arena?

No, I think I know where it might be. Although not how to get it.

LUCY HAD BEEN MORE DRAINED than she realized. She slept until well into the morning, and woke to find Leonoa sitting at the cave's edge, eating stale bread and sipping from a clay jug of water.

Reaching within herself, Lucy checked her power reserves. Still so low! Enough to fly her down, perhaps, and then she could go in search of something to replenish herself. The College of Mages might have magics that she could take. There was plenty of magic in Tabat; she could feel it, a mass somewhere beneath the surface. If she could tap that, she would be invincible.

And she would. She would learn how to tame or steal that power, because she wanted it, and what she wanted was, by rights, hers now.

Where was she to begin her revenge? She thought that she would strike first at Adelina, Adelina who had believed the worst of her and had thrown her out for telling secrets, even though there had been nothing like that. Adelina had pretended to be kind, and then she had been angry, and her anger had been unjustified, which made it entirely unfair and therefore utterly unforgivable.

But when she had been directing the lightning, she had tried to strike the press with it, only to find the building gone already. That was satisfying in many ways and yet utterly not in others. True, Adelina had been injured, clearly, by the loss of the building. But she might have easily reestablished elsewhere. Maybe she had even moved it long before the building had been destroyed. That was intolerable to think of, that she was unscathed.

Tabat held thousands of Humans and Beasts, though. There was no way she could seek them out ...

Unless.

Unless she did something that was utterly unappealing, and pretended to be just a girl again, and went into Tabat to look.

If only she still had Teo! But he had vanished, and if she found him again, she would kill him for leaving her as he had. He owed her, after all. She had been the one who transformed him back into a boy. He should have been very grateful for that, so grateful that he served her without thinking.

Leonoa was lame, and moreover, what if she took advantage of the situation to try and escape herself? The little woman was taciturn and had not said much in all of this, just watching with her sharp black eyes. Currently Lucy had her confined in this cliff crevice above the castle. She could not climb down from there; the only way to reach it would be to fly, and Lucy would have noticed any such attempts at rescue, if anyone had known that Leonoa was there in the first place.

She was an artist, and so she would be useful, later on. Lucy would have her paint portraits of Lucy as the Queen of Tabat, dressed in jewels and furs and silks, dressed as elegantly as anyone in Tabat had ever dressed. Portraits more beautiful than anything that had ever hung in Bernarda's gallery.

So she could afford a little while of being thought less than she was, if it let her find Adelina. She scavenged in the ruins to find suitable clothing, the sort a kitchen servant might have worn, serviceable and clean, but of cheap fabric.

Even so, as nice as her best clothing had been, if not nicer.

She washed her face in the fountain's still waters, and walked down the road to the city.

CHAPTER 22

Sebastiano was torn between following the Fairy and going to speak to the Mages. But a trace of anger at the thought that they might discount him so much that they might not—probably would not—even listen in the first place, drove him along.

He slipped out of the building. He could see Mages setting up equipment in the plaza before it, the machinery that would drain the participants, take their magic so the College could wield its collective might against Lucy. Gratitude that he'd escaped it steadied him—he had been drained once, just a touch of it, in a class demonstration and he remembered the sensation as a highly unpleasant one, as though pieces of him were being turned inside out.

He wondered what the Fairy Queen wanted. He knew that the Fairies had appreciated being freed, but he had not thought that they were intelligent enough to experience gratitude or a need to repay his kindness.

He had been wrong about that, as he had been wrong about so many things about Beasts, because he had accepted the common wisdom: they were less than Humans, they could not help their nature, they could not be trusted, they needed, above all, to be watched over and guided. *We call them all of that so we can justify enslaving them,* he thought, *so we can pretend we are doing it for their own good, rather than ours.* The idea was like gravel grinding in an open wound, undeniably painful.

He followed the shimmer of motion, the almost inaudible whine in the air that was the Fairy. It led him into the tiny square of forest near the main building, and then one of the inner groves of the College of Mages.

Sebastiano had always found this a strange and unexpected place. Sometimes in the groves you heard unknown voices from thin air, and many claimed to have met personages from the past—and every once in a while the future—on its paths. Flowers grew here that grew nowhere else in Tabat—with the possible exception of Milosh's greenhouses—or even the entirety of the continent. There was a bank of talking flowers, which the students were strictly forbidden to get near, because of their unfortunate habit of picking blossoms and attempting to carry them off as pets. The Fairy led him to a grove of trees near that bank, but the flowers were unexpectedly silent.

Fairies covered the branches, but the branches did not droop as they might have with heavier burdens. Instead it was as though someone had shaken glitter on the branches, with the sparkle of the scintillating wings. Constant buzz tickled at his ears, the shrill noise of voices too high and fast for his dull, slow ears to catch them.

He stopped and looked up into the nearest tree. Towards the top there was a movement, and then as he watched, the Fairy Queen—so much larger than her fellows—crept down the mottled bark towards him.

Her wings were atrophied and desiccated, but still beautifully detailed in their glittering, multi-veined complexity. Her face was almost Human, but held a wildness in the sharpness of her nose, the points to her elongated ears. She wore scraps of leaves and nothing more.

"The Mage Sebastiano," she buzzed.

"I am," he said, trying to make it sound like a statement of fact rather than a question.

"You freed us."

"I did."

"Why?"

"Because it was unfair to keep you in there," he said, a little astonished that she would even need to ask.

She tilted her head, considering him. Around them was the constant whine and flutter of lesser wings, the feeling of being watched, like pinpricks pressing in on him.

"You are a Merchant," she said. "Merchants make exchange, one thing for another thing. What is it that you want in exchange?"

"Nothing," he said. "I did it because it seemed right."

"But you had been to see us many times before that. You watched us and did not free us. You did not tap on the glass, like so many, but you watched, doing nothing. What changed?"

"I did," he said. "I learned better."

The Fairy raised her head and for seconds there was a shrill whine in the air, as though all of the Fairies were talking at once, too high to be understood. Then it stopped, abruptly as a door slamming, and the pressure on his ears ceased.

"Your wife has a problem," the Fairy said. "We may be able to help."

"A problem?" he said stupidly. "What sort of problem might Adelina have?" Her face had been strained lately, but that was due to their circumstances, and now there was even more to be strained about.

"You know how we are treated," the Fairy said. "Our bodies are taken, to be eaten or made into spells."

Shame settled on him like a heavy blanket. He should have understood their cause earlier, particularly when Letha had lectured him on it so often. He said, simply, "I do."

"Your wife consumes something made from our bodies, to make her tongue speak better. It is a powder that looks like the metal you call gold."

He was horrified. "Adelina would never be involved in such an unwholesome process." But at the same time, his mind was flicking through scenes: Adelina turning away from her dresser abruptly when he'd come up behind her; her saying, "You make me nervous if you hear me speak, and besides they write it all up in the penny-wides so you can read it at your leisure."; Adelina out on errands and shrugging vaguely when asked where she was going, saying "Quite a few places, really, what should I pick up for you?" And him so touched that she would offer that he would always say something, like a pastry, or a pack of quills, and happily imagined her thinking of it while she was picking it out. And instead she had been creeping off to some shady house to get something that would require sorcery to make.

How would she even have come across it in the first place? What would have led her to try it?

"She has taken so much of it, she craves it now," the Fairy buzzed.

"How do you know?" he demanded.

"Because she smells of it. We know the smell. We are drawn to it, very strongly. A Fairy smelled it on her; others confirmed it."

"Why are you telling me this?"

"You are wise. You understand that we wish to stop this trade. But there is something in exchange for you. Because if she continues, she will take more and more, and she will die. If she attempts to quit without knowing what she is doing, she will die. Do you want her to live?"

"I do."

"Then bring her to us."

"Under what pretext?"

The Fairy's eyes blinked. "Do you need a pretext to bring her?"

"I will do it," Sebastiano said. "But there is also the child menacing the city. Will you help me find out how to defeat her? Because if she is not stopped, everyone will die."

There was more buzzing before the Fairy said, "We cannot defeat her; she is far too powerful."

"No, not to defeat her," Sebastiano said. "To help me find out how to do so. You can let me in the library. Then I can find the books I need." Or thought he could, at any rate. The library was very large and its stacks confusing by design, to prevent the sort of thievery he intended to engage in.

"Tell us what you need us to do," the Fairy said.

Out in the plaza, he had seen the heaps of magical things being gathered to be disassembled for their magic. Minor magics and major artifacts, and many student projects among them. He remembered the weather glasses his friends had made so long ago. He knew how to modify them now, how to create exactly what he needed in order to break into one of the most securely protected locations in the city.

BERTO'S IS DESTROYED, and all the little cages of songbirds have fallen or been stolen. There is trash in the street gutters, leaves and papers and storm-broken twigs, all of it a damp and sodden mass, beaten into shapelessness by last night's pounding rain. One side of the arena is totally untouched by the devastation and the storm, but on the north side, an enormous hole gapes in the side. I'd hoped to be able to pick through ruins, perhaps, and come away with it, although that is perhaps not the cleverest plan I've ever come up with, and unworthy of a tactical Gladiator, really. Brute force lacks finesse.

Which is why I climb the side.

I don't care who sees me. There is so much going on that Alberic's guards will be somewhere guarding his life, rather than his valuables, and most of the arena seems to have relied on locks and chains to keep things safe. It makes sense enough. Who would want to break into an arena? All that is stored here are ceremonial weapons and armor, and the great cloth banners that they fly on fight days.

No one seems to mark me much, or perhaps they simply, wisely, think that there is enough happening in the city without adding to the confusion.

Almost at the top. I pause and look out over the city. Everything looks small from this distance. I look up at the sky but there is only blueness, no hint of clouds today.

Where is Lucy now, and what is she planning next?

Inside the arena, it is flagstone cool and my footsteps echo. No one else is here in the entirety of this building, I think. Only small lives like the little black and white cat I find patrolling for rats in one hallway. She pricks her ears at me, and I kneel down, extending my fingers, and ksh-ksh-kshing under my breath.

She regards me without moving for a long moment and then finally deigns to step forward to sniff my fingertips, then lower her head so I can rub along her neck, feeling the soft rumble of purrs as she bumps her entirety along my knee, savoring the moment. I don't hurry myself, but lean, like the cat, into the moment. It might be one of my last and so why not enjoy it, why not be here, being me?

"Why not indeed?" a voice says, and as I look up, the cat abandons me to circle the ankles of Selene, who stands there, looking at me fondly. How can she be so beautiful that the air itself should burst into flame around her? But she is, to me.

I scramble to my feet, but don't step to her immediately. Instead I savor the sight of her as I savored the feeling of the cat's fur, its bird-thin bones under my touch.

"Are you here to help me?" I ask.

She widens her eyes deliberately, purses her lips. "More than I have already helped you, you mean? There are limits on how much I can do so."

"How close are we to those limits?" I ask, trying to reckon chances, plotting strategies for the fight. How can I hope to battle Lucy without the powers of this god on my side?

She ignores the question, and asks me, "What are you thinking to do?"

"I don't know," I snap. "That's why I'm asking you," and irritatingly, she laughs at me, and even worse, she is quite adorable as she does so and I cannot be angry in any shape or form.

"A hint," I say. "A clue, a word, half of a riddle, something, anything, to point me on my way, because I am not a subtle woman and all of my arguments are made with blade or fist."

"That is not quite true," she says. "I have seen you be subtle enough when it comes to coaxing someone."

It takes me aback and makes me blush, to think that she might have seen all my encounters over the years. How long has she been watching me? And, truth be told, it heats me a touch as well, makes something inside me lick its lips and smile, at the thought that she might be so interested she had spied on me all this time.

"If you cannot lend me power, can you tell me how to regain what I once had? The power of Tabat?" I demand.

Because that is what I need, as well as what I crave. Not so much the power as the connection to the city that I once had. Because now that I am returned, I feel that lack. It used to be that the city and I breathed as one, and now I am severed from that source. Bereft. Because without it, I am still Bella Kanto, but a different Bella Kanto.

"Now you are asking the right question," she says approvingly, and rips it away again with "though that it is all I can tell you about that."

The groan from me is heartfelt and only amuses her.

"Is the armor here, at least?" I ask her. "Can you tell me that much?"

"I cannot," she says, "But certainly no one will mind if we walk together here and see what we can find."

Lucy walked cautiously down the road at first. She thought that if she were discovered, they might attack her, and she was not ready for that yet. The storm had taken most of her energy, and it would take her a while to replenish it, unless she found another treasure trove like the Dryad logs.

There was no one on the road at first, but as she came lower, there were a few people, then more and more. By the time she was off the highest terrace, there was a crowd, and she lost herself in it, pretending to be just anyone, and listening hard in case someone spoke about the disasters she had wreaked or speculated on who she might be. Disappointingly, there was nothing like that in conversation, only questions of times and schedules and meetings. It was very dull.

She was so hungry! She thought that the College of Mages might hold something she could use, and perhaps tomorrow, she would try to harvest that. Perhaps early in the time before dawn. They would be less awake then, and not expecting her. She smiled a little to herself, her head down, and kept walking.

She walked past the arena and grimaced up at its walls. Soon, very soon, she'd come to finish destroying that, if for no other reason than that it might upset Bella Kanto. She did not remember the arena with pleasure. That was where she had first met Sebastiano, and at the time had thought it quite fine to hang about with a Mage eating wonderful food from his basket. Yes, the arena must be flattened, sooner or later.

As she came closer to the North River Gate, there were more and more people on the street. Some were pretending to go about business as usual, but the majority were not. They were repairing things damaged in the storm, or bolstering other things in case there was another storm, and there was a satisfying number that were simply packing up and leaving.

That showed proper respect, that showed they feared her. But they could not be permitted to do so, all of them, or she would be left with no one to rule over. The next time she attacked, she thought, she would destroy all the boats that were left, before they could carry anyone else away and out of her reach.

She wished she had money. Then she could have bought a cookie at the bakery cart she passed. She was tempted to just seize some, fly away, but she forced patience on herself. Things would be all the more satisfying later if they realized she had actually walked among them. That would frighten them, make them wonder when she would be there again. She grinned to herself, looking downward as she walked, in order to keep the expression hidden, but more than one person seemed to edge away from her.

On Greenslope Way, she paused near the windows of Ellora's Daughter Candy Shop. She was close to the College of Mages here, and she could feel the power in it, so ready and ripe for the taking, but not yet, not until she had enough power of her own to reach out and take it. A whisper of magic overlaid the candy knights jousting in the window and she turned her attention there, standing a little back from the crowd of children watching, delighted, and cheering on their favorites.

First one knight faltered, then another, then a candy horse staggered and went to its knees. The children stopped cheering and pressed inward, watching with horrified eyes as one by one, the candy warriors slumped and fell lifelessly. Two of the smaller children began to cry, and a parent hurried over.

Lucy coiled the wisp away inside herself and walked on, feeling like a cat licking its whiskers. Not a lot of magic, but something to add to the store.

As she headed downward and away from the College, she stretched out her sense and stole magics wherever she could: flickers from good-luck charms and household warding spells, the power from magic-fueled mechanisms, and the trickle of magic in the coin the Moon Temple followers wore. While they did not know it, their coins stopped changing, all of the virtue fled into Lucy's store of power.

It was not much, but it revived her, and she realized how deeply she had been drained, and resolved to never spend herself so freely again. What if someone had attacked her while she was so helpless? No, she must always have enough to make an escape, and the signal to escape would be that the means of doing so would be all the power she had left.

At length she came to the ruins of Spinner Press. It looked as though fire had taken it, but it was hard to tell how long ago. Definitely some amount of time, by the weathering of the sooty boards, and the dusty green weeds that had grown up around the edges.

Across the street was a stationer's, and she went in there to ask a bored clerk more engrossed in her penny-wide than the shop's clientele, "Do you know where Spinner Press has relocated to?"

The clerk snorted to herself and turned a page without looking at Lucy. "Relocated? B'ain't relocated anywhere, they're gone."

Gone! That was satisfying in that Adelina would have been hurt by it, and yet utterly not in that Lucy had not played a hand in it. She said, "What happened to them?"

"Place all your money on a bad horse, that's what happens," the clerk said. "Bella Kanto made that press, and then she took it down with her in exile."

Bella Kanto. She remembered facing her down, enacting her vengeance. How satisfying it had been. It was too bad Bella would still be down in the Southern Isles, unable to witness the destruction of her city. Lucy wished that she had had the forethought to bring her along.

"And the owner of Spinner Press? The former owner, I guess that would be. Did she die in the fire?" Lucy asked with a certain amount of hope.

"She's got lodgings down near the docks, on Ravel Street," the clerk said.

Lucy's heart leaped. "What's the building?" she said.

The clerk put the paper down now, to look across the counter at her. "What for?" she said.

"I'm her old apprentice, and I need her to vouch for me to a new master," she said.

That appeared to be assurance enough for the clerk to put down her reading material and search through a drawer of orange paper cards. "It says the first block, the sandstone building marked with three fish, the apartment on the second block, in the back," she read off. She looked expectantly at Lucy.

"Thank you," Lucy said in her grandest manner, pretending not to understand that the clerk thought she merited some coin. It was embarrassing not to have such at hand; was there a way to come across it? She should have looted some of the bodies back at the castle but it was too late to think of that now. Perhaps Adelina would have such a thing on her and Lucy could take them, after she'd killed her.

The thought almost, almost made her falter, as though she were taking a step over a particularly wide stream and was not sure whether or not she might fall in. Killing someone she knew was different than flinging thunderbolts, knowing that there were people she didn't know in the way, somehow.

But Adelina had wronged her. Misjudged her. Had been responsible for so many of her troubles.

She started down the main stairway towards the docks, wishing now that the trams were still running. It was inconvenient to walk when you were used to flying, but she consoled herself with the notion that soon enough she'd be flying again. She could feel herself recharging, now that she had replenished herself a little. She no longer felt weary down to her bones, but she still craved the sensation that she'd had after consuming everything in the caverns below the city. She had felt full then; she had been satiated. Nowadays the power was a comfort and a hunger, closer to her than any of her siblings had ever been.

At that thought, her lips crept back over her teeth in a grin. Her siblings still remained, and vengeance on them would be very sweet indeed.

CHAPTER 23

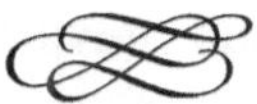

Teo was not sure whether or not the coin was the one the priest had held, and then given to Eloquence, who must have given it to the Temples. It was a coin of Toj, as the one he had lost had been, but did that mean that it was the equivalent, in the eyes of his dream? Perhaps he would dream an answer to that question, once he went to sleep.

He could have stayed for as long as he liked in the Beast camp. They had let him in, vouched for by the fox-women, who had said, simply, "He's as battered by it all as we are. He's just a boy," to the old, half-blind Minotaur overseeing things, and the Minotaur had dipped his great, shaggy head in a single ponderous nod and that had been the end of that.

But the city was in tatters. Buildings had fallen, things were knocked over. People went beside their houses; others stoically went about trying to salvage what they could. On one corner, someone had hung one of the Duke's Peacekeeper mechanical dogs from a useless aetheric lamppost. The body still twitched and spasmed as though from idle energy as Teo edged past.

He knew the way to Bella's old house, up on the Fourth Terrace, so well that his feet followed it without thinking and he found himself standing in front of Abernia's boarding house. He did not think that she would welcome him. He remembered taking the Fairies away, to preserve them for Bella. He wondered where they were now. If they were still alive—how long did Fairies live? Were they as fleeting as butterflies or more like little birds?

He knew how to get into the backyard quietly, through the trade gate there. He sheltered among the pine trees and watched the windows. He could see Abernia moving back and forth, first in one room, then another. Packing. He saw when the carriers came in, watched Abernia take a last look around the kitchen, and then leave. He wondered where she was going to and if she was leaving the city.

He knew how to jiggle the back door's handle to coax it into unlocking, something Abernia had grumbled about needing to fix. It gave way with a click that sounded too loud, and he held his breath for a moment, worried that someone might have stayed behind. But nothing stirred and he let out his breath in a sigh.

First Jilly's, now this. Perhaps it was becoming a habit, housebreaking. Maybe he could just live in abandoned houses for a while. It was dry and warm, at any rate. In all the chaos that the city was undergoing right now, it was as good a way to find shelter as any. He grinned to himself, momentarily feeling roguish and daring, but the growl in his stomach reminded him of reality.

He went into the kitchen. Empty now, the shelves cleared of all food as well as the little ceramic Trade Gods that had once watched over it. Every room on the first floor empty, devoid of furniture. The front rooms smelled faintly of dog.

Up and up to Bella's chambers, the treads creaking under his steps, the railing smooth and smelling still of wood polish. Her former chambers, he realized, as he reached them. All her old furniture gone, everything cleaned out.

But nothing new in its place, either. Just bare floors and barren walls. He crept through the place quietly, trying to avoid any sound of his presence in case any of the lodgers should somehow be lingering. But the house felt empty, as empty as this upper floor.

The tap in the bathroom still dispensed clean water, but not hot, only cold. He cleaned his face and hands as best he could, and dried them on his trouser legs.

He went to the window and looked out over the pine trees of the garden. A flutter of Fairies startled away from the ledge as he appeared there. The Fairies he'd been trying to take away when he'd been taken himself. They must have escaped and returned here, thinking Bella would return and feed them. Finch and Yellow-hair and all the others, waiting for her to come back.

He took sweets from his pack and laid them out on the ledge but the Fairies did not reappear. He could think of no way to reassure them. Abernia must have refrained from having them trapped, as she had threatened to. Or perhaps she had simply never noticed their return.

It served her right, this empty house, devoid of paying lodgers, given how she had turned on Bella, he thought indignantly. She was like all the Tabatians, she had been fickle! More fickle than any villain, more fickle than luck or fortune. Ungrateful. Everyone in Tabat had been bad, down to the bone, except Bella, and they had treated her as badly as they had treated him.

The depth of anger that rocked him at the thought surprised and frightened him. He felt it surge through his body and his body start to respond. He tried to resist it, but the magic, denied so long, could be pushed away no more easily than a boulder rolling downhill. It filled him entirely.

He doubled over, becoming cougar, feeling his bones, his skin, everything about himself change. But this change felt more natural than the one imposed on him by Murga had been. Three agonizing breaths' worth of change and then the cougar stood there, tail lashing, in the puddle of discarded clothes.

And then he shifted back to crouch there naked, shivering with the sensation of the air on his fresh skin, until he reached for his clothes and pulled them back on.

It was like flexing a limb, one he had never used before, so there was barely any muscle to it, but he could feel it. He had his Shifter magic and he could control it now, and the aetheric lights that could have betrayed him, all of them were darkened now. Lucy had done him that favor, at least. He need fear nothing now—aside from her, of course—if he wanted to walk the streets.

He left the house at dusk. The streets were quiet around this neighborhood, but he could hear noises elsewhere, the fast clang of water-carts, trying to put out some fire. Shouts and cries from another direction, sounding like some riot.

"Thought that was you, boy!"

Someone grabbed him by the scruff of the neck, and he twisted away. After his time with Lucy it was hard to be too afraid of Human hands.

Canumbra and Legio, standing back, glaring at him, fists clenched. Dressed more raggedly than the first time he had met them, as though they had fallen on hard times. He felt no sympathy at that thought. They deserved whatever had happened to them.

"Brought us all sorts of bad luck!" Canumbra spat. Legio, lurking just beyond him, nodded grimly.

"Hurting me isn't going to do you any good," he told them. He waited, though. They wouldn't listen, and he was fully prepared for that.

He was hoping for it, in fact.

The aetheric lights were gone. The streets were in chaos elsewhere, in darkness here. And that meant that right now it was not a terrible time to be a Shifter in Tabat. It meant that he could move without worrying about being betrayed as a Shifter in the shadow of the aetheric lights, which would have shown his true form.

"Won't do no good, but it'll make me feel better," Canumbra snarled and closed in, raising his fist, Legio close behind him. Their faces were full of mean anger, blaming him for everything awry in their lives.

This time the change was effortless, as though he was flowing from one shape to another. One moment he was a youth on the verge of manhood, the next a brawny young cougar in its full strength, and his snarl of rage echoed up and down the empty street.

The men both fell back, but not before a swipe of Teo's claws opened Canumbra's face to the bone. They fled, and he forced himself not to follow, though it was hard—they scampered like mice, and bloodlust crawled up his throat and came out as a growl before he shook himself all over and resumed his Human form. So effortless now that straining unsuccessfully to do it seemed like a faint memory.

Things were not all bad in this new manifestation of Tabat.

Up ahead. How could it be?

Eloquence knew that shape, although it was taller now, though just as lanky, just as awkward.

"Teo?" he called.

The boy turned. He wore dirty trousers and an old tunic. His eyes widened as though in fear at Eloquence, but then he calmed as though remembering some reassurance. He held himself differently now. As though some fear had been removed.

Or perhaps he realized that the Temples were destroyed and that there was no point in following them. And what would Eloquence do, if he reached out and caught him? Who would he have taken the boy to? So he stood quietly, keeping his hands to himself as Eloquence approached.

"I thought you were dead," he said. "A Mage checked your coin and said you were."

The boy's hand strayed to his pocket. "It wasn't mine," he said. His voice had changed in the months since Eloquence had known him aboard the Eloquent Swan, grown deeper, even as his shoulders had taken on a new breadth. He was no taller, but he was better muscled now. And held himself with a confidence that had been lacking before.

"Well," Eloquence said, "I'm glad you're not dead." Then suddenly as it occurred to him, "Your parents are here."

Teo's eyes were wide and startled. "Where?"

He cursed the fact that he had not asked them where they were going to next. "I don't know, but somewhere here in the city. They're looking for you."

"Is my sister with them?"

Eloquence shook his head. "I'm sorry not to know where they are. Where are you staying, if I encounter them again?"

Teo barked out a startled laugh, then shook his head. "Nowhere that has an address."

"Then I will give you mine, and you can check there when you can, if that is good?" Eloquence said. It seemed very important to make sure that Teo and his parents were reunited, as though it might compensate for all sorts of things. Despite his disappointment in not being able to have them immediately meet, the fact was that they surely would, given time—Tabat was a big city, but not all that big, not as big as Verranzo's New City.

He made Teo repeat the address back to him several times, so he would remember it. He thought about inviting him back to the house for a meal, but things were stretched enough as it was, and who knew what the girls would make of this stray puppy—they'd insist on adopting and feeding him, and there simply was not enough to go around as it was.

But he felt happy as he walked away from the encounter. The boy was not dead. He imagined the joy his parents would feel. It made him warm. He walked along with a smile and thought of happier things. It made him feel like a new person, someone capable of happiness.

He had been rude to Adelina, and that was because he was so angry at her, and he knew in his heart he could not be so angry if he did not still love her, at least a little.

He had not seen a ring on her finger. Perhaps she and Sebastiano had already parted ways. But it did not matter. He wasn't thinking about that at all.

He would go and talk to Adelina about all of this, and ask her forgiveness, and maybe they could start being friends, in a way that his pride and anger had prevented him from before. It had to be hard for her, after having so much, to have it all stripped away. He thought that more than the physical possessions, the money of it all, the loss of the press would be something that struck at her pride, and her desire to leave a legacy. That was something that had helped fuel her desire for a press, he knew. It was a feeling all writers grappled with, in one form or another.

No, he would go and see her and apologize in gracious words that would make her feel more kindly inclined towards him. He might not linger too long if Sebastiano were there. There was a limit to a man's patience, after all. He might be learning to be a new person but that didn't mean he could leave all his old angers behind quite that easily.

But he could work at it. He was willing to do that at least. And surely Adelina would meet him halfway. Perhaps even want to publish him again, reestablish her press with a volume of his works. That dream had been lost with their falling out, but before then she had said such kind things about his writing. She really understood what he had been trying to do, and an editor like that was hard to find. Together they could reinstate the press and make his book the center of the effort, the sort of book that Adelina might say she had always wanted to publish. He imagined the interview with journalists who wanted to discover the secret of the success of Spinner Press, and perhaps talk with the author whose work had achieved that.

Pleasant daydreams of this sort accompanied him on his way, made him ignore the turmoil in the streets, the suspicious glances people threw each other, and the marks of rioting and smoke on the walls.

CHAPTER 24

$\mathcal{A}$ rap at the door, an unfamiliar knock. Adelina tried to wipe her face as best she could, but knew the tears still showed on her face, that her hair was unsmoothed and tangled as though she had been tearing at it.

Later she would reflect that perhaps it was the misery so evident on her face that had saved her.

For a moment, it seemed an ordinary visitor, a little girl in blue and gold Ducal livery, not particularly clean, and too long in the sleeves. Then she saw Lucy's face, improbable and impossibly there, and smiling at her in a way that turned Adelina's bowels to water and made her mouth as dry as sand.

"L-l-lucy!" she exclaimed, and felt herself pressed back, away from the doorway by some invisible hand that closed around her and did not let her go. Lucy stepped through the doorway and turned to close it, quietly but definitively, with a decided click. She turned the latch to lock it. Then she turned back, and her smile was worse than ever.

"Here we are," she said. "Here we are. Come, we will sit down."

Adelina felt her body steered to the little couch in the front room, where so often she and Sebastiano had cuddled and talked. She wanted to ask Lucy what was going on, or perhaps just to scream, but her lips would not move to shape the sound and all she could manage was a hiss, like a teakettle being smothered.

The sound made Lucy smile even harder. She sat down in the chair facing the sofa, the same one Bella had sat in only a day earlier.

"Are you scared, Adelina?" she asked. "Are you thinking back on all the times you were unkind to me and regretting them?"

The band around Adelina's mouth relented, allowing her to reply, though the invisible hand held her pressed down into the couch cushions, almost uncomfortably.

"I have been seeking you ever since, to tell you I was sorry I lost my temper that once," she said. "But you had vanished from the city and no one could find you. Your brother Eloquence has been looking and looking for you."

"I'm sure," Lucy said coldly. "He and the rest of my family were glad enough to be rid of me. Don't pretend that he cared that I was gone, or that you did either."

"But he did, and I as well," Adelina protested, only to find herself silenced again, as though her muscles in her face could not move to shape the words.

Lucy rose and began to inspect the parlor, her hands folded behind her back. "This is a much nicer place than you deserve," she said. "It looks as though you share it with someone. Your lover?"

"My husband," Adelina said.

Lucy chortled, "Oh, that's a new development." Her eyes narrowed in sudden surmise. "You didn't marry my brother though, did you? Did you break his heart in the process?"

"I did not," Adelina said. "We are adults. I just saw your brother earlier today. He would speak to you; he is eager to do so."

"How does he know I am back?" Lucy demanded.

"You are not the only one returned lately from the Southern Isles. Bella Kanto has returned as well."

Lucy's face betrayed shock at the news. "Bella Kanto? How?" she demanded.

"She said Dragons brought her, although I am never sure whether to fully credit what Bella says."

LUCY WAS MORE than prepared to believe this. This was the Dragons, angry she had destroyed one of their own, meddling, trying to interfere with her works, even though she had killed one of them just to show what would happen if they did so. But they had acted, had brought Bella Kanto northward. Although she wasn't sure what they thought this would accomplish.

"Why did they do it?"

"Who knows, with Dragons?" Adelina said, somewhat reasonably to Lucy's mind.

But she pushed further. "What did they bring Bella Kanto here to do?"

WHAT WOULD HAPPEN if she told Lucy everything? How much advantage would it take away from Bella? Or on the other hand, perhaps if Lucy were frightened enough, she would flee the city and leave it to Bella.

"I think they wanted to warn the city, and Bella was the only person at hand to take," she said.

Lucy nodded slowly. "I killed one of them," she said, less to Adelina than to herself. "It was trying to meddle with me, and it brought it on itself. But they might not understand what I was trying to say. And Bella Kanto was down there." She laughed. "Do you know, I thought at first that you might have been sorry, sorry enough to send her chasing after me? But it turned out to be mere coincidence." She grinned. "I took her your letters, plucked them from all the places they had ended up, searching for her."

"I am sorry," Adelina said. "Believe me, you have no idea how sorry I was when I discovered what had happened, that you had been taken down there."

Lucy's eyes were bright with glee. "Oh, I am sure I have no idea how sorry you were." She took her time with the next words, savoring them. "But I have some idea how sorry you're going to be."

The knock on the door, quick and impatient, startled them both. Adelina opened her mouth, ready to call out, but with a gesture, Lucy stopped her.

"Who is it?" Lucy called out, and her voice was not her own, but Adelina's. Adelina wanted to scream so badly her jaws ached with the tension of not being able to release it.

"Eloquence Seaborn," came the answer, and both of them were surprised by that, so much that Adelina was finally able to call out, "Get away!" only to be stopped again abruptly as Lucy recovered her control.

The door flew open with a crash—had Eloquence slammed into it or had Lucy flung it open with invisible hands? Adelina couldn't tell.

But he stood there in the doorway, looking surprised enough that Adelina thought it had been the latter, and thought it even truer when he stepped in, moving stiffly in that way that meant Lucy had seized his muscles.

Step by step, she marched him in. Adelina's heart ached a little at the sight of him—they had not parted on good terms, but they had once been friends, good friends, on the verge of becoming something even deeper. Then he had blamed her for Lucy's disappearance. And now here his sister was, and transformed into something terrifying. Did he blame Adelina for that as well? He must, else why would he have come here?

He said, hoarsely, "Obedience ..."

"Lucy!" she snapped.

He stopped and swallowed whatever it was he had been about to say. He tried again, his voice soft and cajoling, "Lucy, then ... stop all this, little sister."

"I am not your little sister anymore!" Lucy screamed. "I am big and I am better, and no one can hurt me, ever again!"

"No one wants to hurt you," he said, reasonably.

"No! You sent me away! You didn't notice when the rest of them were bullying me because of Mamma's death! You don't care whether or not I'm happy, just whether or not I'm bringing in money to feed the rest of you!"

"And how is that different from how any of you regard me!" he snapped back. "I didn't go to the Temples and request a pack of siblings I'm to be responsible for!"

Adelina could hear the sincerity in his voice, and apparently Lucy could as well, because she stopped for a moment to gape at him.

ELOQUENCE HAD BEEN COMING up the stairs when he heard the two familiar voices, both high-pitched and feminine, but so different. Adelina's rich and resonant. The other voice a young girl's. He froze. How could this be?

The girl was speaking again.

"Oh, I am sure I have no idea how sorry you were." Then more slowly, as though savoring the words, "But I have some idea how sorry you're going to be."

He struck the door with his fist.

Lucy's voice. The voice he had hoped to hear ever since she disappeared. But now there was an inhuman glee in it that chilled his heart. "Who is it?" she demanded.

He put reassurance and command in his tone, so Adelina could hear that he had the situation under control and cease worrying, as she no doubt was. "Eloquence Seaborn!"

His fist rose to pound on the door again, and then he ceased to have any control over it. The door crashed open of its own accord and his feet marched him into the room.

It was small but cozy, this apartment, and full of books, and it was so like the life he would have wished to have with Adelina that it made him want to weep. But his face was not his own to control, nor any other part of him.

He managed to choke out, despite his traitorous throat, "Obedience ..."

"Lucy!" she snapped.

He swallowed thickly, trying to remove the invisible lump. She was only a child, he had to remember that. "Lucy, then … stop all this, little sister."

"I am not your sister anymore!" Her face was red and full of fury; it swam in his dazed vision like a watery moon. "I am big and I am better, and no one can hurt me, ever again!"

"No one wants to hurt you," he protested. How could she believe that he, her own flesh and blood, meant to harm her?

"No! You sent me away! You didn't notice when the rest of them were bullying me because of Mamma's death! You don't care whether or not I'm happy, just whether or not I'm bringing in money to feed the rest of you!"

That match was the flame that finally lit the bonfire of resentment in his heart.

"And how is that different from how any of you regard me! I didn't go to the Temples and request a pack of siblings I'm to be responsible for!" If she wanted truth, then she could have it.

Lucy was silent and wide-eyed in the face of this, and he went on.

"Did anyone ask me before I was saddled with the lot of you, to make sure you're fed and washed and sheltered? Did anyone say, Eloquence, are you prepared to lay aside your own life in order to take care of children you didn't sire? No. No, they did not."

But the anger in him leapt to her and he regretted his words as he saw them set her ablaze with anger in turn.

"Oh so sad to be the oldest and the one in charge!" she sneered. "Everyone supposed to cater to you." She smiled, and the smile was like cold water running down his spine, a terror so sudden and frigid he almost pissed himself.

CHAPTER 25

We walk through the arena, Selene and I, and it is so full of memories that I wonder that there is room enough for me to breathe. I know these stairs, these hallways. They smell of straw and people and the sausages that are served on the second level. My feet know the dents in the stairs, caused by a thousand thousand footsteps over centuries of the games.

The games. The vast tradition into which I fit. Who is Winter now, who is Spring, I wonder, in the midst of all this chaos? Perhaps they have already died; perhaps they had never been picked.

We walk in silence, but it is a comfortable one. Her fingers brush mine, and I'm not sure which of us initiates the act of twining them together, her skin as smooth and cool as milk against mine.

"You have a question you want to ask me," she says.

I do, but the thought of asking it seizes my throat with terror of what the answer might be. It is a question that has been burning at me for a while. So far away in time, I see her again at the gallery, Bernarda's gallery, that first meeting. Alone in the crowd. No one speaking to her. No one really noticing her, and that itself so strange, because she is so beautiful.

And other places, other crowds, and again, no one noticing her.

As though I were the only one that could see her. I do not know the ways of magic, but that is certainly a possibility, that there is some spellwork upon my eyes that allows me to see her, or some spellwork on her that allows only those she wishes to perceive her, or some permutation of that.…

But there is another possibility.

"Are you *real*?" I ask.

She smiles at me. "Am I real?" she teases. "Am I an illusion?" She raises our linked hands, squeezes mine with hers. "What do you think?"

"I think you are not answering," I tell her. We are still walking this corridor—at its end, we step up the stairway, heading towards one of the upper levels.

"If I were not, how would I have told you about Teo?" she asks.

But I have already considered this. "I might have deduced it without realizing it," I tell her. "The sort of knowledge that comes to you in a dream and tells you what you have known all along, just not that you actually knew it."

"Fair enough," she says, still amused, lips flexing as she regards me fondly. "And what if I am or am not, Bella Kanto? Will it make a difference in how you deal with me?"

I find myself on my knees before her, still holding her hand. "Not a whit, not a pebble," I tell her earnestly, and nothing is more important to me than that she understand this, the absolute and undying truth of my feelings about her. "Not at all."

She strokes my hair, holding me against her for a too brief but still endless moment. Then she draws me to my feet. "Come, let us see what is on this floor."

She does not guide me, not precisely, but I still feel that I am being steered, and it is unsurprising, somehow, when we find an alcove, an unobtrusive door with a less unobtrusive lock that yields nonetheless to a well-directed kick. And therein, more than one set of armor, but I only have eyes for one of them.

A poet I loved once described my armor as "frothed with ice and flowers," and it is nothing so fancy as that. The smith was Thakun

Hammring and it was arguably one of his best pieces, a silver with a rose gold underlay so subtle it was barely a blush. A visor slim and sleek as a shark, crystal lenses protecting the eyes; gauntlets like gloves of icy crystals, plunged to the elbow.

"There you are," I breathe, and take it down from the mannequin it currently clothes.

Selene helps me slip it on, as deftly as any handmaiden, but when I turn to tease her with that comparison, she is gone and it is only me and the little cat, watching from the corner, in this echoing room.

I am Bella Kanto, and I am wearing Winter's Armor, as I have before. Perhaps it will be the last time, but it will happen.

As I leave the arena and step out into the street, I salute the white Moon, rolling on the horizon as though chasing her smaller purple counterpart.

"What next, my lady?" I ask, but she is absorbed with her chase and does not answer.

SEBASTIANO WANTED to wait until dusk, when his chances would be better, despite worrying what Adelina would think when he did not return in time for dinner. She knew that he had gone to the College, and she would know that he was still there, although she might not have been able to guess at what it was that he was doing. But he would have to depend on the chaos on the campus to enable his task.

Burgling. He pushed down all his fears, all the stories that were told to the students about the many, multitudinous measures that the College had installed to prevent not just thieves, but the mischief that students might have otherwise been tempted to wreak. The College was not kind to thieves; if he set off the wrong spell, he might be transformed, or cursed, or even killed or erased from existence. Magic was nothing to trifle with.

Good thing that he had brought what he had. The Fairies had fetched it from the jumbled pile of artifacts, ready to be consumed by the machine, for him. Now he slipped on the spectacles and looked at the building.

Seen this way, it was a daunting blaze of light, each color and pattern representing a different kind of protective spell. But if he could see them, he could undo them, given enough time. And so he set to work.

Hours later, he eased the door open, holding his breath as he did so, and only opening it a third of the way, rather than full-way. There was only so much he had been able to do in his limited time, and the white Moon was already starting to fall towards the horizon. There could have been other things waiting for him, but no alarm sounded. He suspected any magic wards had been disassembled so their energies could be used in the College's gathered effort. They had been siphoning power from Mages all day, had stopped when sundown approached, and he'd overheard that they would be starting again at dawn. He didn't have much time.

He slipped through the darkened stacks, shuffling slowly to avoid tripping over anything and fumbling his way along the bumps of ancient spines. He knew the books he wanted; they were the ones that were referenced in one of the first texts that the students studied when they came here. The history of Tabat, as written by a Mage who assisted. Someone who might know how it was that Bella had become Champion of Tabat—and how she might be reinstated.

The books were bulky, and gathering all of them was not possible. Instead, he chose the first few, and the last few, and two grabbed at random from the middle. It was a hefty amount of weight, and he had to make three trips in order to get it all outside.

He thought about getting a wheelbarrow, but in the end simply lumbered along, praying that either no one would see him or that they would think it quite normal to see a man overburdened with books on the College grounds.

Somehow, impossibly—perhaps the Fairies were flying interception for him—he got to outside the College and hailed a pedal cab on Spray Way. The driver quoted him a price three times what it should be, citing the weight and the fact that there were few pedal cabs still willing to go about their business, but Sebastiano paid without demur.

He would have rushed up the stairs, but the books slowed him. He arrived at their door to find it wide open. He was eager to give Adelina the books; between the two of them surely they would be able to figure out how to defeat Lucy.

He dropped his armload at the sight in the small apartment—Adelina and Eloquence (why was he here?) facing off against Lucy, who looked as she always had, a small girl on the threshold of adolescence. But her face was white with anger, and the knowledge that she had power enough to kill them all without thinking about it made him stop dead.

Lucy and Adelina were staring at each other. Lucy was speaking towards the pair.

But Eloquence's eyes met his. Those eyes spoke volumes. They said, protect Adelina, and there was perhaps a touch of censure that he had not been there to do so, even if he were here now, when it was too late.

Sebastiano nodded once.

Lucy noticed nothing.

She said, "You sent me off to the tanner's and then when I found a place that suited me better, you kept me from it."

Eloquence said, "I've left the Temples, truth be told. I've realized that all they wanted was our money, that we were sheep for them. At least that's what's come to my mind."

That startled Sebastiano. He had not thought the man capable of such nuances of thought, no matter what Adelina had said in praise of the prettiness of his writing. Pretty words were one thing, philosophy another.

ELOQUENCE COULD NOT THINK how things had come about in this: facing down his sister, his small sister, and she failing to recognize that he was the head of the household and respect him. But she had already demonstrated her power over him, and he had to be wary of that. But surely she could see reason if he could only find the right words to persuade her.

"Your sisters will be glad to see you," he said. "We thought you dead, and realized how precious you were."

He did not expect what happened next. It startled him to be raised into the air and then hurled into the wall with blinding speed. He crashed into a shelf of books and came tumbling down with it.

Despite his daze, he could see that Sebastiano had moved next to Adelina and that Lucy was ignoring the two of them, eyes fixed on her brother. He tried to sit up, despite the stabbing pain that told him ribs were broken, and spoke to her, trying to seize all her attention.

He was her brother, and she had worshipped him, like the other girls, he knew that. He'd taken advantage of it before, and he could again.

"You were always my favorite," he told her, "but I couldn't acknowledge it in front of the others." He tried to smile with love in his eyes.

And he rose in the air and smashed into the wall again. He cried out, and agony made the world black for a moment. When he opened his eyes, Lucy was staring avidly, stare locked on him as though drinking down his pain.

But Adelina and Sebastiano were gone and that was what mattered. He had done that good thing, at least.

And now he could think about saving himself. "Lucy, I realized when you were gone …" he started, and then he met the wall again.

"I DON'T CARE what sorts of realizations you've come to, or what you've learned while I was gone," Lucy said. Her brother looked like a crumpled doll where he lay among the pile of books. She had seen Sebastiano—who would have imagined that was who Adelina had married!—and Adelina fleeing, but she had let them.

Later she would be able to track them down and they would have their turn with her. Let them run in terror; that would make things even more entertaining.

"I care about what you let the others do to me while I was still here," she told Eloquence.

"What?" he said, and sounded startled. But could he really be? He had lived in the same house with them. How could he have been utterly oblivious to all the cruelties they had visited on her in retribution for Mamma's death?

No, he could not have been that stupid. He must have known what they were doing. She could feel her teeth grinding at the thought and with an effort, she stopped and forced a smile.

"We should go see everyone," she said sweetly. "The whole family,"

In the distance they could hear the clanging of an alarm bell.

She could tell that he expected her to flee, but she smiled. "Come, Brother," she said, even more sweetly. "We must go."

ELOQUENCE FOUND himself walking without ever deciding to put one foot in front of the other, despite his bruises and broken bones, which ground together agonizingly as he moved. He was a puppet, a marionette that moved at someone else's will—Lucy's. He felt as though he had turned to water, unable to say or do anything other than the impulses that flowed through him and which he performed as though their origin lay inside him, rather than in some outside force.

It was like walking in a nightmare, and the pain of each step made his surroundings swim feverishly, like smeared paint strokes. The windows leered at him like amused faces, the pavement turned and twisted underfoot, squirming and trying to make him trip.

Lucy walked beside him, her fingers firm on his, holding his hand. To anyone looking at them, they might have seemed parent and child, the older leading the younger, rather than the reality of the other way around. They went down the stairway and into the street.

Lucy pulled him into the shelter of an alleyway to let a fire cart rumble past, then forced him to keep going along Printers Row. The alarm bell kept clanging but it was apparent by now that no one was coming. The city was in chaos and there was no one to keep order.

He tried to speak and couldn't. All he could do was roll his eyes to try to catch her attention.

Which he did. She said to him, "You always had plenty of words to tell me what to do with. Now I think maybe you cannot talk for a little while and will have to keep your ears open to hear what I have to say for a change."

After that they walked in silence. It was up two terraces to their house, two long stairways, and the journey was an eternity of pain and dread. He had no way to let his sisters know what was approaching, but his spirit shrieked in silent agony. It was clear Lucy was angry, and equally clear that she had no boundaries, and that anything could happen as a result of that anger.

Whatever was to come would not be pretty.

CHAPTER 26

Adelina and Sebastiano hid in a stairway nook as Lucy and Eloquence left. She clung to her husband, and let him think her shaking was because of fear.

How was it, even now, now that Lucy had marched her brother away, no doubt to kill him and the rest of her family, now that Lucy might return at any moment to kill her, that all Adelina could think of was the drug and how it could still this terror in her nerves? But where could she go, in these days of chaos, and find such a thing?

"We cannot stay here," Sebastiano said. "We will take the books to my parents' house and study them there."

"But what if Bella returns looking for me?" Adelina protested.

"That is a maybe, and Lucy returning is a certainty," he snapped.

"There are things here I cannot leave behind," she said. "I need to pack before we go to your parents. Perhaps you could go ahead and tell them that we are coming. Perhaps return with a servant, if they have any left in all this mess, to help carry what is needful."

"Adelina, this is insane!" he said. He seemed about to say something else, but bit it back with obvious effort.

But if she had an hour or so to herself, she could go back to the teahouse that Jilly's friends had frequented. Surely by now one of them would have received her message, which had described what she wanted in oblique terms, but ones no one familiar with Jilly's other trade would mistake. She would not ask what it was he was avoiding saying—she didn't want to know, it would just complicate things.

Sebastiano grabbed her hand. "We must go," he said. "Look through the books here with me, and we will each take a sackful. But we must go, Adelina, there is no denying it."

She wavered. Surely she could convince him, if only she could find the right words. But he had folded his arms, and she could tell there would be no moving him. She thought about picking a fight, stamping off. For a moment it felt like a plausible enough solution.

But that was her craving steering her. She recognized that with more than a touch of shame.

ELOQUENCE STRAINED EVERY MUSCLE. He pleaded with the Moons, and told them that he would give them anything if they would stop this, would return to worship and never doubt again, be a man who devoted all his life and all his words to the Temples, putting the entirety of his gift at their disposal.

The emotion that kept seizing him at intervals, in between fear and anger, was outrage. Obedience was not behaving as she should. She was not respecting his position as the head of household, let alone realizing that everything he had done was for her good, for the sake of her own soul.

And if she had stayed at the tanners where he had prenticed her, none of this would have happened, and everything would be as it should. But instead Adelina had encouraged the child in her outrageous temper and stubborn independence.

What you let my sisters do to me, she had said.

Well, what could have been as bad as all that? They were ordinary girls and they had always squabbled. It was normal for girls to quarrel, and when you had so many of them, it was constant.

But creeping out behind all that anger came the memory of how

Obedience had been acting those last few days before he'd sent her off. How she'd flinched away from Mercy when she'd seen them. How she had suddenly seemed the clumsiest of children, collecting bruise after bruise.

He had a sinking feeling he had failed her as a brother, and that he was about to pay for that failure.

They were turning into his street, approaching the shabby house with its curling paint and slipshod roof. How many of the sisters would be home? He prayed that they would have gone on an outing, errands, to worship at the Temples. Anything that would have removed them.

Simple houses flashing by in the hallucinatory pain. No neighbors in evidence. Perhaps the Moons had saved them, had led them to be elsewhere.

His house. The three steps up, each one a new surge of torture.

Obedience—no, not Obedience, Lucy, Lucy, Lucy, someone entirely new, because Obedience would never have done these things —beside him, still smiling. As she had all the way.

Sometimes in the past when bad things had happened, he'd consoled himself with thinking about using them in his writing, but he would never do that with this, could never do that with this. He would never come back to these moments if he could possibly avoid them, would drink himself blind if it would stave off these memories so he could never relive them.

Everything was fragmented by now, an effort to stay conscious, darkness calling him. His body was full of pain, as though Lucy's inexpert attempts to control him had done so wrongly, straining muscles in ways they should not have been strained.

Mercy there in the doorway, face so astonished to see her sister that her eyes and mouth were perfect rounds, like a drawing in a penny-wide.

He lost consciousness for a little while.

When it returned, he was in the front room with Lucy and all but one of her sisters, he could tell that by counting, but he could not focus enough to figure out who it was, nor how much time had passed, and he could not turn his head to see them. The air smelled like kitchen smoke and sour garbage; he had told the girls to keep better order, but they never did.

Lucy held him like a vise, and judging from what he could see of the others, did the same to them. There was early morning sunlight in the room, and summer heat beginning to kindle, and two fat flies like blots of darkness circling in the window, oblivious to what was happening in the room.

Lucy made them go to the kitchen, fetch out the last of what they had, and bring it to her. She ate it greedily, more than she should have been able to consume, while they stood frozen, forced to watch, straining to speak.

When she was done, she belched and patted her stomach, then released the invisible gag on everyone's mouth. A frenzied flood of words, apologies and reproaches and exclamations, washed over the room, but Eloquence kept silent. He knew nothing any of them could say would convince her.

All he could do was watch, tears streaming down his face.

Lucy raised a hand and everyone was cut off mid-word, unable to speak again.

"I have been thinking what to do with you," she said. "So many different things!" She grinned, baring her teeth. One of the girls pissed themselves; he could not see who, but heard the spatter of liquid and smelled the urine.

"So ready to do that. What a pig!" Lucy said, laughing. Then, softly, to herself, "Yes, that's it. What a pig."

The girls began to dwindle, shrink in on themselves. Then there were crumpled masses of fabric on the floor, each with a fat pink piglet, confused and squealing, in the middle.

The smell of pig shit overrode everything else as several voided their bowels in panic. Clambering out of the fabric, there were squeals and the clatter of hard little hooves on the bare wooden floor. The front door swung open at Lucy's gesture and the piglets ran out en masse, squealing loud enough to alert the neighborhood. Windows swung open to discover what was happening.

"What will become of them!" Eloquence cried out, heartbroken.

Lucy turned to him, still smiling. "They will run!" she laughed. "And people will try to catch them, how funny that will be!" She threw back her head and laughed. "And then!" she laughed. "And then, when they catch them—" She broke off and the grin she gave him was savage and cruel and not at all like his Obedience. "Do you know what they will do with them then, Brother?"

She leaned up and hissed the answer into his face, "They will kill them and cut them up and eat them!" And she laughed again, a sound that turned everything in him to water, until he thought that he might simply slide down to the ground and die. *If only I could.*

She laughed. "I think I will keep you. For now. I have you, and I have another pet. The two of you will keep me company. I am bored with pretending to be ordinary. I am not ordinary and never will be again. We will go home now."

THEY FLEW east over the salt marshes and when they had gone far enough, Lucy circled around. She intended to fly towards the marshes every time there was a chance that the College of Mages might have seen where she went.

Let them try to track her there in that sea of long purple grass that waved far above the height of a Human head. That was the place many fugitives escaped to, including Beasts, and there was good reason that they went that way, because in the swamps, hunting dogs and Dragons were baffled by the water, and could not be used to hunt them down as they normally would have.

Yes, the salt marsh seemed like a dire enough place that they would believe that she was living there, and they would never guess her true location, just below the castle in the cliff face.

THIS IS WHAT ELOQUENCE KNEW—THE jostling, jarring, jerking back and forth lurch that was flight with Lucy. She yanked him this way and that, and laughed when he again and again cried out in terror against the dizzying swoop of distant land as they jolted up the cliff face. Then he was roughly thrown into a space in the cliff, a cave dug into it. Already inhabited by a little woman who looked familiar, all huddled up in herself against the wall.

She ignored their entrance, but Lucy was having nothing of that. She gestured and spun the woman around, pinned her against the rocky wall like a butterfly, splaying out her limbs with painful suddenness. Like Eloquence had, she cried out in terror and pain.

"What's the matter with you?" Lucy demanded.

"I need food and drink," the woman faltered. She was richly dressed, but the garments were long bedraggled, crumpled and stained, torn at the neck and hem. She was smaller than Lucy, much smaller, and her form was twisted, he realized, not because of anything that was Lucy's doing, but because that was the way of her.

"Food and drink!" Lucy said scornfully. But she took three angry steps to the cave's mouth and launched herself off into the air without a word, lunging downwards.

The woman sagged and Eloquence hastened over to her. She slid down onto her heels, sitting again, and considered him. Her face reminded him of Bella Kanto's, he realized. Was he just still obsessed with the woman who he privately thought had been a major factor in the failure of the relationship between himself and Adelina? But no, it was definite, the resemblance. But he refrained from blurting out any question about that.

"Are you all right?" he asked instead.

She surprised him with a laugh. "I have been in the Duke's dungeons and now I have been plucked from them by an unpredictable child who seems uninclined to hurt me, at least, but equally likely to kill me from neglect. How is your day faring?"

He didn't laugh. This was not a time for such levity. "Why were you in the dungeons?" He considered her. It could not have been for anything too menacing, she seemed small and ineffectual.

"He did not like my art," she said. "It is a Ducal prerogative, to not like art, but it is less so to have an artist imprisoned because you do not like the subject. But there you have it."

There had to be more to it than that. "What was the subject of the art?"

"The rights of Beasts," she said serenely.

He was shocked and appalled to the point that he pulled back from her. "You are an Abolitionist!"

"Guilty as charged," she said, still with that maddening gladness.

He found himself lecturing her. She did not understand her error, of course. "Surely there is enough chaos in the city without adding to it by proposing the upending of the natural order?"

"Is it the natural order?" she countered. "Or one that the Humans have advanced, in order to disguise the exploitative nature of the relationship?"

He could not help but think of the Dryads, what seemed like years ago now on the Eloquent Swan, chained to the boat's railing, weeping, weeping as the boat steamed along. It was a phenomenon that bothered every sailor, but you learned to harden your heart to it after a while, because even though they resembled Human women so closely, that was not what they were. They were Beasts, and incapable of the higher thought of a Human.

His mind skittered around the thought that they were taken so their logs could be burned, so their bodies could be used to fuel the engines of the city.

The little woman was watching his face. He summoned rationality. "Perhaps we should be introducing ourselves and working together to escape just now, rather than setting ourselves at odds."

"That seems reasonable enough," she said. "I am Leonoa Kanto."

"Ah, so you are related to Bella Kanto? I thought so by the look of you." He could tell that pleased her a little; and indeed, how could it not please any woman to be compared to the charismatic Gladiator that had held so many Tabatian hearts in her hands?

He continued. "I am Eloquence Seaborn."

She was studying his face. "You have a familial resemblance yourself," she observed.

He drooped his head in shame. Of course she would notice the similarities between Lucy and himself, how could she fail to mark them, particularly if she was an artist? "She is my sister."

"Oho," she said. "I have heard a great deal about her other sisters, and less about you, though I would venture she holds you in higher regard than them."

"She killed them," he said simply. The words wrenched him, and now he was standing no longer, but seemed to have fallen to his feet. "Or close … she turned them into animals and sent them running."

"Oh, my friend," she said, and could not help but move forward at the sight of the pain on his face. They wrapped their arms around each other, seeking the relief of that embrace and simply held each other, there in the face of the cliff.

Lucy returned within the half hour, laden with two baskets that she threw onto the floor of the cavern. "You two seem to have made friends," she said scornfully. She gestured at the baskets.

Eloquence went to investigate them. One held two waterskins and the other seemed to hold the contents of a pillaged bakery cart, nothing but pastries. He guessed that she had simply swooped down and seized one. He brought the pack over to where Leonoa sat and opened it so she could take her pick.

She eyed the mass of pastries with a slightly surprised eye, and finally reached forward to extract two nut rolls. He brought her a waterskin as well. When he took a cookie from the pack, it suddenly jerked away from his hands and went flying to Lucy.

"You should have offered me some first," she said angrily. "Rather than waiting on her." She took two sweet rolls and then sent the pack flying back into Eloquence, almost knocking him down.

"I am sorry," he said with a weary surge of regret. How had everything come to this? His sister had been sweet and loving and had worshipped him, he knew that. "Obed … Lucy, we need to talk. What has happened to you?"

Her eyes burned blue and terrifying, full of an unearthly fire that burned his heart to ashes with fear. "Now you finally call me by my name, and it is too late. What do you care? You put me out into the streets. Why should it matter what happened to me after you threw me away?"

"Because you are my sister," he said, but she was having nothing of it.

"Then you should have taken better care of me," she snarled. He thought she was about to transform or kill him then, as she had the girls, but she did not, just made an inchoate, incoherent noise, and flung herself back into the air, vanishing into the sky.

He crawled back over to Leonoa with the pack and they sat there, shivering and huddled together for warmth, eating sticky pastries in silence.

CHAPTER 27

*A*delina heard Sebastiano make a sound, deep in his throat. She looked up from her book to see him staring down at the page before him. It was the oldest of the books he had stolen, a great tome bound in greasy-looking leather, almost outsized. Its cover read "First Records of the College of Mages, established by Ellora."

"Ellora founded the College of Mages?" Adelina said, intrigued. "I have never heard that."

Sebastiano shook his head absently. "It's not that."

"What then?"

He spun the page around so she could read it, and she swiftly scanned the text, then read more slowly, then stopped on a sentence. Her eyes rose to meet Sebastiano's. "Is this true?" she asked.

He shook his head. "I've never heard it spoken of. But it is marked here as something never to be spoken of."

She traced the sentence with a finger and read it aloud, "As we know, when a Mage comes to his last days of power, the magic he is imbued with will shape him in turn into one of the nobler Beasts, such as a Unicorn, a Griffon, or in very rare cases, a Dragon." With an impatient little gesture, she pushed the book away. "Ignoring the assumption that all Mages are male, which is an unfortunate habit of you and all your colleagues, despite Ellora's example, this is something that means ..."

"It means that the lines between Humans and Beasts are even less solid than we pretend."

"Of course they are not solid," she said. "We have created them to advantage ourselves."

"You have been speaking too often with my mother."

"Your mother is the most sensible of all your family," Adelina said. "And that makes me ask: what will we do with this knowledge?"

"Spread it," Sebastiano said instantly.

She laughed at him. "You have been speaking with your mother too often as well, because that is the act of a true Abolitionist."

"No," he said. "I'm come to realize, she is right. We live in a system that grinds up Beasts and feeds them to Humans, often literally." He looked at her hard before going on. "That is wrong and unjust. We pretend this city is noble, but it is a hollow shell, built on evil practices."

She shook her head. "It is not just a Human city," she said. "It is the city of the Beasts that live here as well. That is the Tabat we are trying to save, not the structures that overlay it. The place where so many of us have grown up, the place that has sheltered us all our lives. We can acknowledge that it has done so, but that can be tolerated, as long aswe are willing to change things. Good intentions are not enough, change must happen if things are to improve."

"Agreed," he said. "But all of this is moot unless we can save it from Lucy. And these books have nothing in them so far."

"Not quite," she said, tapping the book before her. "This one does talk about Ellora, and says that in the process of making her creations —the caverns and the gardens and so much of the structure that underlies Tabat—she did tie things together. And she tied them to the games. That's how Bella happened to become who she was. She was the champion the city had been waiting for, and the longer she stayed in that position, the stronger the belief of the citizens—and her own power—grew."

"Do you think the Duke knew something of this, and that's why he worked to bring her down?"

"No," she said with definitiveness. "The Duke is a petty and venial man, and he disliked Bella having the power that she did. What I suspect is someone else pushed him in that direction, knowing that it would destabilize the city."

"Murga," Sebastiano said instantly. "He is a Sorcerer."

Adelina shuddered. "Are you sure? Perhaps he is using some artifact or thing of power."

"No, I should have realized it earlier."

"And why destabilize the city?"

"Because he thinks it the best way to secure the rights of the Beasts. Kill the Humans, or at least any not sympathetic to their cause, and make Tabat entirely Beast-run. No doubt with Murga in a position of power for having facilitated it."

"So how do we connect Bella with Tabat's magic again, so she can set this right?"

He tapped another book. "It is a question of belief. She must believe in the connection with the city, and the city itself must believe it as well, if we can find the right representatives for it. Done right, her link to its magic might be reinstated."

"Surely there is more to magic than belief."

"There is, but it is definitely part."

"We should discuss this with Bella," she said. "Perhaps I should go out and look for her."

"The streets are more dangerous by the hour," Sebastiano said. "If you go, I am going with you." His face was resolute and she could tell there would be no convincing him.

I TAKE the armor back to Adelina's with me, thinking of the place as hers and hers alone, which is why I find it mildly off-putting to walk into the devastated apartment and find her in her husband's arms, talking pretty talk to each other, and all the while piles of books on the table being neglected.

"What's happened?" I ask, and find out Lucy has been there.

There is a lot of talking and talking and talking at that point, some of it more to the purpose than others. Throughout it all, though, my anger smolders that Lucy has been here, that she dared to menace my Adelina. And most angering of all, it was not I who saved her. I don't mind that she clings to Sebastiano's arm, keeps him in touching distance. She has been frightened, sorely, and he is a comfort to her. I don't begrudge him that at all. Not at all.

Well, perhaps a little.

And it is irritating that he seems to know the most about magic, or at least is the most willing to pontificate about it. But I am forced to admit that perhaps, since he is the only one of us that has actually studied magic, he is worth listening to.

And, to be fair, he does some listening in turn. He attends carefully to my account of what happened in the islands and asked me questions about Lucy's appearance and her actions that demonstrate his attention to the details. I am glad to have him as an ally, although perhaps not as a romantic rival.

But then I look at Adelina, sheltered in the crook of his arm as he speaks. Even as he is talking to me, he does not forget about her, keeps his arm around her in comfort, keeps an eye on her. He is as shaken as I was at the thought of losing her. Lucy could have destroyed both of us, perhaps, with a single blow at Adelina.

I tell them everything that has happened. Or most everything.

I do not tell either of them about Selene. Is it that she is my secret? Or that I am still not entirely convinced that she is real? The gods do not walk among us like ordinary people, do not play at Human emotions. Those are simply stories. And if she is real, my white Moon, then are all the Trade Gods that the Merchants worship real? Is this world full of invisible entities that I have somehow never perceived before this time?

And if that is so, how can I trust anything at all?

I still do not feel entirely myself, do not feel like the old Bella

Kanto. Perhaps I never will. Would that be such a bad thing? There are plenty that would miss the old Bella Kanto, but perhaps the new one would be better than the old one ever was, with or without magic.

I can see why she likes him, why she even loves him. The two of them in conversation is a medley of rapid-fire exchanges, one throwing out an idea and the other grabbing it, elaborating and embellishing, before tossing it back. He knows magic, but she knows how magic has affected history. Soon they are in waters that I have never swum, speaking of matters that I know nothing of. I fall silent, listening. It is not a familiar sensation, but it is not unpleasant.

Adelina finally turns to me, and says, "We must figure out how to renew your connection with the city."

I say Alberic was the one that severed the relationship when he pronounced me exile.

"Do you remember anything about that?" Sebastiano asks. "Was there any physical sensation, a moment that you knew that the magic was gone?"

I shake my head. "I had been under a certain amount of physical strain," I say dryly.

"They tortured her," Adelina put in. I remember when she came to visit me, and I barely had been able to look at her. I try to push the memory away but it resists.

"Perfectly understandable," Sebastiano tells me after a brief hesitation. "When did you realize that the magic was gone?"

"On the journey," I tell him. "I began to age in a way that I never had before."

I flip a glance at Adelina, who surely must have noticed all the changes in me. She knows exactly what I am thinking, for she says, "You are still beautiful, Bella, you know that quite well."

"Of course," I say. "I do not know that I could ever doubt that without becoming something other than I am."

"It is reassuring to me that you have not changed," she says, and there is banter in her tone, some of the old fondness. Sebastiano's eyes narrow, very slightly, but he says nothing. She turns to him and asks,

"Is this something that might be in a book that is still in their library? You said there were plenty of others."

"Perhaps," he says, "but I do not know where it would be, and a book explaining such things does us no good if we cannot find it."

"There is something else that you may want to think of," I say. "Lucy is taking her revenge on the city, and you say that she has taken her brother and will have wreaked it on him by now. That means she will be looking for new targets. She has already proven that Adelina is one of those targets, and I cannot help but think that the College of Mages, which rejected her, will be one as well."

"So you are saying that I should get there as soon as possible, before she razes it to the ground," he says. He is speaking half in jest but he's taken aback when I nod at him.

That is exactly what I am saying. Am I the only person here who realizes what she is capable of, even when they have seen so much destruction already?

"You are thinking of her as if she was still a little girl," I say. "She is not. She is something much more than a little girl."

Adelina says, "She was prepared to kill me, I think. Eloquence took her away, and I do not know what price he paid for that intervention." She looks at Sebastiano. "I know that you do not like him. But he does not deserve to die."

How many rivals for Adelina's attention are there nowadays?

A *rat-a-tat* at the door. I leave Adelina and Sebastiano arguing and go downstairs to open it. There is a figure there standing in the doorway, familiar but unexpected, golden-winged. She wears a cloak that hides her wings and it occurs to me that walking the streets and seeming to be a Beast may not be as safe as it once was. If it ever was.

She sweeps past me. "I need to speak with all of you," she says. I follow, but this isn't right. How did she know to come here, how has she tracked me down?

She goes upstairs to Adelina and Sebastiano's apartment as though she already knows the way, which also isn't right, because how does she know them? Has Adelina formed a friendship through Leonoa, but did not mention it to me? Surely not, or if it would have come up when we were discussing how she had been taken by the Duke.

"They said you had gone up to the castle. Did you find any sign of Leonoa?" Her voice is high with worry and hope, and it makes me feel a little more kindly to her, that she feels so strongly about my favorite cousin. I shake my head.

"I found nothing of her up there, which tells you nothing either way, I am afraid," I tell her, and I am sincere, as is her thankful nod. "If I find out anything, I will send to tell you, and if you learn anything …"

"I will also send to tell you," she says immediately and without hesitation. Our eyes meet, and there is acknowledgment there of tension in the past—although I am still not sure of the source—but we are allied in our feelings for Leonoa.

Adelina offers Glyndia tea and sandwiches, but she shakes her head. "There are searchers still, up at the castle. I am going to go and help."

She hurries away and I shrug in answer to Adelina and Sebastiano's silent looks of question.

"Lucy marched Eloquence away," Adelina said. "Someone should go and see what there is at his house."

"I will go," Sebastiano says before I can. "You will be safe enough here with Bella." I am surprised and perhaps even a little irritated by his complacency, but very well, he can be the one to go face whatever horrors Lucy has created, and I will stay here safe and eat sandwiches with his wife.

So many threads, Sebastiano thought, hurrying along and trying to sort through the bewildering mass. Murga and the Duke, old Mages becoming Beasts, the Beasts themselves, Bella Kanto and his own Adelina, and now her apprentice Lucy, the child he'd befriended only earlier this year when he'd found her entering his box at the arena. He'd fed her, and enjoyed her prattle, had enjoyed everything until he'd taken her home to the pickle-faced Eloquence. He made a face at that last. Eloquence was Lucy's brother, so by some kind of reasoning, this whole situation with his out-of-control sibling should have been his to deal with.

Eloquence's house was not hard to find, but the front door stood open and there was no one inside, just a bewildering litter of clothing and pig shit, and tracks leading out the door.

Two urchins were skulking nearby. He offered them coin to tell him their stories, and extracted a bewildering mass of details about pigs and flying people. All he could gather was that Lucy had taken Eloquence away, and something about pigs, which was why the children were lurking, "in case more come out."

He could make nothing of it and returned home to say as much, to find Adelina and Bella sitting on the sofa, talking. But when he looked at his wife carefully, he could see lines of strain around her eyes, and a tightness to the way she held her mouth. She moved restlessly, fingers touching the sofa's arm as though to reassure herself of the fabric.

It was good, Adelina thought, all this talk, this figuring things out. And happiness, to be there with both Bella and Sebastiano. But at the same time, she could feel the drug creeping up on her, fingering its way along her limbs, leaving a feeling behind like bees crawling on her skin.

"What's wrong?" Sebastiano asked, and she realized she had been lost in contemplation of that sensation.

"Nothing," she stammered, and saw Bella's eyes narrow at the same time that Sebastiano's did.

He said, very gently, dangerously gently, "Is it the drug, Adelina?"

The shock of it was as though an immense bandage had been ripped off and the new air was searing at the revealed flesh. She wanted to say, "What drug?" but it was clear that he knew much more than she had thought he—or anyone—had ever guessed at.

Bella was silent, looking thoughtful. Had she known about this already, or was she using her usual tactic of looking as though she knew everything while actually comprehending very little?

"I understand why it appealed to you," Sebastiano went on, his voice implacable. "I had always wondered at your love of public speaking—it seemed so out of character for one of a retiring nature, content to be seen only in her writings. But the drug made it possible for you. To please your mother at first …"

She flinched at that. Yes, it was exactly why she had done it in the first place, in her desire to finally secure Emiliana's approval. But it wasn't why she had kept at it, she would have to admit that. It had been the heady rush of having her words go out and sway people, feel the words pulling their attention to her, sweeter than even the most glowing review, somehow. That had been the greater part of the addiction, that rush of pleasure.

And she had been too long without it. She could feel something in her body yearning for it, craving it so much that three-quarters of her attention was pulled to that urge.

Still … To be exposed and embarrassed like this.

"Don't get on a high horse with me, Sebastiano Silvercloth," she snapped. "You and your fellow Mages have been ingesting the magic of Beasts to the point of literally becoming magic. Is that not a drug? And you, Bella, tell me you're not addicted to the adulation of the crowd, that you didn't suffer withdrawal from it as strongly as any dreamweed addict."

"This is not you speaking," he said, although now there was a quaver to his gentleness that made some mean, small, petty part of her soul rejoice.

"It is!"

"It is not," Bella said. "Trust the two who love you best in all this world, Adelina."

"You left me!" burst out of her before she could prevent it.

"It was not in my heart to do it," Bella said, more apologetically than she would have ever believed Bella could sound. "But the Duke sent me away, Adelina. He exiled me."

"I know!" Her fists were balled up, pressed to her chest. She turned away from them, unwilling to look at those kind, reproachful faces that wanted nothing but the best for her. "But everyone has secrets, both of you. Can you not leave me mine?"

"Not when they are hurting you, love," Sebastiano said, and the heartbreak in his voice was what made her swing back around to him, to step forward and be drawn into the comfort of his arms.

"Who supplied you?" Bella asked. "Are they no longer around?"

"Jilly Clearsight."

Bella frowned. "I know that woman. She is tied up with unsavory characters." She paused, considering. "What did you mean, that the Mages become literally magic?"

She gave Sebastiano an apologetic look. He shrugged. "It's true," he said. "We have found that when a Mage dies, he—or she—becomes one of the major Beasts."

"Is that change reversible?"

"I would not think so, but who am I to know? All of this is news to me."

"Will you become a Beast, eventually?" Bella said with interest.

"Bel!" Adelina twisted around in her husband's arms to give Bella a scandalized look. "How can you ask something so … so …"

"Personal?" Sebastian said dryly. He said to Bella, "I doubt it. I have not taken in a fraction of what the older Mages have. And now that I understand all this, I intend to eat none of it going further." He gazed down at Adelina. "But, my love …"

"What?" she demanded.

"The powder you have been ingesting is magical," he said. "It comes from the flesh of Beasts."

She retched at the thought, an immediate revulsion. "What? Surely not!"

"It is made of Fairies, Adelina," Sebastiano said. "Their bodies, dried and crushed."

It was disgusting. It was appalling. But somehow she knew it was true. How else could it have felt so powerful, so heady?

She could bear it no longer. She ran to the kitchen and hung her head over the wash basin, heaving, until the contents of her stomach had been emptied.

"The Fairies said withdrawal is dangerous," Sebastiano said. She had not realized he had followed her into the room. "That you must do it slowly."

"I cannot do that," she said. "All I had is gone, and no matter where I look in the city, I can find no more."

He handed her a tiny paper packet. "They have given me enough that you can wean yourself from it slowly."

He studied her. "It is made from their own bodies, Adelina, you understand that? And they have given up enough that you can survive."

"What do they want in return?" she said. The paper packet was so real in her hand. She longed to open it immediately, consume the contents, but she would hold onto her dignity in front of Sebastiano. She hated him more than a little for having found out, for telling her what the drug really was, for having no addictions of his own.

He did not answer her question, but said, "Bella has gone out again. I think to give us privacy. She is more tactful than I would have thought, your Gladiator."

There was a question underlying that statement that made her heart hurt. She reached out with her free hand to touch his sleeve. "Not mine," she said. "The only thing that is mine is you."

His face cleared. "Always," he said.

eo had left Maisie and her rabbit with the Beasts. While the rabbit was not one, not being intelligent, it was a magical animal and would be in peril if Humans found it. The fox girls were happy to oblige, gossiping with Maisie, holding the rabbit and petting it in a way that told him the rabbit would be far safer with them than with him.

When they had met last, she had told him that Murga was acting even more strangely, talking to himself in his rooms at night, losing his temper with the circus members. "If I had a place to go, I'd leave too," she had confided. Her look made it clear that she was grateful to him for having brought her to stay with the Beasts. He hoped it would be the refuge that she thought it was.

Just in case, he told her about Jilly's house. Warned her that she should not be seen going in and out, at least for now. But it would be a safe place for her to shelter.

He also told her about his time with Bella. Maisie made a face. Murga was obsessed with Bella Kanto, she said, even had all the old penny-wides. But she'd also revealed something that he thought might be useful.

"There's an old Centaur that he goes to visit," she said

unexpectedly. "I spent a week trailing him—you'd be surprised, all the places he goes, and the faces he puts on. But he wears his own face to visit him, and goes into the stables where he is kept, and they sit together, talking for hours. That's the only person I've ever seen Murga smile, really smile, at."

Bella was the key.

He ran through the city in his cougar form, and no one dared step in his path. City guards were nowhere in sight. He paused at the top of the Tumbril stairs, ignoring people shrieking and running away from him. He raised his head and sniffed the wind. All the smells of Tabat, and the smell of Lucy there too somehow. And then, like a scarlet thread winding through it, a scent that he knew, that made his heart beat faster with the knowledge that she was there, somewhere. Bella Kanto.

With a snarl of joy, he bounded forward, chasing the scent ever upward, ignoring everything else, including the panicked shouting of the crowd. Lucy was wherever she was, he thought, but surely Bella would put her down. She was Bella Kanto, after all, and that was enough to conquer anything.

A shadow swept over him, and he paused long enough to gape with the rest of the crowd at the huge blue and gold zeppelin centered in the sky overhead. Then it moved on, and he was back in sunlit astonishment. How could such a thing fly? No doubt there was some magic in it. It must have been sent by the College of Mages, sent to aid in the attack.

The sight heartened him. Bella would not be alone in her fight against Lucy. There was less doubt that she would win—a doubt that he did not want to admit he had been harboring.

THE DUKE HAD FELT himself useless all this time, but now he would finally act, he decided. There was no point in hiding—and in his own city, no less! No, he would act with the decisiveness that had served his ancestors so well when settling Tabat. He knew where the zeppelin was kept, only two terraces above the Peacekeeper headquarters. Two still-loyal Peacekeepers accompanied him.

"It can't go up without a full crew," the engineers said in answer to his demand.

"I don't care," he said. He knew how to fly it, he'd made sure of that because it was enjoyable, maneuvering the vast entity and letting the trained harpoonists fly as they would. The Peacekeepers would man those guns, and he would fly. Three of them was enough. They usually held more crew in case of disaster or fire, but he would roll the dice and gamble that such a disaster would not come. How could it? He was the Duke, he was the hero of the people. Stories showed that such people never fell.

He watched the huge heap of cloth slowly filling from the magically augmented tanks. This zeppelin could have taken down a Dragon, he thought. The girl wouldn't stand a chance.

They boarded and took their stations, feeling the uneasy movement underfoot, so like and unalike all at once of being on a boat.

The Duke settled himself in the tiny basket where the ornate brass controls were, a cabin made of gilded wickerwork reeds. They were sturdy enough, but there was a feeling of fragility about the whole thing that he had never noticed before. He steeled his jaw. This would be his moment. Tabat would witness his glorious victory and the city would be his again.

Creaking underfoot as the vast gas balloon slowly filled with the heated air from a hulking brass and crystal contrivance that sat in the center of the hangar. Near it were what might be the last three Dryad logs in all the city, their essence slowly pouring into the machine, the bark graying and losing all its luster as the magic seeped away.

A lurch from the zeppelin, and another, and he could feel they were no longer touching the ground.

Men with ropes towed the zeppelin along towards the hangar door, fighting to keep it low enough to slip out with another awkward, upward leap. The Duke spoke through the brass speaking tube near his elbow. "Are you ready?"

"Sir, yes sir!" the Peacekeepers chorused back.

"Good men." He touched another control, and the slow drift upward took on momentum. He would steer along the eastern terraces, taking advantage of what cover they provided in order to gain altitude. He had never fought a battle in the air, had never really even thought about it, but he had gone hawking, and knew altitude meant vision and speed in the attack.

This was his day, the day that he would save Tabat and cement his hold on the city. It would be a glorious day, one unlike any other.

WE COLLIDE IN THE STREETS, and I step back in surprise. "Teo?" I say.

"Bella!" He is all puppy enthusiasm, hugging me.

"How did you get away from Lucy?"

"She wasn't paying any attention when she was destroying things. So I slipped away. I bet she's angry." He makes a face to demonstrate his lack of interest in encountering an angry Lucy. "But I never told you who turned me into a dog."

"The Duke," I say. But he shakes his head.

"He's a Sorcerer, I think. Not the Duke. Murga, who owns the Autumn Moon. I've seen him be all sorts of other forms. He was Miche. And a woman with wings."

That hits me hard. "Glyndia?" I say.

He looks bewildered, but I am thinking of Adelina and Sebastian, standing face-to-face with a Sorcerer and not even knowing it. What if she—or he, what words fit—returned after I was gone? "Come on," I say, and grab him by the shoulder so he is pulled along with me. "Tell me what you know as we run."

When he reaches the part about the elderly Centaur, I miss a step and come down hard on my ankle, almost turning it. Could Philip be involved in all of this somehow? But there are plenty of Centaurs, and elderly ones to boot. Still. If Philip is alive, what could he tell me about his time after Jolietta, how he came back to language and meaning? If it is him. If it can be him.

Adelina and Sebastiano are not at home, but I find no signs of struggle. I will let them take care of themselves for now. My mind is reeling with all this news.

Teo says, "My parents are here, somewhere in the city. I need to keep looking for them." I do not object and he slips away. He will come back when he can.

I don't want to believe what he has told me at first. It cannot be, that Philip has been alive all this time. I looked so hard for him. Why wouldn't he have looked for me? I was enough in the public eye that he would have been able to find me easily. Did he think I would become like Jolietta with age? That thought hurts me. And he himself —Centaurs have shorter life spans than Humans. Their hearts give out more easily, and they age fast, towards the end.

So I go to the place that Teo has described,

It is an old stable. I know this one—the owner has always been kindly (to the point of softness, Jolietta would have said) to Beasts. It is on the outskirts of town. There is someone sweeping the stable yard and I hail them. A young woman, her hair pulled back, her face dirty. It takes me a few moments to recognize her as the daughter of the owner. He's dead, she tells me flatly.

"I was hoping to see a Beast here," I say, finding myself faltering. Her eyes narrow.

"Who?" she says flatly.

"His name is Philip," I say, and her face shutters further.

"I had not thought you would turn to Beast-hunting for the Duke," she says.

"That is not it at all. I know him from long ago."

Her eyes are still suspicious. "If I should go and tell him Bella Kanto wishes to speak to him, what will he say?"

"I do not know at all."

THE STABLES SMELL OF HAY, and horseshit, and the good strong smell of horse. The old Centaur is standing in the sunlight, head drooped, dozing. For a moment I think it's not him, but then he opens his brown eyes and it is Philip, my Philip, regarding me with a fond look.

"Bella Kanto, champion of the city," he says. "Look at you!"

I had expected hatred. Recrimination. So long ago I told Jolietta that he had learned to read and write, and that caused her to burn out his mind. But he seems hale enough, hearty enough, although he has lost the harshness that once lurked behind his expression.

"We have both gotten older," he says. "Perhaps wiser, perhaps not. Come and sit for a while. Tell me of your travels."

I find myself pulling up a small three-legged stool that is in the corner, and settling into the sunlight beside him.

I ask the obvious, and he tells me that he escaped under the care of a Human who was curious about the results of gentling and if it could be reversed through natural treatments.

"He was a kindly man, but dispassionate in his science," he says, and trails off in a way that makes me wonder why he phrases it exactly like that. Jolietta was dispassionate, in her own way, and it was not a good one. It was not a quality that I think of accompanying "kindly."

"I made my way up, eventually, to Verranzo's New City," he says at length. "Have you ever been there, Bella? I read of no adventures taking place there, and I believe I read them all."

That admission takes my breath away, and somehow I burn both with embarrassment of thinking what he would have read, would have thought of me over the years, and a fierce pride that he has taken the time to watch me—to see me, when I could not see him, all this time.

"I have never been up there," I admit. "The Duke forbade all travel there."

"And you obeyed him in that? Intrepid Bella Kanto?"

"It seemed easier not to pick that quarrel," I admit. "Of all the people who have been able to wear me down over the years, it has always been Alberic the most adept, with his threats and promises, and all that he can offer in those promises."

Philip's lips curl at that, and I regret the admission. But he might as well have the truth of me, the truth that Adelina hid in all those stories. I am not the noble figure she painted me, though at times I might have lived up to certain, more dashing aspects. But like any other being, I made compromises in order to live.

I am who I am now, though, and it is the same old me that has always been here, always challenging and accepting the world all at once. Searching for some meaning to my existence and thinking I had found it in being the heart of Tabat.

"Will you be its champion again?" Philip asks, as though he could read every thought that has been passing through my mind.

"I do not know that the city wants me anymore," I say frankly. "I was thrown out for things that were not true, but most of the city's folk seems to have believed it." I think of Abernia, my landlady, and her eagerness to eject me and all my belongings.

"Not all of them, surely," Philip says, and I shake my head.

"No, not all," I say. "Not my cousin Leonoa, nor my friend Adelina. But enough of the others to hurt, to wound me deeper than any physical blow ever did." My eyes seek his. "And I say that as someone who has endured blows. They tortured me, in the questioning, and I came apart under that. But Tabat's scorn …"

"Ah," Philip sighs, and there is sorrow in his tone.

"I did so much in their name, over the years," I say. "And when they celebrated me, it was sweeter than any candy, more intoxicating than any drink."

He smiles at me. "And you did love candy, I remember that." He says it with a fondness that catches at my throat.

"So how have we come to all this?" I ask. "You went to Verranzo's New City, where I have never been."

"Aye, and saw a different way there. A place where everyone works and lives alongside each other with no thought as to who is who. Only their merit, only the fruits of their hands matter. There are artisans there cleverer than any of Tabat's, and it is because of that lack of division. The Mages there work wonders."

"If it is all as good as that," I find myself arguing, and hear the words in my head as though they came from Alberic's lips, "then why does not the notion spread all through the world?"

"The answer is that it is doing so," he says. "More with every passing day. Had Alberic actually succeeded in exiling you to some frontier town, you would have found it much more egalitarian than you might have predicted. When everything depends on simple survival, when you are together in a hostile world, many differences can be overlooked."

"You are saying Tabat is the only hold-out," I scoff.

"Not that. The Rose Kingdom has its own ways, as you know, and the Old Continent will always be ruled by sorcerers, or at least till the last of them dies, centuries from now. But Tabat is the largest place that still holds to the old ways, no matter how modern it may style itself."

I make a face. "This is not how anyone speaks of the world."

He outright laughs. "Anyone that you know, which is Tabat, and the places it rules over. You should have spent more time on the One Story city—you would have found things there much changed as well."

"It was all chase and escape there," I say.

"Will you tell it to your friend, so that she will write the story, and I may read it in all its detail?"

"Maybe," I say. "If we all survive these next few days."

"The child," he says. "Murga goes to challenge her soon."

The words startle me. "You are with him?"

"Not with him," he says. "Adjoining him. We have disagreements on how things should be done, how the city should be changed. But I agreed to let him try his way, which I knew would be a compelling one. Riots would leave the city more ready to work together in the aftermath, I thought."

"You knew what he would do to me, as part of his plan."

Philip's eyes are clear and guileless. "I did, Bella. Sometimes one makes sacrifices if they think it worthwhile."

I cannot reproach him. Not when I betrayed him myself, so many years ago. So I just nod, although I can feel the tears in my eyes.

He reaches out to cup my face. "Does it change our friendship now?"

I shake my head, but barely, letting myself feel his hand. "It does not," I say.

We sit in silence for another moment, but time is so precious right now that I cannot squander too many moments, no matter how sweet, how welcome, how longed-for they have been.

"Will Murga win against her?" I ask.

He pauses before he answers me. "I do not think so," he says, reluctantly. "I did not reckon on whatever she is."

"Some ancient force," I say. "Forgotten. Buried. And then put in the hands of a child. How could you predict that?"

My wry tone forces him to laugh, but he sobers quickly. "So are you asking how she is to be defeated, Bella?"

"I am, if you know."

"I do not know, in the way you want me to know. But I think that perhaps it is you."

"Me?" I say, startled.

"If you can reconnect to the magic of Tabat."

"That is what my friends believe as well. But what is the means of doing that?"

His shaggy hair obscures his eyes as he shakes his head.

"You are of no help," I say severely, and he laughs at me.

"This has all been a gamble, Bella," he says. "But things could not go on as they were. You know that as well as I. Humans depended on Beasts to the point of exploitation, and rather than admit that, they vilified us and infantilized us. Said we had to be watched over for our own good as well as theirs. You saw what that made Jolietta become. Would she have been so hard if she had not been forced in that direction?"

The thought that Jolietta might have been something other than what she was startles me to the point of breathlessness. "She did what she did to you, and you do not blame her?"

"I can blame her while knowing there were forces shaping her," he said. "You yourself became a Gladiator and fought plenty of Beasts in the arena."

"They were there to fight," I stammer, and he shakes his head again. "Forced into it," he says, and I know it is true, and somehow it diminishes every such victory, makes it a hollow and tawdry thing.

"You were not the champion of the Beasts. And so you were not the champion of the entire city, and that made you vulnerable," Philip says.

"Vulnerable to your plans."

"To Murga's. And my plan was always that if you were pressed hard enough, you would become that champion. What did exile teach you?"

What did I learn? That I was vulnerable, certainly, but more than that. Once I was outside Tabat, once I was no longer part of it, sitting in my cabin aboard the Stooping Hawk, I thought differently about the furnaces, and the things the College of Mages use. And on the journey with Scylla, away from the Long Slow City, I thought of how the Duke named some Mers Humans and others Beasts, depending on how it advantaged him. How it fed his pockets.

I learned the divisions we Humans have created are not as sure as we pretend they are. I learned that the moon itself could come down from the sky and urge you to do the right thing. I learned that friendship lasts over leagues, over decades. Over lives.

I have left Winter's Armor at Adelina's, but do I need it? After all, am I not Bella Kanto?

Philip says, "Are you ready?"

"I am ready to try," I say.

CHAPTER 29

Teo ran in Human form this time, and didn't even know where he was going, let instinct drive him upward along the terraces. He was happy that he had seen Bella, but now he had other errands. He'd been told to find his coin, but it was with his parents, and they were here, somewhere in the city.

He rounded a corner. For a second he could not believe his eyes.

He had not thought he would ever see their faces again. And yet, here they were, on the street looking at him. A little older, as though the trip had worn them down, a few more fine lines around his mother's eyes, his father's bristle of a beard a brushstroke grayer.

He gaped to see them, stopping dead, but they did not hesitate. His mother's face lit as though she had been expecting him to step around the corner at any second (somehow he thought that maybe she had, ever since she first set foot in the city) and she rushed forward with open arms, his father quick after her.

Teo felt himself happily lost in the comforting tangle of their arms, an almost purr rising to his throat that drew first a startled look from his mother then a smile in answer to his happy nod.

His father rested his head atop Teo's, a comforting and familiar weight. They smelled right, even here in the heart of the city, smelled of woodsmoke and fir trees, and sycamore, and the little herbs that Teo's mother habitually laid among their clothes to ward off fleas and moths.

He finally broke away from the tangle long enough to say, "How are you here? And where is Elya?"

His heart sank at the sobering of their faces. His father shook his head, and said gruffly, "No longer with us. We had her for three white moons after you left, and a handful of days. And then the fever returned and took her away and both of you were gone."

He shrugged uncomfortably and jerked a thumb at Teo's mother. "Near gone with worry, after all that, and finally I said, why not stop fretting and start walking? And so after a while—and plenty of stories along the way, I'll be telling you—we are here, and looking for you."

"No one at the Temples could answer any questions, nor that fellow who the priest trusted you to," his mother said indignantly. "This is a poorly run place, and not one welcoming to strangers at all."

"There are good things here and there," he said, grinning at her. "I'll show you some of them."

People around them were no longer watching the happy reunion but instead looking upward, into the sky. Teo followed their stares and swallowed.

"After we get away to safety," he amended, watching Lucy, hanging far above the city.

A few moments later there was a brief flash of light, so bright it dazzled his eyes. Everyone recoiled. Then the laughter began, and though it was thunderingly loud, though it filled his ears, he recognized its source. Lucy was laughing. His heart sank in his chest.

LUCY SAW the zeppelin rising over the city skyline and it made her throw her head back and laugh. What did they think such a thing, made of air and fabric, could do?

Then she caught sight of the two brass guns riding its front and her eyes narrowed. What did they shoot? Physical objects would be easy to elude.

No, it would be something else, something magical. It was trying to move upward, to get above her, and that was easily thwarted.

Keeping just above it and out of reach of the guns as she judged them, she moved with it.

Like an avenging hawk, she hung in the sky. How pretty it was, this fat feathered bird, all adorned with blue stripes and golden feathers. In front a vast figurehead shaped like a golden Griffon's head, enchanted to the lightness of air. How could anything so beautiful be anything but an ornament?

But she had miscalculated. Both guns spat out lightning, and while one shot went wild, another caught her solidly in the midriff.

She tumbled backward in the air, losing altitude before she recovered herself and stopped her fall. Breathless and angry, she realized another hit like that and she might not be able to recover.

It was unbearable beyond belief to think that the Duke would score a victory over her.

The blazing anger of that thought leaped from her hands to strike at the zeppelin's ribbed midriff.

First there was a black spot on the blue fabric, and then it became a circle of nothingness, fire licking away the delicate fabric, making it disappear to show the delicate wooden skeleton underneath.

The zeppelin lurched, tried to right itself while the balloon still existed, then slanted abruptly as it vanished. Unimpeded by clouds, it plummeted.

Falling, the Duke screamed anger. It was unfair. It was all so unfair.

Unlike Lucy, he had no remedy for his anger, which only lasted until he struck the ground.

It was at this moment that the College of Mages struck.

They had been preparing and preparing, but the Duke's impetuous attack had taken them unawares and they'd had to scramble to catch up.

They'd shoveled everything into the machineries, breaking it down to the constituent parts, extracting all magic. They looted the small museum, feeding in its stuffed mermaids and plumes of Fairy feathers. They plundered the student dormitories, confiscating all the small magical devices that made life in those stringent surroundings bearable: bedwarmers and ever-shining lamps, a kettle that heated itself, and hundreds of little cosmetic spells, from wart remover to hair pomade.

They took every book in the library and fed it to the machines, whether magical or not, on the theory that it would have absorbed plenty of magic from its fellows. The fruit from the glade of ever-bearing trees, the golden roses from beneath the Dean's windows, the enchanted teapot that served his morning chal.

The released magic was absorbed by the white globe in the center of the circle of machines. It grew brighter and brighter, and the air whined as though overloaded with power, smelled of freshly forged steel tempered in blood, made everyone's hair stand on end, their teeth grind, their intestines spasm.

Seven Masters waited for the right moment, standing near the growing, glowing globe. They were the best the College had to offer, the most skilled among them, and they were all filled with the confident assurance that they would win. What they were dealing with was surely just another type of Beast, and Beasts were meant to be dominated by Humans.

Thunder crackled in the sky from Lucy's vicinity; the zeppelin fell like a discarded toy. Its flaming frame landed on the eleventh and twelfth terraces, smashing the houses and railings and trees there, and setting fires leaping through the neighborhood.

Seven voices shouted in unison, seven left hands lifted. The globe detached from the ground, floated upward. Slowly and haphazardly at first, then with growing speed that became purposeful, arcing upward towards the speck that was Lucy, moving faster and faster.

She saw it coming long before it hit and she opened her arms to it, let the globe of light collide with her, driving her backwards several feet through the air, and then closed her arms around it as it dwindled and the shine of it transferred to her, as though every inch of her were outlined in incandescent fire. She was like a Phoenix, she thought, and laughed, filled with the joy of her power and her flight.

The laugh was magnified, so it thundered over Tabat, a laughter gleeful and demented and threatening, all at once, so many hid as best they could, while others walked the streets shouting that the end had finally come. Five elderly Humans and one Satyr died, their hearts bursting.

Tabat trembled and waited for whatever was next to come.

Hovering in the air, Lucy eyed the city like a platter of treats laid out. She saw the great silver hoop that had once been the waterfall in the Duke's plaza. There was magic still, steeped in the metal, magic worth consuming.

She swooped down from the sky like a hawk striking, then stopped with effort, looking at the plaza and the figures that stood there.

SELENE HELPED me find Winter's Armor, and I take it back to Adelina's apartment. There, as I put it on, I can feel a little bit of strength returning. Not the flood of power that came with being the city's champion, but a trace of that, as though it clung to the armor.

Adelina and Sebastiano assist me, not as expertly as a dresser in the arena would have, but I direct them when I need to, tell them to tighten that strap, adjust that buckle. It is like putting on my own skin, this welcome weight, as though it were an outgrowth of my body.

I wish that the trams were still in working order—how am I to get to Lucy? But even as I think that, standing in the doorway of Adelina and Sebastiano's building, there is a tumult on the street. Glyndia driving one of the circus carts, drawn by two zebras that seem annoyed by the whole arrangement.

"Murga," I say.

She sags a little. She—or he, or they, or however this being styles itself—did not expect me to know. They are Glyndia, and Miche, who shared my bed, and Murga, who tried to raise the Beasts against Tabat.

"I can get you to where Lucy is," they say. "Together, perhaps, we can defeat her."

"You've given up on your pawn, the Duke," I say.

Glyndia—for this is the form they maintain, perhaps afraid that if someone on the street sees them turning, they will call out an alarm—shrugs. "We have a common foe," she says. "Is that not enough reason to form an alliance?"

"An alliance requires trust, and I do not trust you."

"If you wish to walk all the way up the stairs in order to confront her, you can," she snaps. "And arrive so out of breath you fall over when she looks at you. Or you can take advantage of my offer, and we can attack together and in the process perhaps both survive where individually we might fall."

It is an offer that makes sense. There is no other way to get up to where Lucy is on the uppermost terrace unless by Dragon wing. I do squint briefly, hopefully, up at the sky, but the Dragons perhaps feel that they have meddled enough in Tabat's existence, because none of them are in evidence.

And so I climb into the cart, avoiding the snap of teeth one zebra makes in my direction, and clamber onto the driver's bench beside Glyndia, who clutches the reins in her clockwork hands.

"Well?" she says to Sebastiano and Adelina. Before I can protest, Sebastiano nods, and helps Adelina up into the cart bed.

"This is dangerous!" I protest.

"Many aspects of life in this city are currently dangerous," Adelina says. She looks less haggard than she has, and I hope it is true. Finding out she was addicted to something—my Adelina, whose worst vice I would have said to be spiced chocolate—that is a hard hard thing for her to realize.

Did she fall into it because of pain over my departure? Was it that I had not been there to support her when she made her first speech?

Sebastiano had told me a little of what had happened—its effects, and how the withdrawal would affect her—when we had a moment together, and the thought that I had somehow caused it eats at me now, gnaws me like a mongrel with a scavenged bone, determined to crack it down to the marrow.

"Drop us off at the College of Mages," Sebastiano says. "The Fairies have told me how to find you an ally there."

Glyndia snaps the reins. "Haw!" she barks, and then we are thundering over the cobblestones with little regard for our fellows in the street. Startled faces shout indignantly as we flash by, and more than one person is forced to dive out of the way.

I have never traveled so fast while not in control of my means of travel, and I clutch at the seat as we rocket along, hitting every rough spot. We come to Greenslope Way and almost slide sidewise as Glyndia navigates the hairpin turn, slowing only a scant measure before picking up speed as we hurtle up towards the next terrace. She barely pauses outside the College of Mages to let Sebastiano and Adelina tumble out.

"Where are we going?" I shout over the clatter of wheels on the cobblestones.

"The Oracular Pig said to take you to the Duke's plaza!" she shouts back. "Everything collides there!"

Despite the terror, I find myself grinning, almost laughing in exhilaration. At last, I am finally going to face an actual foe, not nameless shadows working against me in the dark. At last, I have a chance to avenge myself against everything that has been done to me. To face those who have made me a pawn in their games.

At this thought, I do glance sideways at Glyndia, who played a part in the circumstances that put me into the hands of the Duke's torturers—but she notices nothing in her focus on keeping the cart moving at its utmost speed.

The zebras are lathered with foam, and I shout something about not pushing them too hard and Glyndia shouts back that it is not the time for kindness, a saying that makes me think Jolietta would have gotten along with this person very well, in their ruthlessness and willingness to overlook the needs of others.

But sometimes you have no choice in your allies, and your enemy is what matters. Lucy has proven herself my enemy not just in attacking me, but in attacking my city. The city that has chosen me.

WHEN THE FAIRIES told Sebastiano what to do, he had protested at first. It was cruel; it was grave robbing.

But they had persuaded him. And so he and Adelina hurried together to the glade where Fewk was buried, in order to dig the Griffon up.

There were Fairies with them, sent by the Fairy Queen, who also accompanied them. The Fairies were hard to see in the air; they were shimmers and gleams, and Sebastiano thought that when he had glimpsed one in the past, it had always been by the Fairies' choice.

He remembered the fierce Fairies that Milosh had shown him— had it only been a few months earlier, back when the world seemed normal? He wondered if they had survived, or if when Milosh had died, his creatures had been put down. It didn't seem like a hobby many others would care to continue, but who knew.

Adelina was speaking to him. He shook his head to clear it and looked where she was pointing.

He could see the blue and gold zeppelin falling from the sky; the distant glint that was Lucy was difficult to discern in the hot blue sky's dazzle.

"That had to be the Duke," Sebastiano said. "A stupid, desperate attempt."

"Our attempt is desperate," Adelina whispered to herself.

Sebastiano looked at her. "Yes," he said. "Desperate. But not stupid. It is our best guess, arrived at between Human and Beast ..." He made a slight bow in the Fairy Queen's direction and the hum of her wings buzzed acknowledgment.

"It all depends in the end on Bella, though," Adelina said.

He nodded. "She has been the city's chosen champion before. Can she reforge that bond? That is the only way she will defeat Lucy, with the entirety of the city's magic behind her."

They had brought shovels from one of the gardener's sheds. The campus was empty, except for heap after heap of ash. Sebastiano had refused to stop to examine any of them; he knew very well what they were: Mages consumed in the process of trying to attack Lucy. If any survived they were not here. He thought they might have fled; the campus had a stillness in it that he had never felt before.

"Is this the only part I play?" Adelina asked as they dug, and it was the Fairy Queen that answered her.

"You are one of the things set right," the tiny shimmer in the air buzzed. "You had fallen and now you are climbing back. The city cannot be redeemed unless it acknowledges its faults. Its addictions. They are part of it. You will stand for the city. You know its story better than anyone else."

"Perhaps," Adelina said. "But I only know one version."

"You know many, and you pick and judge and present so people can understand. You know the city. You will write this story."

"It may take me a lifetime to untangle, but I will." Adelina mopped sweat from her forehead with the back of her sleeve, then lapsed into silent effort.

It felt like an eternity at first, the digging—how could they possibly accomplish their mission in time to help Bella?—but then their target began to dig itself out.

He had expected rotting flesh, but instead the body was uncorrupted, only covered with a fine golden fuzz that might have been some sort of lichen or might have been something else altogether. He could smell the freshly dug earth, but there was no scent of rot.

His heart hurt. This was not fair. It was too much to ask of him.

But he spoke the words the Fairies had told him.

One by one seven Fairies sank into the golden fuzz and it brightened with each touch. It had consumed them, Sebastiano thought, then amended it. They had sacrificed themselves so the Griffon could move again.

But not live. He was afraid to look it in the face, afraid to see no recognition there. He put his hands over his face as though to contain his tumultuous emotions.

Then a familiar nudge at his sleeve, and he reached out to pet behind the feathered ears, and felt his heart fill so completely that tears ran down his face.

He fumbled in his pockets but there were no apricots; he had split the last of his dried apricots for breakfast with Adelina.

"Here," Adelina said, and gave him some honey candy.

He fed them to Fewk one by one, petting him as he did so.

The books had told them that such creatures were ancient Mages, Humans transformed by their consumption of magic. He presumed the Sphinx had been a similar creature, and he wondered who she might have been.

"Fewk," he said, drawing back. "Fewk, are you …"

He faltered. The Griffon's eyes were filled with amethyst light, but they were still his eyes.

"Your friend," Fewk said. "I am your friend."

From far above them, they heard laughter.

"We must hurry," the Fairy Queen said.

He knelt so both Adelina and Sebastiano could get on his back, and the remaining Fairies and their Queen swirled into place near the feathery neck. Sebastiano was worried that the weight would be too much, but Fewk seemed untroubled by the load.

"Hold on tight," Sebastiano said, and midway through the sentence, Fewk beat his wings, an urgent swift flap that sent them upward into the air, then another, and another, propelling them upward at a speed that took Sebastiano's breath. He tightened his hold on Adelina and the Griffon, and realized with pride that his wife, unafraid, was craning her neck in order to see as much of the city from this vantage point as she could. Trying to commit it to memory, he thought, and grinned at her when she caught his eye and she grinned back.

They were flying upward to probable death, but it was a glorious trip, no matter what. And he could think of no better person to share that probable death and current glorious flight with.

CHAPTER 30

long time ago, I stepped into a winter garden and challenged the Universe to do with me as it would, said *I am the instrument. Play me, play ME!* And it did, and now I fling that challenge down again, and the Universe leaps to meet me.

Selene stands there waiting for me as I reach the plaza below Lucy. I clamber out of the cart, looking at her and ignoring Murga. Or Glyndia. Or Miche, or whatever it is they want to call themselves. I don't care what their true form is.

Can they see Selene? I neither know nor care.

"I don't know what you are," I say to the white Moon. "Whether you are in my head, or something born of the world beyond it, but either way I love you, and I am yours, and I will live to be worthy of you all my remaining days."

"And if I charge you with the care of my city?" Selene asks. "Tabat, so long ago established in my light?"

"I will always belong to the city," I say firmly, "because the two of you are one, are you not?"

"Clever Bella," Selene laughs. She reaches her hand upward and moonlight reaches down for her hand, pours along her in a sweep of light, rears like a serpent about to strike, and then seizes me.

A door opens in my soul, one I had not known was so firmly barred until now. Like a dam bursting, giving way, magic roars in me.

I know this feeling, but I have never realized it while it was still with me. Only when it was gone did I realize what I had possessed. Now it rushes through me, fills every muscle, every vein, until I might burst from joy and power. I close my eyes and breathe in, letting myself bask in it for a few seconds.

"There is not much time to delay, Bella," Selene's voice says. Is it inside my head or outside? I'm not sure anymore in this dizzying wash of power.

"I know," I say, and open my eyes. I look up to the sky and the distant Lucy. "How will I get to her?"

"Your friends are here, and they have brought you wings."

I turn and there are Adelina and Sebastiano, climbing down from the back of the biggest Griffon I've ever seen. And one which shines, a soft golden light that seems to come from somewhere beneath its feathers.

It looks at me, and I look back. I am not much accustomed to fight while mounted and I do not relish the thought of trying to learn it now.

"No," Murga said. "The two of you will fight together." He shimmers and is Glyndia again, her face proud and arrogant as ever, almost diffident as she walks towards me. She reaches out not with her clockwork hands, but with the golden sweeps of her wings. They enclose us like a cocoon; they smell like honeysuckle. I feel the wings embrace me, and then an unexpected weight on my back.

Glyndia steps back but the wings remain, somehow fastened to me. I flex them and feel their readiness.

Adelina reaches me.

"You are the city's champion," she says to me. She rests her hand on my cheek for a moment, and it is unexpectedly warm, unsurprisingly soft. She steps back and Sebastiano follows, bowing to me. "You are the city's champion," he says, and there is a reverence in his tone that feels ceremonial.

The Fairy Queen buzzes around me. *You are the city's champion*, she says in my mind. *You are acknowledged by Beast and Human, and one caught in between the two.*

Selene's hand on my cheek. "You are my champion."

The Griffon clacks its beak in challenge and nods to me. What better battle companion than the emblem of Tabat, the brave bright creature that is its sigil? I flex my wings and almost lose my balance, but beat them again, and the Griffon echoes me and together we leap into the air and the air takes us up.

Three huge wing flaps, and I am in the air. Another three and I can see the city starting to spread itself out underneath me, long terraces leading down to the sea, stitched together with staircases and tram lines. Another three and we are high enough that Lucy notices us.

The girl looks down as we drive upward towards her, and when she realizes who it is, she smiles.

"Bella Kanto, one more try!" she laughs. "I have destroyed Dragons, Bella. I'll eat you up." She gnashes her teeth as though in demonstration.

I don't waste breath on replying, concentrating on gaining ground and achieving a higher elevation. Lucy's eyes narrow and then she realizes my intent and tries to move upward herself, forestalling me, but she is too slow, too late.

I come down on her like a slice of white moonlight, swinging my blade. Lucy raises a forearm, and the blade rings off it as though it were made of steel.

The blow's impact still forces Lucy back and off balance, an aerial sidestep stagger that the Griffon takes advantage of, striking from below and sideways, driving its beak at her, claws slicing. They skirl off her skin, not drawing blood, but silver sparks fly out from the point of impact, and Lucy screams, although I am not sure whether it is in pain or in anger. Perhaps both.

Then Lucy recovers herself, pulling back. She flings a lightning bolt and the Griffon dodges its sizzle in a near collision that comes so close that an updraft carries the smell of singed feathers to me.

We hang in the air for a split second at the same height, eyeing each other. Then the three of us swoop together again in a tumble too fast for any onlooker to track.

The Griffon fights well until a blow from Lucy hits its shoulder and cripples it. It spirals downward, the intact wing fluttering to break its fall. She yells something incoherent and triumphant at me and dodges my blade this time.

She holds up her hands, her fingers ablaze with crimson fire, and flings it at me, too fast for me to dodge. But it splashes harmlessly off me and I hear Selene's voice in my head. *Get yourself together, Bella. I can only do that once.*

I am the city's champion.

I am the city's champion.

"I am the city's champion," I scream at Lucy, and swing my blade, and the words and the blow hit her at the same moment, catch her in the gut so she folds around the blow, and falls some twenty feet before she catches herself.

Battle instinct has kicked in, drives my every moment, strategies drilled in by decades of combat. *Don't give her time to catch her breath. Hammer her. Hit that first spot of impact, it's a point of weakness now. Push forward, forward, don't let her recoil away and out of striking distance.*

Blood on my blade, but it is not Skye's blood.

Blood on her fists.

And then.

She falls, and from the height she is falling, there is no chance that she is alive after she hits the ground.

I sway in the air as all the blows catch up with me, and I begin to feel them. My wings take over, adjusting, flexing into the shape that carries me in a slow spiral toward the ground, where Adelina and Sebastiano and whoever Glyndia really is all stand around the fallen Griffon.

CHAPTER 31

The city, seen from the point of view of a hypothetical pigeon:

The buildings that once housed the Brides of Steel are now a public school, one where both Human and Beast children go to learn their letters and their numbers. They are not taught anything of fighting; the weapons racks and sparring dummies, the targets and the longbows, all gone. The kitchen garden is intact; it helps the school serve the children lunch during the day, a kindness in these days when everything is still scarce.

Myrila still runs the place, with all her cleverness at stretching coins to cover the needs of students. It is a harder fight now, but Adelina has been writing another book about Bella, and Bella has promised her share of the profits to the school.

The Sea Gardens are gone, flattened, and the gardeners that once tended the lilies there have moved on to other plants, elsewhere.

Down at the docks, ships come and go from across the world: the Southern Isles, the Old Continent, even the Rose Kingdom. The Water Humans who once ruled most of this trade have been forced to give way for their Beast kindred, and Scylla's city grows in power and trade. She sends Bella letters from time to time.

Bella is rebuilding the city with the aid of the Beasts. Envoys have come, some from Verranzo's New City, to offer their help in learning to create a city where none are slaves. It will be hard, but it will be worth it. Sometimes in the evenings she goes to see Philip, and they sit together by the firelight, alone but together, and talk about the world in low, amused voices. Every once in a great while, they hold hands while they are talking.

Scylla has written that she is sailing soon for Tabat, and Adelina is looking forward to comparing notes, despite Bella's assertion that anything she said would probably be a lie to test Adelina's gullibility.

Fewk is buried in the Duke's plaza, with smooth white stones carved with his name and the outline of a Griffon. It is considered lucky to walk across it, and some name the practice "Calling Tabat's luck."

There is a little white stone building dedicated to Bella's former student Skye. A place on a terrace where one may shelter from the rain, or two may find themselves in each other's arms. Bella paid for it, but she never goes there to sit. There are blue irises planted all around it.

Sebastiano has founded his own school, which teaches magic and merchanting together, despite the disapproval of the College of Mages, and Adelina writes the history of this new city.

Sometimes Letha comes to visit Adelina and Sebastiano in their tiny apartment, which is so full with happiness, and one small child, a daughter, named Bella. Unlike her namesake, this Bella is studious and quiet, happiest sitting beside her mother or father, lost in a book. They have not given her any of Adelina's penny-wides to read yet.

Leonoa is painting mural after mural of this new city, showing Beasts and Humans together as they have never been before. They are paintings full of joy, rather than the somber patience of her first paintings. Murga has not been seen since, only Glyndia, whom Bella treats with caution.

Eloquence's sisters, no longer pigs, are scattered across the city. Two found shelter with another family. Others are past the apprentice stage now, and both stay with their fellow juniors. One signed on board a ship, the *Glamoured Gannet*, and is currently bound for the Southern Isles, while another works for Letha and Corrado as head of their maids, a mingling of Humans and free Beasts.

There is still scarcity. Trade is coming back to Tabat, but slower than it might have if everyone approved of Beasts having rights. There are plenty of cities on this continent that still hold to the old ways, and over on the Old Continent, there is no word of similar uprisings.

But one thing there is in abundance: kindness. At first many of the Humans were shamefaced or even downright against the idea that they had a part in oppressing their fellow beings. But some learn, and teach the others, and the Beasts are surprisingly patient.

Teo has returned north with his parents. There he has wriggled down a rocky chimney overgrown with brambles and re-emerged in his rocky crevice, overlooking the river far below. He doesn't feel the need for solitude as keenly as he once did, but it is pleasant to be alone with his thoughts. No one teases or torments him nowadays—even the bully Bjort is cowed by his wider experience and Teo has tried not to make the most of it.

Perhaps he'll travel again someday, go back to Tabat to visit Bella or even up to Verranzo's New City, to see what life is like there. His parents are happy to have him home, but they also know he's at the age for leaving.

Will he leave? He doesn't know. Lidiya the herbalist asked his opinion on an unknown herb today, saying he might have encountered it in Tabat, and indeed he had. That was good, that was very good. And his uncle had said they could go hunting together soon, perhaps tomorrow. So maybe yes, maybe no. A question for another day.

He shifts into cougar form and makes his way home, running for the joy of it.

Far above the world, the Moons roll in the sky as they always have, three of them, dancing, and beneath them beat Dragon wings. There are songs in the sky and some of them are about Bella Kanto.

APPENDIX ONE

TRADE GOD NAMES

(An Incomplete Listing)

Abkerdomma, Trade God of Full Disclosure
Abvioti, Trade God of First Impressions
Angrajekna, Trade God of Beasts
Angrato, Trade God of Cargo
Arilkepgioti, Trade God of Apprenticeship
Arilkepyaotu, Trade God of Mentorship
Arilworyaomi, Trade God of Future Marital Alliances
Chalwoarma, Trade God of Lustful Influence
Chayanyata, Trade God of Medicines
Diahmo, Trade God of the Balanced Ledger
Domkepdepru, Trade God of Books
Domkepko, Trade God of Negotiation
Domkepku, Trade God of Publishing
Domkepthka, Trade God of Persuasion
Dompri, Trade God of Communication
Ehworhaoti, Trade God of Negotiating Marital Alliances
Enbi, Trade God of Need
Erilgioma, Trade God of Influence Through Childhood Friendship

Fayapprima,Trade Godof Prevented Losses
Giobi, Trade God of Friendship
Hazba, Trade God of Mortality
Ihobvioki, Trade God of Public Display
Keppro, Trade God of Work
Kepterto, Trade God of Tailors
Kepverma, Trade God of Tanners
Landmo, Trade God of the Southern Isles
Marbu, Trade God of Chance
Mompru, Trade God of Food
Plarworki, Trade God of Political Connection
Rilriliworhaomu, Trade God of Hypothetical Marital Alliances
Rupru, Trade God of Ritual
Uhcoemo, Trade God of Exiles
Uhfawyanbi, Trade God of Danger, Loss, and Gambles
Uhkephelmi, Trade God of Small Mistakes
Uhkepyaoki, Trade God of Family Misfortune
Uhmarko, Trade God of Unlucky Finds and Unfortunate Meetings
Uhyanyapri, Trade God of Rot
Uhviodommu, Trade God of Bad Reputation and Taint
Viodomki, Trade God of Public Reputation
Vioyaovi, Trade God of Filial Display
Woryaoto, Trade God of Filial Ties
Yalunkwanko, Lady of Nighttime Doings
Zamhruku, Trade God of Entertainments
Zampri, Trade God of Advertising
Zimjekma, Trade God of Magic Knowledge

APPENDIX TWO

STORIES SET IN TABAT

"Broken All My Boughs and Brittle My Heart," *Unlocking the Magic*, 2019

"The Bumblety's Marble," *Paper Cities*, 2008

"The Dead Girl's Wedding March," *Fantasy Magazine*, 2006

"Events at Fort Plenitude," *Weird Tales*, 2008

"Every Breath a Question, Every Heartbeat an Answer" (novelette), *Beneath Ceaseless Skies*, 2020

"The Ghost-Eater," *Thirteen: Stories of Transformation*, 2015

"Hoofsore and Weary," *Shattered Shields*, 2014

"How Dogs Came to the New Continent," Patreon, 2015

"I'll Gnaw Your Bones, the Manticore Said," *Clarkesworld Magazine*, 2007

"In the Lesser Southern Isles," *Black Sails*, 2007

"Love, Resurrected," *Beneath Ceaseless Skies*, 2011

"A Merchant Has Maxims" (novelette), *Unfettered III*, 2019

"Narrative of a Beast's Life" (novelette), *Realms of Fantasy*, 2008

"Primaflora's Journey" (novelette), *Beneath Ceaseless Skies*, 2015

"Sugar," *Fantasy Magazine*, 2007.

APPENDIX THREE

FLASHES OF TABAT

The following series of brief pieces were written to publicize the second book, *Hearts of Tabat*. They primarily appeared as part of my Patreon.

SPINNER PRESS ADVERTISEMENT

Advertisement plastered on Spinner Press's reading wall:

Bella Kanto's most notable adventures, now available in a special omnibus edition of the Tales of Kanto! Color plates include portraits of Kanto in both Winter's Armor and standard arena gear.

Edition includes:

The Conquest of the Heliotrope Sorceress: When danger threatens the port of Cayne, Bella investigates to find sorcery at the heart of it all! She must battle a foe more adept with magic than blade, a mysterious figure clad in purple. Thrill to Tabat's most seductive hero as you've never seen her!

Bella and the Pirates: Shipwrecked and bereft of her memory, Bella rises to power as the Black Belle, Pirate Queen. Will her memories return before she attacks Tabat itself? Includes a list of Tabat's most notable pirate hunters!

Bella in the Land of Fungus: Trapped by a landslide in the caverns of Qat, Bella has no choice but to travel deep into the earth, where she encounters the strange race of Beasts living there. Shiver as you explore new lands with Tabat's most intrepid Gladiator!

Bella Arrives at the Brides of Steel: At fifteen, Bella Kanto is a year too old to enroll in the school her heart has brought her to. How will she persuade the leaders of the school to break tradition and admit her? Read the very beginnings of Tabat's greatest hero!

Bella and the Thornwalkers: To remain Champion, Bella fights some of the most exotic Beasts ever brought to the city, including a treacherous Shifter, a Dragon, and a crop of rare Thornwalkers brought back by a southwestern expedition. Includes basic fighting tips from Tabat's foremost Gladiator!

A BRIEF TREATISE ON MAGICAL ENERGY AND

THE PRACTICE OF EATING BEASTS,

Being A Primer for Elementary Students
of the College of Mages
by Sebastiano Silvercloth
(private publication of the College of Mages)

To understand the basic principle behind this practice, one need look no further than the custom of keeping Oracular Pigs, common among larger Merchant households. Since such Beasts are capable of seeing only matters in their own physical future, they must be kept in places where their warnings of fire, attack, or other household disasters will involve the household, such as outside but near the kitchen, or beside outlying buildings of importance.

When the time comes that the Pig foretells its own death (or shows signs of concealing such a prophecy), it is slaughtered and prepared for a feast in which the entire household takes part. The Pig is consumed in the belief that its oracular powers may be acquired; some gamblers swear by a diet of such flesh.

Absorption of magic energy through ingestion of the flesh that held it is at the heart of many magical rituals. In truth, the roast pork and other meats are of little use to the consumers in the manner they desire. Luck is not a transferable quality. But it does advantage them in other ways: such consumption is known to increase lifespan dramatically, to prevent some illnesses, and cure others. The longevity of many of those able to afford the practice is augmented, while those with flatter purses lead lesser lives.

Some Beasts and animals are much richer in magical energy than others, depending on their race's characteristics. Almost every by-product and physical bit of a Dragon, for example, is highly valuable in that regard. The wings, which are typically removed from captive Dragons, are dried, while the meat is powdered and used as an ingredient in the alchemical cooking for which the Chefs of Tabat are famed. The leather is employed in the construction of aerial apparati and some armors, though the cost of such is prohibitive enough to keep them from the ordinary soldier's wardrobe.

Dryads are similarly prized, for once they have taken on their ultimate form of a rooted tree, the wood of their bodies becomes steeped in magic over the course of season after season, and yields great quantities of energy when treated and burned in special furnaces. Such fuel supplies much of the energy that drives the city and gives its citizens the rich life we enjoy, and the trade boats are always on the lookout for Dryad groves, in order to collect the substantial bounty the city pays for their trunks.

For the most part, though, the effect created by partaking of a Beast or magical animal's body is slight. Both Fairy blood and honey are faintly hallucinogenic in nature, but one would have to ingest vast quantities, such as the blood of two or three dozen Fairies (depending on the ingestor's body weight and susceptibility to the drug) to experience anything appreciable. Still, the creation of dishes incorporating such substances has become an art for which Tabat is famed throughout the world. This reminds us that such knowledge may well be turned to practical purpose without suffering scorn. While pure Magicians pursue abstract knowledge, others help keep the College and city functioning through their willingness to put aside such lofty pursuits.

DUCAL CORRESPONDENCE

Addressed to Alberic, 10th Duke of Tabat, Commander of its Navies and Armies, and Peace Keeper in the fourth month of winter of Year 299 of Tabat's Rule

We trust that this letter finds His Grace well. Because we are so keenly aware of the interest the Duke finds in our works, we have set aside a costly resource in the form of a skilled scribe, in order to furnish the daily reports His Grace requires, although the number of them may be better reduced to fit within our budget.

"Translation: give us more money and fewer demands," Alberic, 10th Duke of Tabat snorted.

Our foremost researcher, Master Mage Faustino, has prepared quarters for the Manticore we spoke of. In this endeavor, he is assisted by the College's own Sphinx, who has taken the Manticore under her figurative wing, and who evidences great interest in each and every proceeding having to do with her newly found friend.

"Gibbledy gibbledy gibbledy. They can never get straight to the point."

Theories regarding the wellspring of the Manticore's unwonted aptitude differ. Some credit the raising by the Beast Trainer (who is unfortunately no longer available, having perished in a recent training accident) and say that he perhaps bathed the egg in the light of certain salubrious stars, or introduced fluids designed to increase its intelligence while it was still an embryo, via the mechanism of a slender needle inserted through into the shell, such as Master Mage Faustino has recently attempted, perhaps with better results sealing the gap than he has experienced.

Still others credit the breeding, saying this is no true Manticore, but rather one adulterated with the blood of a more intelligent creature, or a sport, such as Nature gifts us with from time to time. They propose various ways to investigate its parentage, whether through costly time mirrors or expensive rituals allowing the ghosts of its forebears to be questioned. Of course, we are extremely lucky here at the College of Mages to be the only establishment capable.

"Would it were not so! If they had rivals, I'd patronize them at ten times the cost just to be rid of these sniveling, timorous, mealy-mouthed and never certain, doddering old fools!"

Mage Rehallow (*"That conservative old fart!"*) continues to worry that its combination of mental faculties, magical potential, and brute force represent the vanguard of a new race of intelligent magical creatures that will undertake the overthrow of Humanity. (*"The man's been rowing that leaky rowboat of an idea since before I was born! At one point, he thought earth elementals were undermining the city and funding a revolution with plundered gems!"*)

As always, (*"There they go again!"*) we have checked the signs and portents, using what we have learned of reading the future (*"Reading my peach-colored rear!"*) in order to reassure His Grace of the future happiness of his realm. (*"Oh, this should be good."*) However, portents are cloudy and ominous at this time—events are in such turmoil that nothing can be predicted with accuracy. (*"For once they're right."*)

We urge His Grace to pay attention to ensuring that he and his surroundings are magically cleansed each hour (*"More incense and muttering."*), that he adheres to the purifying diet prescribed by Magus Rehallow, (*"Old fool!"*) in order to avoid repetition of last week's distressing events, and that each night where he lies down to take his repose, he focuses on the patterns, or mandalas, we have furnished or else take three drops of our prescribed elixir in a small glass of tepid—not hot!—milk.

On a final, lighter note, your Grace may recall the Fairy Champion Quickblade, who defended the Duke's Honor in the last Spring Wars. He requests a boon of you, that you endow the College with a fund to ensure the hive is always supplied with sugar.

Master Mage Faustino, Diligent Scholar of the Fence of Illumination

"Feces of Illumination, them and their mysterious names! What's the next letter then? Indeed? That one next, then."

To Master Mage Faustino, Diligent Scholar of the Fence of Illumination

His Grace bids me tell you that under no accounts must any experiments be undertaken that in any way jeopardize the Manticore—if this slows down the investigatory efforts, then so be it.

As to the matter of the bill for the feed for the creature, it is His Grace's understanding that the circus known as the Moon's Accomplice should be paying for that creature—it is an expense that they were already due to incur, and they are being paid well for the loss of their creature's time, as well as being housed in prime territory within the Inner Walls of Tabat and allowed to take in monies from the crowds there. Accordingly the Duke wishes to decline responsibility for this bill, but remains ready to pay the bills for the circus already agreed upon.

It is his understanding that the profits from the ship Saffron Bloom are to be split and that the ship is due to harbor soon. Is there any word of its arrival?

As to the Fairy, have it drowned in honey and sent to the Ducal Table for enjoyment. His Grace has had enough of insolent Beasts.

Scribe Hasten, for Alberic, 10th Duke of Tabat, Commander of its Navies and Armies, and Peace Keeper for the General Good

An Instructive Listing of the Pests of Tabat, being Pamphlet #2 of the fifth series of "A Visitor's Guide to Tabat," Spinner Press, author unknown.

The newcomer to Tabat will find the pests they are accustomed to: fleas, lice, and rats are no strangers to the city. But several creatures indigenous to the area may cause the unwary traveler distress.

In late-summer nights, the gold and orange wings of phoenix moths will be visible in their mating swarms. Despite the beauty of the phenomenon, the creatures are destroyed whenever possible, for the flames created when they deposit their eggs and immolate themselves in order to harden the casings can lead to larger fires.

Marsh flies are prevalent on the city's eastern side when the wind is from that quarter. The fierce bites of these insects have been known to drive even the most placid creature to the brink of madness. Citronella and other scented candles and lamp oils are the most popular remedy for these creatures, along with bed netting in the summer months.

Parasitic Fairies have, for the most part, been eradicated, but clusters of the minute Fairies known as slavemakers still exist in the farmlands. While they rarely if ever make their way into the city, those traveling in the areas directly around Tabat should be aware of the danger they pose.

Mandrakes are neither animal nor Beast, but rather a plantlike intelligence found only on this continent and capable of ambulation in their early stages. Mandrakes kill larger mammals, using the corpse as a plant in which to root themselves and propagate and are, like parasitic Fairies, only a danger to those venturing outside the main city.

Due to Tabat's damp weather, a myriad of molds thrive in untended corners. Scarlet mold, toxic to animal and Human, may appear and is invariably accompanied by black mold worms, whose bite produces severe hallucinations.

A HANDBILL POSTED OUTSIDE FIGGIS' BAKERY

Now available at Tastesweet's Emporium: Seventeen Varieties of Fairy Honey, including the following:

Tastesweet's Midwinter Amber: Comes with the traditional drowned Fairy preserved in the jar and a scattering of midwinter spices. Five gold galleons per household jar.

Tastesweet's Invigorating Infusion: Spiced with spectral peppers from the Southern Isles, Frenzy Fairy honey of a most delicious flavor will rekindle affections of the flesh and revivify even the most winter-jaded appetite. One golden galleon per gill.

Tastesweet's Calming Mixture: Equal parts of high-grade Fairy honey and Dryad sap are infused with soothing herbs; this mixture is identical to the one employed by Physicians for invalids and the habitually nervous. Three silver galleons per gill.

Tastesweet's Occult Lozenges: Fairy honey mingles with two parts blood of Oracular Pigs (guaranteed not culls) to create a blend famous for enhancing lucky instincts and premonitions. As used at the Fuchsia and Heron, where it is a favorite of poets, musicians, and actors. One golden galleon per household jar.

Tastesweet's Traditional Syrup: Suitable for the frugal household, this sweetener consists of one part Smallholder Grade Fairy honey to fourteen parts cane syrup and is used by commercial establishments throughout Tabat. Three silver skiffs per household jar.

Included with each purchase free and gratis as a token of gratitude for your patronage! Two noughts, each valid in trade for a Tastesweet's Secret Recipe Honey Candy!

An Instructive Listing of the Notable Markets of Tabat, being Pamphlet #4 of the first series of "A Visitor's Guide to Tabat," Spinner Press, author unknown.

The Rain Market: To the north and east of Tabat lie the great marshes, half salt water, half fresh water. While the struggle to drain them and transform them into cropland presses on each year, the vast marshlands, a mix of salt and fresh water, seem unthreatened. The grasses that grow here are colored, like most of the marsh's vegetation, by the purplish and green clays and minerals that underlie the marsh. Their pliant grasses, colored from lavender to dark purple and shades of olive, grow in abundance and are harvested for the purpose of making the tight-woven rain-gear that fills the Tabatian square known as the Rain Market.

Open come rain or sunshine, the Market sells, beyond its hats and shell-shaped overcoats of woven grass, baskets and other containers in whatever size or shape you might need. Bring the object there and they will weave a basket to hold it, from spiky pine-fruit to a glove-shaped case from a wooden prosthetic hand of the sort the 5th Duke wore. Clatter chimes, lengths of hollow reed strung on cording and meant to be hung from windowsills or bank tills to scare away sea-ghosts, are sold here exclusively in this Market in the shadow of the Slumpers.

Also near the Slumpers are the shops that sell its wares: tiles and china and porcelain goods. At the very edge of Rose Way is the complex of shops devoted to brownie wares: miniature dishes many use to coax brownies into their houses as well as other wares designed for smaller Beasts and animals.

Spice and Fish Square, only a block away from the main dock, supplies goods just unloaded from fishing and Merchant ships. The freshest sea fare can be found here and many vendors are prepared to cook your dinner on the spot. The air smells of brine and rot and smoke, and the nearby alleys are scattered with fragments of scales like silver spangles underfoot.

The Stable Markets are housed in what were once the city stables, since relocated to the northern edge of Tabat. Sitting on the Fourth Terrace, the building is filled with swarms of tiny shops selling this, that, and the other thing. Some stalls have existed here for generations while others are new traders, come with merchandise they want to dispose of quickly, if sometimes not cheaply.

The Midnight Market, located on the lowest terrace within sound of the sea, operates only from dusk to dawn, in the spaces that will be occupied by traders, Merchants, and sailors during the day's daylight hours. Anything and everything can be purchased here, and many of the vendors, as in the Stable Markets, are Beasts acting as representatives for Human masters.

"An Educational and Instructive Listing of Notable Statues of Salt Way," being Pamphlet #17 of the third series of *A Visitor's Guide to Tabat*, Spinner Press, author unknown.

Lining the incline of Salt Way as it runs uphill towards the College of Mages at its terminus are ninety-nine white marble statues, each depicting a major citizen during the reign of the 3rd Duke. At the time of their creation, sculptors vied to be among the thirty-three artists chosen to handle three statues each, and one former worker in oils, Brynit Firaubo, converted his medium to stone specifically for the event.

Visitors lacking time for a leisurely perusal of each statue (supplied in Adelina Nettlepurse's complete guide to the statues, *A Complete Guide to the Statues of Salt Way*, also available from Spinner Press) can, by using this list, obtain a representative sampling of the tour sufficient for conversational purposes.

Beginning at the foot of Spray, at the very entrance to the street, are the Duke's husband and daughter. The statue of Eryk Kanto holds sword and lantern, signifying his status as an Explorer, while his daughter Alba holds a crown in her hands, foretelling her coming reign.

Three blocks up is Figgis Doughmaster, the fattest man of his time in Tabat and a renowned chef who served the Duke before opening a chal shop, the Fuchsia and Heron, and a series of bakery carts that now service the entire city. His bulk makes the statue a favorite for the birds that cluster here, including flocks of parrots and Fairies escaped from the gardens on the College of Mages' grounds.

Notable singer Vyra Serena, another two blocks up, has become a patron saint for those who seek success on the stage or in love. Floral garlands can often be found hung around her neck, and superstition promises the lover who makes such an offering only the best of luck.

Merchant Fisia Nettlepurse watches over the road a half block up. She founded many of the businesses around the docks, such as the chal shop the Salty Purse, and civic improvements such as the Sea Gardens. Touching her toe is regarded as good luck for those down on theirs, and her appendage has been worn away over the years until she is clubfooted, but it is also considered a surefire method of revealing those with evil intentions.

The statue of Jack Buttertouch, also known as Sparkfinger Jack, is considered ill luck to visit. Visitors will know the statue quickly; its features were defaced and removed six months after its installation after his horrific crimes were discovered.

At the very top of Spray Road, the 3rd Duke and the head of the College of Mages, Ellora Two Sails, face each other. She was responsible for some of the basic magics that shaped Tabat: smoothing of the harbor and the creation of the Sea Gardens, and the implementation of the sewer and underground farm system that yields what is euphemistically called "Ellora's fruit."

"An Instructive Listing of the Fashions of Tabat," being Pamphlet #2 of the first series of "A Visitor's Guide to Tabat," Spinner Press, author unknown.

Tabat, like any city, has fashions that distinguish it, often shaped by the city's history and resources. To look like one of the natives, you may want to purchase one or more of the following to wear.

Feather cockades, worn pinned to the breast or on a hat, represent a long tradition in the city. The explorers of the early expedition Perseverance found a river of feathers, cast off by vast flocks of waterfowl. They brought back sackfuls of the varicolored feathers to the city and it became customary to show one's support for one expedition or another by wearing the cockades. In recent times they have become associated with different political powers in the city and with the coming of the elections, they are widely used to indicate one's party affiliation.

Rain market hats, wide-brimmed and tightly woven of purple reeds, are seen in abundance on the streets of Tabat and are as functional and cheap as they are picturesque. Some sellers sell hats with designs or slogans painted upon them, often distributing the latter at political rallies.

Great-coats, woven of wool or made of dyed fur, are traditional gear for Merchants, Explorers, and others who travel widely. Their styles may vary from year to year in matters like buttons, pocket cut, or thickness of piping, but generally they remain the same in overall look.

Dandies of either sex prize the fine lace gloves produced by the Altos factory, where they are woven by the large spiders exclusive to Altos use by order of the Duke. If on the street outside where they are housed in early morning or evening, linger to hear their haunting song.

An Instructive Listing of the Street Foods of Tabat, being Pamphlet #5 of the first series of "A Visitor's Guide to Tabat," Spinner Press, author unknown.

The visitor to Tabat will find themselves faced with a multitude of new things, and the food of the city is no exception. Carts and food stalls in particular supply many of the daily food needs of the populace.

No matter where you go in the city, you will find the bakery carts. Most belong to the Figgis Bakery, but you will also see some from smaller and independent bakeries. They sell a multitude of breadstuffs, including several pastries unique to the city: two and twos, large flatbreads which are half one color, half another; hyacinth cookies with their distinctive purple icing; and jelly cups.

Close to the docks, particularly around the Fish Market, vendors sell all varieties of sea food, cooked on the spot and fresh from the boats that have just brought it in. Many of these use the seaweed spices Tabat is famous for: ironbite with its metallic peppery taste; summer salt; and the mix of dried fish and seaweed that forms the basis of chal. Look for kerik, the sweet purple nodules of seaweed that are harvested in late summer, for a particularly exotic treat.

Sweets are usually flavored with honey from bees or Honey-mothers, or a touch of Fairy honey for those with more expensive tastes. Of late, though, the Southern Isles have been sending sugar to Tabat, expensive and rare, and a dusting of such atop a pastry or cake is considered to render it the height of culinary sophistication.

An Instructive Listing of the Major Gardens of Tabat, being Pamphlet #4 of the second series of "A Visitor's Guide to Tabat," Spinner Press, author unknown.

Despite the city's fierce weather, the cliffs that shelter it on the northwest and western side create pockets of weather that allow its gardeners to coax fruit and flower that normally would not be found here. Additionally, the presence of the College of Mages ensures a perennial crop of young Mages ready to earn their coin by turning them to a patron's use, creating marvels like a moonlight garden whose flowers change aspect according to the positions of the three Moons in the sky, as is rumored to be located in the center of the Moon Temples' complex, unknown to any but their priests.

Accordingly those interested in the botanic, the scenic, or the complete experience of Tabat should allot time in their schedule for the following.

The Duke's Gardens: Appended to the Ducal castle, the grounds are open to the public on even-numbered days and feast days but are always closed during the Games. Often select Beasts and animals from the Ducal menagerie are brought out for display. Cost is a silver ship per adult visitor, with children at five per ship. Hours are dawn till the seventh evening bell.

Tabat's Heart: These vast gardens stretch through the middle of Tabat, cutting across all but the top and bottom terraces. Tram lines and staircases line the western edge, allowing access to the paths across as well as the many sub-gardens and fountains. Admission is free and the parks are always open, but are patrolled by mechanicals after midnight until the first morning bell.

The Sea Garden: Built into the western cliffs at the water's edge is the Sea Garden, full of corals and in the summer tanks of sea creatures and Beasts, including singing Whales and Dolphins, and a display of venomous sea serpents. Admission is free in the winter and a copper ship throughout the rest of the year, with a discount for schools and educational groups. Hours are from the last night bell through the first evening bell. Open all days except Games.

The Gardens at the College of Mages: Filled with plants, animals, and Beasts collected from across the world, these gardens are renowned in scholarly and academic circles. Points of interest include the Fairy hive in their central hall, which also acts as a museum, the caged Mandrakes, their Sphinx amid its xeric landscape, and the Hypnotic Garden, which features narcotic and soporific plants and animals and which can only be entered with a guide, who wears a white silk mask and is prepared to wake the visitor if he or she succumbs. Admission is a silver Merchant for two, and includes chai in the Dancing Cup across the way from the College's grounds.

Famous for their aromatic and ornamental plantings, the grounds of the Nettlepurse estate are open every Fifteenth Day. Cost is a Nettlepurse nought. Hours are the third morning bell through the midnight bell. Go in the spring in the evening to see the humming moths that are an all too brief yearly phenomenon, or visit the Cypress Maze in order to view the reflecting pool in its center.

If you have additional time, we recommend the flowering tree groves of the Piskie Wood (to be visited only in the daylight hours, and wear bright clothing to avoid the Piskie hunters who practice their livelihood there.)

An Instructive Listing of the Flowers of Tabat, being Pamphlet #3 of the fifth series of "A Visitor's Guide to Tabat," Spinner Press, author unknown.

Winter roses were originally created by Ellora Two Sails as an ornament for the winter months. Their magical nature makes them expensive, but capable of blooming during the coldest weather.

The iris, particularly the blue and gold variety that grows so thickly along the canals, is Tabat's signatory flower, its colors matching those of Tabat's flag.

Tulips, brought with the original settlers of Tabat from their homeland, have been developed into a wide variety of colors and shapes. Forced tulips in little pots are a traditional good-luck gift exchanged during the first few weeks of spring.

Marsh blooms include the rare Siren flower, believed to be a variant of Mandrakes, which are prized despite the dangers of their collection.

Beloved first sign of spring, primaflora are tiny blue flowers which grow low to the ground and invariably bloom on the first day of Spring.

An Instructive Listing of the Major Artists of Tabat, being Pamphlet #5 of the series of "A Visitor's Guide to Notables of Tabat," Spinner Press, author unknown.

Tabat's art tradition is well established, and not a mere copy of the practices and schools of the Old Continent, as has been charged against the artists of Verranzo's New City. Tabat's artists build upon the traditions of the past while innovating and creating anew in a way that reflects the diversity and history of the city. When making conversation about the city's art, it is useful to know the names of its leading figures.

The cousin of famous Gladiator Bella Kanto, Leonoa Kanto is a figure in her own right, known for an eye that catches remarkable depth of detail and a willingness to speak about her work and how it relates to the day's influences unmatched by other artists.

Descendant of a long line of sculptors and artists, Coe Firaubo has produced statues that adorn the Ducal gardens and the College of Mages grounds, where his most famous work, "Truth defeats the Serpents of Falsehood," is situated.

An artist who has only recently risen to prominence, Etaya Wain uses nothing but natural elements in his artwork, employing homemade dyes and natural substances, many of them specifically taken from the north and celebrating its influence on Tabat.

Tailuaba Cloudseeker chooses to draw on supernatural influences (and magical animals) in the creation of her work, and both her subjects and her methods reflect her former training as a Mage.

All of Tabat has lately been buzzing about unknown artist Flora, whose work is made of dried flowers, stuffed Fairies, and other creative taxidermy. The work is sold through Bernarda Manycloaks' gallery, which has refused to disclose anything more about the artist and his or her work.

A GLIMPSE FROM THE COLLEGE OF MAGES

In the lull between bells, the campus walks were deserted and their scent trails stale, the pupils all in their classes this late morning. They worked them hard at the College of Mages, and no student would have a break until after a lunch of bread and fishy oil and the moments they could snatch for chatting, flirtation, naps, or mischief, before they were forced to plod on to other debates in other classrooms.

The sunlight was weak in this place, a thin draft of heat unlike the fierce burn of home, particularly in late winter. The Sphinx lay on a stone slab outside the Hall of Instruction, wishing for the comfortable give of sand and listening to the voices from inside: an instructor teaching her first year pupils about the Lists.

The Sphinx combed her hair with a paw. Black strands, dull from infrequent brushing, had fallen in front of her face—discolored claws slid through them, dirt-darkened to a matching color. A fly crawled across her tawny flank, and her limber tail swatted it away as she listened.

"How do we know," a student asked, "what is Beast and what is Human?"

The instructor's voice was mild, although she had answered this question before at the lecture's beginning. "The races that are Human and the races that are Beasts are set forth in the Lists."

"What if the listmakers were wrong?" a student asked. There was brief, shocked silence at the words before the instructor said "We do not believe that they were wrong."

The words' quiet conviction made her hackles rise, the fine fur at the nape of her neck, where it shaded between hair and mane, bristle. Irked and restless, she rose, abandoning her puddle of sunlight to move along the gravel paths of the College, in and out of the pine and cedar shadows.

An itch between the pads of her paws, furry grooves full of sensitive hairs, told her that somewhere in the crypts below the College, Carolus was teaching a class on summoning ghosts. There was electricity and regret in the air, and spiritual energy stirred on the breeze, pulled here and there by forces of attraction and repulsion.

A wiggle of ectoplasm circled her ear, an incipient ghost trying to figure out whether or not it wanted to be born. Another flick of her tufted tail, as big as a fat feast carp, dispelled it back into shredded wisps, and it did not re-form as she passed out of range.

She patrolled along the high iron fence that kept the townsfolk out and the students in, intricate ironwork that held containment sigils, woven together so thick and strong that passing through the gates felt like sliding through velvet and steel curtains, heavy weights catching at her. She resisted their impediment to pause outside, surveying the street.

Only one passerby paid her much attention—some Northerner newly come to town, country dust still thick on him and his eyes wide with wonder at the city's nature as it unfolded strange thing after strange thing. Including her, who he eyed with trepidation as he moved along the street. He was a mouse, a boy who would snap beneath one pounce.

She watched him with her wide golden eyes, knowing their unnerving nature. Outside the city, Beasts were more dangerous—her uncanny fellows stalked the Humans through the wilderness, and claimed hundreds each year—but she had become civilized in her role as the doyenne of the College of Mages. She was legendary to the students—generations had tried to evade her detection when sneaking in or out of the grounds. Though she was forbidden to harm them, they acted as though she would. As though she was still dangerous.

Perhaps she was.

AN AUCTION HANDBILL

A flyer, kept carefully folded, in the top drawer of Bella Kanto's dresser. Dated some twenty-five years earlier, the paper crumbling and worn, and never looked at since being placed there.

VALUABLE GROUP OF ASSORTED BEASTS AND ANIMALS
Trained by Renowned Beast Trainer Jolietta Kanto, Her Estate
Will Be Sold At Auction
On the 12th Day of Autumn, at the Black Dome
At 2nd Afternoon Bell

Two serviceable male Minotaurs, of approximately twenty-five years, trained in simple guard duties and of proven loyalty and good breeding.

One stout Satyr, capable of gardening and light field work.

One hearty Centaur female, trained in cookery and housekeeping.

One Oracular Pig, of unremarkable accuracy.

Two hands of small hunting Dragons of good bloodline and health, with two females currently in brood.

Brace of Riddling Deer, elderly.

One Dog-Man, incapable of breeding but trained for fugitive-hunting.

Sold For No Fault; With The Best City Guarantee
Sale Positive And Without Reserve
Terms: CASH

HOW DOGS CAME TO THE NEW CONTINENT

This is, of course, but the briefest preface to a longer, more detailed study. To my best knowledge, I am the first Scholar in either Tabat or Verranzo's New City to set down the history of dogs on this continent (aside from the sundry jottings of Beastkeepers). I have written hastily, despite its lack of decorum, in order to pay tribute to my cousin, closer than any brother, recently deceased. In these pages, I will answer the charges made against him as well as myself and my father.

The following 1512 pages contain detailed lineages for the city's significant dog lines, along with accounts of their exploits and advances. While I have neglected many of today's lesser breeds, Appendix G lists the current species available, ranked in order of popularity, from teapot poodles to the dangerous miniature basilisk/greyhound mix. It is indicative of the softness of our society that the lapdog known as Mops tops the list.

At any rate, this work is indeed a scholarly effort, but also one that details the lineage of the heart dearest to me in all this world.

When the man the history books know only as Verranzo's Shadow Twin established the city of Tabat, he opted for differing territory than his brother Verranzo, whose New City lay on the Eastern Seaboard, in advantageous but sometimes dangerous proximity to the Old Continent.

Taking separate ships, both brothers had fled that dangerous land, driven away by Sorcerers. They hoped to establish cities on new shores. Verranzo picked an island to the north, along the eastern coast. Fertile land, inhabited by Centaurs, easily driven west into the mountains.

His twin chose a far more southerly site. Local tribes feared the place, and claimed an earlier Sorcerer had visited there and thrown an existing city into the depths. If true, this would have been the only known visit of a Sorcerer to the New Continent before its settlement, but no signs remain to corroborate the story. The cliffs sheltered a sizable inlet, while quarries and forests close at hand offered ample building material. Within a year, early settlers cleared the northern forests of infestations of Fairy hives as well as ill-natured little scrub Dragons and the spotted panthers that hunted them.

As the city grew, the Shadow Twin guided another member of his party, the Duke of Whisp, knowing himself childless, and Whisp proven fertile seven times. In time, he passed all power to the Duke. The Duke had come from his lands with wife and mistress and all his household, including a pack of greathounds.

These greathounds had always been a part of the Ducal household. Their breed was reserved for royalty: shaggy hounds standing shoulder high, brindle brown and capable of taking down a lion. Such a greathound guarded each Ducal heir's crib. The dogs watched over the babies as carefully as any nursemaid. The children grew shoulder to shoulder with the hounds. If rumor held true, they ate from the same plate.

Several of these hounds accompanied the Duke, therefore, as he went about on daily rounds of the city.

Much work presented itself in those early days. Tabat grew quickly as refugees from the Old Continent landed and set to building the city to come. The Duke planned the city with an eye that looked to the far future. This was laughed at when crews found themselves building sewage systems, canals, and avenues through the wilderness, but in the century to come, the Duke's layout would prove his remarkable foresight.

Over five years, the eastern swamp was drained, creating rich farmland. Deposits of fine-grained alluvial clay were discovered among the stumps, and the first factory began to produce brick and roofing tile in the region later become known as the Slumpers. Neighborhoods sprang up and found themselves efficiently and neatly arranged. Along the cliffs, terraces were smoothed, and staircases and winding roads laid out in careful order.

Between the cliffs and the forest, Merchants funded the brick houses of trade town, posts and warehouses that handled river traffic as well as overflow from the sea docks.

The Duke's vision focused on the promise of trade made by the two great rivers that met the sea near the city. The continent-cleaving Northstretch river emptied out in a waterfall spilling down a ridge and over the Lazylake to the sea, while the looping Lazylake River, upshore so broad that a boat in the middle often could glimpse neither bank, here narrowed, plunged beneath the ridge, and then anticlimactically ebbed its way into the marshlands. A few traders made their way up and down it, but the founders of Tabat knew that their furs, medicinal herbs, and gems only hinted at trade to come.

With this in mind, the Duke set up expeditions while his counterpart oversaw the construction. The first five years, the Duke, his dogs, and his troops roved the territories by horseback and in small boats around the burgeoning city, mapping and documenting. Those first maps, with meticulous notations and annotations of land grants, hang in Tabat's Hall of Law.

A year later, two exploratory parties set out, each numbering a dozen and named for a quality of soul, *Mercy* and *Tenacity*. A pair of Ducal greathounds accompanied each. This action diminished the pack to ten, a risk, yet the Duke wished to signify his investment in the exploration's fruits.

Mercy's greathounds were Cavall and Laurens, both young males. They accompanied the leader, a Scholar-Warrior named Mikka Fenmerry, and a handful of soldiers. The youthful group enjoyed their trip along the river's western edge, drinking wine and living off fish and game they caught and gathered fruit, more and more bountiful as summer wore on and autumn approached.

Fenmerry's journal details wonders: hot springs and the sulfur-colored snakes living in their waters; a talking face carved into a hill side; vast quantities of game; plants rumored to cure snakebite and miscarriage and greed (none of these survived their trip back to Tabat, alas); an ancient road of gray stone, warm and greasy feeling to the touch; ghosts that rode horses; flower-bearing clouds and an island which floated in the sky.

Fenmerry estimated the island might have been as much as a mile above them. They shouted up, but it appeared unoccupied, although both dogs barked as though scenting prey or predators. Vegetation was visible on its sides, but they were unable to obtain samples. They walked through its shadow for three hours. Future expeditions never sighted the island again.

The final incident is unjournaled, and known only from a survivor's account.

Scout Pippin Epselm, making his way back to the city four months later with companion and sister Weiga Epselm, stated that he and the others came to a marsh, where crocodile-headed beings lived in grass huts. These huts were built atop great wooden legs, which walked about at the direction of the village's shaman.

The huts proved the expedition's undoing, for at the comical sight of two huts walking to a new location, they erupted into laughter. The unfamiliar sound enraged or frightened the natives, so that they fell upon the expedition and killed all but two. The dogs stayed behind them, fighting, their fate unknown until decades later.

Epselm's story of the attack the group had brought upon themselves was used to caution future expeditions, urging them moderation in all emotion, no matter the circumstance. The calm placidity with which leaders to come were wont to meet death was a point of pride in the history lessons, and inspired generations.

The second expedition's dogs were Pomene and Maue. *Tenacity* was led by a soldier named Ann Natterly (who may or may not have been the same as a pirate of that time, Tattered Nan). She and her crew ventured as far as the central plains, where they traded for furs and spices, as well as many plant specimens, which were transported back to the city along with Natterly's maps and journals, and seeded the current Ducal gardens.

Natterly herself remained behind in the settlement that would eventually become Cloudmarch and raised a family that became leaders in that city's government and banking. Again, the dogs did not return to Tabat, although three of Pomene's pups were shipped back to the Duke the following spring.

The second flight of expeditions was mounted by more Merchantly minds. Outfitting took at least a year—in the second's case, a year and a half. The first, *Valor*, was jointly funded by the Duke, Verranzo's Shadow Twin, and a Merchant consortium; the second, *Perseverance*, by Merchant family Silvercoin.

Khanda Kanto led *Valor*. Able second Nella Call organized the outfitting and saw the expedition equipped with a variety of supplies, including: trade goods (blue, white, and green glass beads, fireworks, cloth, and liquor); powdered soup in oilcloth packets, dried apples, figs, pears, and raisins, four pounds of baking powder; tea, coffee, pepper, bags of corn and flour; sacks of dog biscuit; twelve glass-bubbled messenger demons; waterproof brass compasses; notebooks, inks, and pens, along with watercolors for what Kanto called her "miserable talents in this regard"; waterproofed playing cards, and a case that doubled as backgammon or chess/checker board; fishing tackle, including line ranging from one pound to 100 pound, with fishhooks sized accordingly.

The poet Tullus accompanied them. Kanto's journals deemed him "a poor shot, prone to whining while pretending not to do so," although she warmed to him by the trip's end, and more so when his *Khanda's Ballad* was published.

A Mage, Aloy Taskter, also accompanied the *Valor*. While Verranzo's New City outlawed any form of magic use, Tabat was more lenient. Both the Shadow Twin and the Duke spoke out about the difference between clean magic and evil sorcery, which twisted the mind until it was incapable of knowing right from wrong.

The remainder of the expedition were soldiers and two scouts, all in all numbering fourteen Humans. Only *Valor* was accompanied by Ducal greathounds, a mated pair, Artos and Gwenhyfar. They traveled westward along the coast, hoping to eventually reach its end.

The second expedition, *Perseverance*, was led by Aldo Silvercoin, seconded by Josef Honey. While it had no Mage, it did take a matched pair of Minotaurs, whose brawn was eminently useful in pulling boats along the river, and who also proved invaluable in impressing the tribes of the interior.

Back in Tabat, little was heard from the expeditions except for a monthly demon-carried message from the *Valor*. Accounts of the latest adventures spread quickly, and when word came of one soldier's death, the city declared a day of mourning.

At the time of the last message of the dozen, they thought the western coast within reach, but the land was dipping southward, so they could not estimate their time of arrival. No word had returned of the *Perseverance* except for two messages carried back by fur traders, which simply stated their arrival at Cloudmarch and then at a place where the river split, and where they were debating which fork to take.

At this point, a year and a month after the *Valor*'s departure, the expedition later to be known as "The Beast's Expedition," set forth, organized by an independent Scholar, Fabula Nittlescent. Where earlier expeditions sought to map which lands were inhabited by Humans and which contained only Beasts, Nittlescent's expedition thought to find lands where Beasts had formed their own governments. Such early Abolitionist thinking was seen as aberrant at the time. Several plays satirized the expedition and its improbable mission.

While Nittlescent's findings were discredited almost immediately upon publication, many of her writings and observations would be used by Abolitionists in following decades. She observed that many of the interior Beasts mirrored Sorcerer-created versions on the Old Continent, raising the question whether the Sorcerers had actually created or summoned them.

Although no Ducal hounds companioned Nittlescent's expedition, it contained two dogs from the Southern Isles, whose like had not been seen on either Old or New Continent before. They were striped deep red and orange and black, with thick fur particularly evident over their shoulders, given to eating carrion. Nittlescent had acquired the pair, which she called Paprika and Cinnamon, on an earlier voyage to the Isles, and they were devoted to her and her manservant Jandro.

Nittlescent's expedition chose to not follow the routes laid out by earlier travelers, but rather struck out across the vast interior plains, inhabited by buffalo and mammoth. Hers would have the most success trading and negotiating with the tribes and other Beasts she encountered. By the end of the trip, she had noted seventy-two different groups.

Like other expeditions, Nittlescent's group encountered Shifters. Where the others had steered clear of such creatures, Nittlescent infiltrated the groups, recording their location, numbers, and whatever customs or other information she could gather, in a special journal. Like others of her generation, Nittlescent feared the threat to the natural order posed by the Shifters, and devoted later years of her career to helping wipe them out.

At the time the first expeditions set out, Tabat's citizens numbered over four thousand, an equal number of Beasts living beside them. Like their owners, these early Beasts labored to build a city for the ages. The site for the Ducal castle had been located, the stereotomy of its block drawn out, and the first granite blocks quarried and cut with simple margins and pulled via mule team to its destination.

By the time *Perseverance* returned, the Duke's pack had grown to thirty, and the castle walls were taking shape.

Where *Valor* had chosen to go via horse and wagon along the coast,

Perseverance chose the river. They traveled along the Lazylake's northern shore, hoping to reach the western mountains and find a way across them.

They rode in sturdy pirogues (the boats' construction created their departure's delay, for they had hoped to launch before *Valor*), but when the wind was against them, they resorted to poling or having the Minotaurs tow the two boats from the shore. The pirogues proved invaluable. Depending on the territory, each could make six to ten miles per day.

Two weeks in, *Perseverance* found itself floating in the midst of a sea of feathers, a glittering mass of white, black and gold covering the water's surface for nearly a mile. Turning a bend, they found themselves among cliffs covered by birds in their summer molt: white pelicans, and golden songbirds, and a host of black swallows of a kind no one had seen before. The noise the birds made was so deafening that the crew stopped up their ears with lumps of tallow lest they be driven mad. They gathered bushels of the feathers, and at their next trade stop, sent back several sackfuls, which were used to make feather ornaments for Tabat's elite.

The most troubling report that returned with *Perseverance* was word of many Shifter tribes inhabiting the interior, co-existing with Beasts.

On the Old Continent, the delineation between Human and Beast had been clear-cut. On this expedition, Explorer Aldo Silvercoin found himself faced with a puzzle this continent would pose for its new inhabitants, when it became clear that the tribe he was trading with were not Human, but Shapeshifters.

Early on, the tribes did not hide this fact from explorers, but rather changed form freely before them. While knowing themselves in the midst of dreadful peril from such abominations, Aldo and his fellows remained calm, and escaped, although all recorded how shaken they had been by the encounter.

Word traveled before them though, and they found themselves surprised by Shifters more than once. They learned to distrust all large animals—even the herds of elk, buffalo, and mammoths turned out to have Shifters in their midst. Debate sprang up in the councils of Tabat as how best to deal with the menace such creatures posed.

The expedition was not a complete success. Upon reaching a place where the river forked into three separate tributaries, they chose one fork and followed it into a series of high walled canyons. There winter snowed them in. They lived a miserable existence, subsisting through trade with Centaurs living in the mountains. The Beasts traded them corn and dried meat, but the expedition found themselves at the mercy of politics—showing one too much favor would send others into a rage.

Things got sticky when the Humans stole several elk from a hunting party. The presence of the Minotaurs saved them. The Centaurs held their two fellow Beasts in awe. An elder one said they had met such beings far to the north in earlier days. The Minotaurs were thereafter used to exact tribute from the neighboring tribes.

When spring came, as the expedition made plans for return, the ungrateful Minotaurs snuck away on a moonless night. The Centaurs refused to assist in their recapture, and the expedition left soon after, tracing their route back and arriving much thinner than they had left.

The Duke observed that if they had had a hound or two, the Minotaurs might have been recaptured.

When messengers brought word, another year later, of *Valor*'s return, crowds formed to meet the expedition, which was unprepared for the heroes' welcome awaiting them in the city, where their legend had grown with each sporadic report of their progress.

Classes in Tabat's schools were canceled for three days, and the brass band that had been preparing for the expedition's return since the previous year was finally given their chance. Merchants churned out replica "Explorer's Hats," complete with a rainbow of feathers in a fanlike formation at the front, the first of what would become Tabat's signature feather cockades.

Valor's cargo was of the utmost importance to the Duke and his government, which had invested heavily in its outfitting. Their expectations were met. It included gold and silver bars; sea and freshwater pearls; pelts of many unknown birds, animals, and Beasts, including two Selkies; ten gallons of water from a healing spring; plant seed, root, and cutting specimens; song-opals; a clutch of Dragon eggs; two gold and blue macaws; crates of phantasmerie collected from tribes; and rock specimens.

They also came back with inlaid bracers of chitin of a type prized to this day, although only a few pieces remain.

Notable among their finds were the purple reeds that are used in dyeing. Transplanted to the marshes, these would spread and overtake less hearty vegetation, until the marshes shone lavender and cobalt in the sunset. The poet Tullus observed of Tabat's marshes that his heart was "less lonely there than any place on this earth."

But most important were journals and maps, particularly when combined with *Perseverance*'s. Space was laid out in the half-completed castle's main hall for what would eventually become the Great Map, showing the continent's entirety.

Valor reported it had traveled along the coast, finding alkali flats and poisonous nymphs, as well as a city of intelligent wasps, who were eradicated by means of sulfur smoke and salt of lead. At times they were forced inland to find a place where they might ford larger rivers, but whenever possible, they stuck to the water's edge, mapping as they went.

Khanda Kanto spoke of hatcheries of Harpies, who screamed at them in an unknown tongue and flew high above them in order to void their bowels, causing the explorers to move along and leave the creatures' territory uncontested.

On the salt flats, while looting the wasp city, they spotted what seemed to be humanoids dressed in spined armor, but were unable to track any down. Finally, the dogs brought a representative of the species back to the city, and they discovered it to be an ambulatory cactus, sized like a ten-year-old Human, but covered with bristles and thorns that made it difficult to handle.

They were forced to bandage the mouths of the hounds and use spears to force the beast into a cage. They tried to speak to it, but it made no sound other than plaintive whistling. They gave it meat and water; it ignored the meat but drank down the water eagerly.

In the morning they found the cage broken and the humanoid gone. Khanda gave the Duke a handful of thorns broken off in the struggle to escape. *Valor* had seen nothing more of the Thornwalkers, who would harry later settlers with warfare that stopped at no barbarity.

For the most part, their dealings had been peaceful. *Valor* had made contact with dozens of tribes and gathered word, where it could, of what lay inland. Khanda's interest in linguistics led her to fill notebooks with rudimentary grammars, subject-verb order diagrams, and notes on tribal similarities.

Like *Perseverance, Valor's* members found themselves in an odd situation. In the few Human settlements they visited, the men were often in high demand for the infusion of new blood it brought into families. Both expeditions left an impressive number of bastard children behind.

More problematic were the tribes of Beasts, not to mention tribes who appeared Human but turned out not to be. While procreation rarely results in offspring, many Humans shun such contact, deeming it to be unlucky and unseemly. The men of *Perseverance* took it upon themselves to defend the prowess of Tabatians, for the most part. Only one Beast/Human offspring is known to have resulted from this —the child was raised by the College of Mages and its descendants still live in its menagerie.

But even more than the Humans, the dogs had been in demand, for many tribes hoped to crossbreed them with their own hunting animals. They had proven surprisingly fertile too—on *Valor's* trip back, they encountered instance after instance of puppies greeting them. The Duke remarked that the dogs sported a remarkably smug demeanor.

In the craze for all things expedition-related, dog ownership became highly fashionable, although only the Royal Household and those favored by it had greathounds. Several traders took to dog breeding and established the varied lines of Tabat, beginning with mastiffs and finally arriving at the terriers, poodles, and sundry ornamental dogs plaguing us today.

Fabula Nittlescent's expedition returned to little fanfare, but much interest on the part of Tabat's government. More than any other expedition, she had established trade possibilities, having found no tribes overtly hostile to her and her party.

Weather, however, had proved their enemy. They found themselves at first greatly enamored of the plains they traversed. Plentiful game included the mammoth that supplied not just meat but hide, bone, and tusk. The soldiers whittled spoons and pipes from the latter; a display of them hangs in the city Museum.

Nittlescent kept careful records of the species she encountered; of her some three hundred illustrations, over sixty proved to be Beasts, animals, birds, plants, and mushrooms of types not yet cataloged by science. Unfortunately her family saw fit to sell her drawings immediately after her death, breaking the collection up. Some examples survive in private libraries; the majority are housed in the Duke's archives.

Future expeditions discovered the fate of the missing Ducal hounds, as well as the puppies they had sired or whelped. In the north, Cavall and Laurens had bred with local wolf packs, which had formed an alliance with the local tribe of Shifters. Over generations, these interbred until some Shifters took on canine, rather than lupine, form.

Many dogs made similar accommodations with native Beasts, particularly Centaurs, who bred packs sired by Nittlescent's dogs, now known as prairie dogs. Trade in these dogs has always been strong, as with the other dogs bred for specialized tasks, such as tracking or rat-killing.

In Tabat, the Ducal pack continued generation by generation. (See Appendix L for a complete listing.) But unknown to the Duke, some dogs brought back from elsewhere were not what they seemed.

When I was a lad of five, my father brought me a puppy, which the Duke had given him for his services, one of the highest honors in Tabat. I named him Cavall in honor of a story I had heard at my nursemaid's knee, and he and I grew apace together. But he matured more quickly. By the time I was thirteen, he had saved my life on three occasions: once from snakebite, once from drowning, and a third by Mandrake. My father loved him as well as I did, and called him in jest a second son. More than once I saw him regard the dog with affection mingled with deep gratitude.

Throughout my childhood, I knew my canine brother a match for me in intellect, although he lacked the power of speech. He comprehended it as well as I did, and I would talk to him by the hour, telling him all my hopes and dreams.

When I reached adolescence, my companion fell ill. He was put in the stable, where the stable keeper nursed him. Over the next two days, I went to visit him whenever I could, and sat reading to him from a book we had both been enjoying, a detailed account of *Valor* and its travels. We made our way from the wasp city to the western coast while he lay panting, white froth around his eyes.

That midnight my father roused me. His face was troubled. We went to the stables. My dog was gone. In his place lay a boy my age, blond where I was dark-haired.

He opened his eyes and they were Cavall's eyes. He struggled to sit up, pushing away the blanket covering him. Naked legs beneath it, spindly and thin as my own adolescent limbs.

"Easy, Son," my father said, and laid a hand on his shoulder. At the touch, the youth calmed and sat looking between the two of us, his expression trusting.

"Cavall?" I whispered.

He smiled at me and half-croaked a response. As though the sound he made frightened him, he flinched back, then recovered himself. "Ca-vall."

The stable smelled of dogs and horses and the bitter medicine that they had dosed him in dog form with.

"He is a Shifter," my father said. "Do you understand what they are?"

"Someone who can be both Human and animal."

He shook his head. "An animal that uses magic to take Human shape, which means it is a Beast."

He looked sadly at Cavall, who tried to croak again but was not understandable.

"Shifters are killed on sight," he told Cavall.

Cavall nodded. Pushing the blanket away completely, he tottered to his feet, then to my father. He moved more gracefully by the end, smoothly enough that he simply rolled over at my father's feet.

He lifted his chin to expose his throat to my father's knife.

I interposed myself before my father could act.

Never have I been as eloquent as I was that night, pleading for my brother's life. I reminded my father how he would have lost me three times over, were it not for Cavall. We could hide his infirmity, I said. I would personally take charge of it. In Human form, he could be my cousin, sent south from Verranzo's New City.

And so Cavall came to be in my household, where we shared all things, and have done so all my life. In dog form and in Human, he has run with me and guarded me from all perils.

When I was twenty-three, we traveled together to Verranzo's New City. There are many Abolitionists there and we attended several lectures. After one, I told him that I would be glad to fund him if he chose to seek out others like himself.

He laughed, and asked me how well I thought he would acquit himself in the wilderness? He told me he had grown fond of the advantages that civilization offered and preferred to stay with me. He made me chuckle, positing ridiculous examples of how he might live in the wild, but he was earnest when he told me he preferred to live with me.

Only a few times have I denied what he is. The first to a young lady we both admired, who inquired of me if I did not think him (she referred to his Human form) a little "odd." I denied this strongly, and praised him to her. It only occurs to me in retrospect that this was her way of telling me her preference. My life has been marked by such dunderheaded moments, though Cavall has saved me from many of them.

Have I wronged Tabat by keeping him safe from its hunters? Have I damaged the order of things, encouraged abomination to walk on this earth? But how could one who loves me so be capable of anything but truth and honesty?

It was, and still is, a hard choice, one I struggle with daily.

But it has been taken from me. I am forty now, and while Cavall was still my age when he walked in Human form, in canine shape he grew gray muzzled and slow-walking.

Finally, last night I knelt beside him for the last time in that shape he could not forsake, as much as I implored him to.

He licked my hand. He closed his eyes.

His last breath shuddered from him, but even then he grinned as only a dog can, promising to run before me and find the path.

All that I have left of him is this tribute, this work. Does my acceptance of him make me an Abolitionist and even worse, a traitor to my race? Perhaps it does, but I have known a devoted soul, and it was as Human as my own.

And so to all the Cavalls of this world—run freely and love deeply, my friends, and know that you will be loved in return.

ABOUT THE AUTHOR

Cat Rambo's 300+ fiction publications include stories in *Asimov's, Clarkesworld Magazine,* and *The Magazine of Fantasy and Science Fiction.* In 2020 they won the Nebula Award for fantasy novelette *Carpe Glitter.* They are a former two-term President of the Science Fiction and Fantasy Writers of America (SFWA). Their most recent books are space opera *Rumor Has It* (Tor Macmillan, 2024) and story collection *All the Pretty Little Mermaids* (Hydra House, 2025).

For more about Cat, as well as links to fiction and popular online school, The Rambo Academy for Wayward Writers, see their website: http://www.catrambo.com

f X

IF YOU LIKED ...

If you liked *Wings of Tabat*, you might also enjoy:

Rise of the First World
by Christopher Katava

Oshenerth
by Alan Dean Foster

The Saga of Seven Suns, Veiled Alliances
by Kevin J. Anderson

OTHER WORDFIRE PRESS TITLES BY CAT RAMBO

BEASTS OF TABAT

Beasts of Tabat
Hearts of Tabat
Exiles of Tabat

Our list of other WordFire Press authors and titles is always growing. To find out more and shop our selection of titles, visit us at: wordfirepress.com

www.ingramcontent.com/pod-product-compliance
Lightning Source LLC
Chambersburg PA
CBHW020359110726
47899CB00006B/1775